Dear Reader,

The editors at Harlequin and Silhouette are thrilled to be able to bring you a brand-new featured author program beginning in 2005! Signature Select aims to single out outstanding stories, contemporary themes and oft-requested classics by some of your favorite series authors and present them to you in a variety of formats bound by truly striking covers.

You may notice a number of different colored bands on the spine of this book. Each color corresponds to a different type of reading experience in the new Signature Select program. The Spotlight books will offer a single "big read" by a talented series author, the Collections will present three novellas on a selected theme in one volume, the Sagas will contain sprawling, sometimes multi-generational family tales (often related to a favorite family first introduced in series) and the Miniseries will feature requested, previously published books, with two or, occasionally, three complete stories in one volume. The Signature Select program will offer one book in each of these categories per month, and fans of limited continuity series will also find these continuing stories under the Signature Select umbrella.

In addition, these volumes will bring you bonus features...different in every single book! You may learn more about the author in an extended interview, more about the setting or inspiration for the book, more about subjects related to the theme and, often, a bonus short read will be included.

Watch for new stories from Vicki Lewis Thompson, Lori Foster, Donna Kauffman, Marie Ferrarella, Merline Lovelace, Roberta Gellis, Suzanne Forster, Stephanie Bond and scores more of the brightest talents in romance fiction!

We have an exciting year ahead!

Warm wishes for happy reading,

Marsha Zinberg

Marsha Zinberg
Executive Editor
The Signature Select Program

SIGNATURE SELECT
COLLECTION

LORI FOSTER
DONNA KAUFFMAN
JILL SHALVIS

MEN OF COURAGE II

HARLEQUIN®

TORONTO • NEW YORK • LONDON
AMSTERDAM • PARIS • SYDNEY • HAMBURG
STOCKHOLM • ATHENS • TOKYO • MILAN • MADRID
PRAGUE • WARSAW • BUDAPEST • AUCKLAND

ISBN 0-373-83642-2

MEN OF COURAGE II

Copyright © 2005 by Harlequin Books S.A.

The publisher acknowledges the copyright holders
of the individual works as follows:

AN HONORABLE MAN
Copyright © 2005 by Lori Foster

BLOWN AWAY
Copyright © 2005 by Donna Kauffman

PERILOUS WATERS
Copyright © 2005 by Jill Shalvis

This edition published by arrangement with Harlequin Books S.A.

® and TM are trademarks of the publisher. Trademarks indicated with
® are registered in the United States Patent and Trademark Office, the
Canadian Trade Marks Office and in other countries.

www.eHarlequin.com

Printed in U.S.A.

CONTENTS

Dear Reader,

Before tackling this book, all I truly knew about the military is that it leaves me awed, proud and humbled by those who give so much to our country. In many ways, the military life feels like a different universe from mine, so I had to query a lot of people to get even the smallest facts straight. Every single person was so giving, so kind and patient, that I have to give them credit for helping me to complete this book.

First of all, I have to thank talented author Catherine Mann and her incredible husband, Lt. Col. Robert Mann. Without them, this novella wouldn't have happened. Big hugs to you both!

Thanks also go to Major Charles F. Rinkevich, Jr., USAF Chief, AFOSI Officer Assignments, who answered a lot of e-mail questions and helped me to understand different decorations, how and when they're worn, and even sent me pictures of various medals.

Other contributors were Amy Case, an honorably discharged veteran of the USAF, and Major Thomas P. Coppinger of the New Jersey Air National Guard, or NJANG. Both Amy and Tom filled in a lot of blanks whenever the odd question arose or a tiny fact was needed.

A lot of the research I collected never made it into the book, but it certainly gave me a better understanding of the relationship between my two characters based on their backgrounds and experiences. Everything I learned proved invaluable—so again, my most humble gratitude for your assistance.

Lori Foster

AN HONORABLE MAN
Lori Foster

CHAPTER ONE

CHAOS REIGNED in the classroom as the kids returned from their second recess. Liv Amery listened to the comforting sounds of their bustling activity, the scraping of chairs, the continued childish chatter. The cold mid-May weather had made their small faces ruddy, and had resulted in several runny noses. Wind-ruffled and still wound up from the recent play, they were utterly adorable.

Only an hour remained in the school day, and then the kids would head home. She had just enough time to finish going over the math lessons. Giving them time to remove their jackets and settle in their seats,

Liv retrieved several papers from her desk. When everyone had quieted, she stood and went to the chalkboard, ready to start the afternoon lessons.

That's when she heard it—the even, very precise cadence of military footfalls echoing down the tiled hallway. She'd grown up hearing that sound, the memory of it buried deep in her heart. But hearing it now, here in an elementary school, nearly stopped her heart.

With one hand raised, a piece of chalk still in her now limp fingers, she faced the blackboard, listening as those steps came closer and closer and finally stopped at the door of her third-grade room.

Heart pounding, throat tight, she began silent prayers. A visit from the military now could only mean one thing, and the idea that her most dreaded nightmare could have happened, that she might have lost him before she'd ever really had him…. No. She couldn't accept that.

Then her senses picked up more subtle nuances. Not just any military walk, but one so familiar that, almost on cue, her stomach did a small flip and her lungs expanded with relief. They were telling reactions, an inbred response to one particular man.

Hamilton was okay. *Thank you, God.*

But because he'd come unannounced, not to her home, but to her school, her uneasiness remained. *He* was fine, but his visit here today could only mean one thing.

Wanting to shut out the moment, Liv started to close her eyes, and the door opened. With a mix of dread and awful yearning, she turned.

There he stood: Lieutenant Colonel Hamilton Wulf. Tall, strong, commanding. Exactly as she remembered him.

His brown eyes zeroed in on her face and stayed there, as probing and intimidating as ever. He wore no smile of welcome because this wasn't a social call.

Shaken, Liv pulled her gaze from his and looked him over, making note of the hat tucked under his arm, his polished shoes and the razor-sharp crease in his dress blues.

Hamilton was fine—but her father wasn't.

Knees going weak, Liv felt herself swaying, and suddenly Hamilton was there, his big hands warm and steady on her shoulders, keeping her upright. Close to her ear, he murmured, "Come with me, Liv."

He didn't wait for her agreement before finding her purse under her desk, pulling her sweater off the back of her chair, and leading her quietly, efficiently from her classroom. Her fractured senses scrambled to understand the situation, to absorb the enormity of what she knew to be true.

"Easy," Hamilton said, redirecting her thoughts with his presence. "Just keep walking."

Liv became aware of Betty Nobel, a teacher's aide,

taking charge of her students; aware of the children staring in wide-eyed wonder at the awe-inspiring figure Hamilton made, and aware of the strained hush in the air.

When they reached the front lobby of the school, the fog lifted and she pulled up. From as far back as Liv could remember, the military had ruled her life. But she'd finally broken free, and no one, not even Hamilton, could come back and start directing her again. She'd known this day would come. It had only been a matter of time. She'd prepared herself, living in dread day in and day out.

She could handle this. What choice did she have?

Hamilton waited while she dragged in two deep breaths. His hand remained on her elbow, his gaze steady and unblinking, the force of his will settling around her like a warm, heavy blanket.

Liv tipped up her chin to see his face. Although she already knew, she wanted it confirmed. "It's Daddy, isn't it?"

The second her gaze met his, Liv felt the old familiar connection. She felt his sympathy and his understanding and his need to comfort. It had always been that way with Hamilton, regardless of how she fought it.

His expression remained stern, but his voice sounded oddly gentle. "Outside, baby. Then we'll talk."

Liv looked beyond him to where another uniformed man and a uniformed woman stood on the front steps. They both appeared to be younger than Hamilton, probably in their early thirties, while Hamilton now edged close to forty.

Being a military brat, Liv automatically sought out the truth. She noted the young man had a religious symbol where Hamilton had wings, and the woman carried a small medical bag.

A chaplain and a military doctor. Did she need any more confirmation than that?

"Come on." Hamilton's arm went around her, pulling her protectively into his side and before Liv knew it, he had her outside in the brisk wind with the blinding sunshine in her face. Slipping on aviator sunglasses, Hamilton hustled her to the car.

Indicating the doctor, he said, "Liv, these are friends of mine, Major Cheryl Tyne and Captain Gary Nolan."

They both nodded, their gazes respectful and sympathetic.

"Father, Doc, meet Weston's daughter, Liv Amery."

Liv tried for a smile, but had no idea if she'd succeeded. Major Tyne settled behind the wheel while the chaplain opened the rear door. Hamilton urged Liv into the back seat. Before she'd completely seated herself, his body crowded in next to hers, giving her no room to retreat, no room to react. He was so close, Liv breathed in his familiar scent, felt the touch of his body heat everywhere.

With a strange tenderness, especially considering his size and capability, Ham put his arms around her, gathering her to his chest.

She waited, breath held.

"I'm sorry, Liv."

Odd, how she'd held out the faintest, most ridiculous hope. Now her hopes sank and around her distress, she felt burning anger. *"No."* She tried to push away from Ham, but his thick, strong arms kept her close. "No, no, no—"

"Shh." His hand cradled her face. "He had a heart attack, Liv. There was nothing anyone could do."

A heart attack? Surprise silenced her. The military hadn't taken him as she'd always feared? But how could his health have failed him when he'd always prided himself on being in prime physical condition?

It seemed…ironic. And so damn unfair.

Sick to her soul, Liv slumped against Hamilton, felt his hand stroking through her hair, his breath on her cheek.

Visions of her father—strong, proud, coldly distant in his discipline—warred with the image of him struggling for breath, a hand to his chest. "Did he…?"

"It was quick, baby, too damn quick." To Major Tyne, he said, "Doc, take us to my motel room."

"Sure, Howler."

Howler? She hadn't heard Ham referred to by his call name in a very long time. Some day, she'd find out why they called him that.

But for now, while her thoughts might be muddled, she still knew she didn't want to go anywhere with Hamilton. She needed solace, to cry in private, to deal with her grief where no one could see or judge her.

She needed to find her backbone, to dredge up her independence. "My class…"

"I took care of it."

She stared up at him, and even though he still wore the aviator glasses, she felt snared by his gaze.

Hamilton lifted a hand as if to remove them, and Liv caught his wrist. Sunshine flooded the car windows, making her squint. But Hamilton's eyes were especially sensitive after so much time flying high above the pollution, being overexposed to the sun. He needed the glasses, and she knew it.

Diverted, his hand again settled against her cheek, his thumb stroking over her jaw. "You're not alone, Liv."

A near hysterical sob threatened to break free. Of course she was alone, just as she'd always been.

Shamefully, she felt mired in self-pity—and she hated that Hamilton always knew her most private thoughts. Her mother had died when she was young, and the military had owned her father. His death was a crushing weight on her heart, but she doubted she could miss him any more in death than she had in day-to-day life.

Looking out the window in an effort to compose herself, Liv whispered, "You're wrong, Ham. I've always been alone."

Her statement bothered him, and he tightened his hold. "Don't do that, damn it. Don't buck up like a good little soldier. You don't have to, not with me."

Liv didn't reply. If she spoke, the tears would come and she'd be even more humiliated.

But her lack of reply didn't deter Ham. "Listen to me, Liv. I'm here and I'm staying." Before her hopes could fully surface, he burst her bubble. "I have two weeks leave."

As if two weeks could matter in the scheme of things. Deep inside herself, pain twisted and prodded. Memories raced through her mind, memories of past years, of lost opportunities.

When he pulled her toward him, Liv rested her forehead against his chest. Typical for a man to think he could handle anything in two weeks. In so many ways, Hamilton was like her father—confident, capable, a man other men looked up to.

A man forever lost to her because the air force was his life.

Hamilton tipped up her chin. "I know that look, Liv. I know what you're thinking." His hand opened, his fingers curling around her nape. "I'll be here with you, to help with the arrangements, to talk to, to…be with. If you need or want anything, if there's anything I can do, you only have to tell me."

Liv closed her eyes, unable to bear Hamilton's close scrutiny. Want anything? She'd wanted *him,* but she couldn't bear the constant moving or the constant worry she associated with the air force. She'd seen so many military marriages break up. Good people on both sides, just unable to handle the pressures of separation. Often the wives had no family close by for support. And she knew firsthand what a tough way it was to bring up kids.

She wanted constancy and close friends and a husband who came home every day. She wanted kids who felt secure, who wouldn't have to go through what she had.

So she'd resigned herself to life without him.

Just as she'd resigned herself to life without a father. As a colonel with the Office of Special Investigation, Air Force Intelligence had taken Weston to some pretty spooky places over the years, and kept him away from her for long periods of time. Too long, and too many times. Liv couldn't go through that again.

Already Hamilton had been in Kosovo, Afghanistan

and Iraq. He'd even flown in Desert Storm as a newly trained pilot in a B-52. Sometimes, ignorance was bliss, and where Lieutenant Colonel Hamilton Wulf was concerned, the less she knew about his duties, the dangers he faced and the volatile situations he willingly put himself in, the better.

Once long ago, she'd been wildly in love with him, hopeful of a future, her dreams filled with the possibility of a tidy house in the suburbs and all the trimmings—kids, pets, rosebushes and a picket fence. They'd both been military brats, and even though Hamilton was nine years older, she'd been closer to him than to anyone else in her life.

After her mother's death, Hamilton was the one she'd turned to. When her father had missed her birthday, a gift had always arrived from Hamilton. And when a boy had broken her heart, Hamilton had been there, convincing her that she was better off without him.

When she'd turned twenty-one, he'd kissed her for the first time…and kept on kissing her. She'd had boyfriends and a few serious flirtations, but kissing Hamilton had proven a revelation. For the first time in her life, she'd felt like a woman.

Liv had asked him to make love to her then, but he wouldn't. Instead, he'd just driven her crazy with desire, showing her how it could be between them without ever fulfilling the promise. For years, they'd played that ridiculous game, until at twenty-seven, Liv had made it clear what she wanted—and what she didn't.

A military life fell in the "didn't want" category, and that had effectively ruled out a relationship with Hamilton. Not that he'd given up on her. Stubborn to the core, he insisted on thinking he could have it all without consideration of her wishes. He made no bones about his feelings—he still kissed her on the rare occasions when Liv softened enough to let him, and whenever duty kept him from her, he stayed in touch with correspondence, cards and phone calls.

It might have been enough, except that year after year had passed, promotion after promotion—and still he'd stayed in the air force. Her heart broke each and every time.

Now at thirty-seven, as a lieutenant colonel, a B-2 stealth-bomber pilot, and second in command of a B-2 bomb squadron, Hamilton was career air force through and through, and Liv couldn't seduce him away from his first love: flying.

The reality crushed her and made her more determined to live her life without him.

With a sigh, Liv pushed herself upright, away from Hamilton's warmth and the lure of his comfort. She *was* alone, and she had to deal with her father's death without allowing Hamilton to get too close.

Hamilton sighed, too, the sound ragged with

exasperation, but he said nothing. He was the most contained, enigmatic person she knew—which made him perfect for the military, but difficult to understand in a relationship.

Liv's father had admired Hamilton's cool regard, while forever accusing her of being too emotional. And she couldn't deny it. She *was* passionate about her work, determined with her students, and despite everything, she'd loved her father so much that now she felt physically wounded.

She wanted to be alone, but at the same time, she wanted Hamilton to stay close and keep on holding her. *Forever.*

The drive to his motel took them within minutes of her home, which was a ten-minute drive from Denton Elementary. She could travel the entire length of the town in less than a half hour. But right outside of town, better hotels existed.

She should have guessed that Hamilton would be staying close by in the shabby lodging rather than putting any distance between them. His organizational skills had served him well in the military. But they would not color her life.

"I want to go home, Ham."

He looked at her, his eyes shielded by the reflective sunglasses, his expression impossible to read. "Not yet. We have some talking to do first."

Shaking from the inside out, Liv whispered, "I don't want—"

But he'd already opened his door and stepped out. Seconds later, he strode to her side of the car and with both Major Tyne and Captain Nolan in attendance, Liv refused to make a scene.

Hamilton opened her door and helped her out. He didn't move away from her or give her any space. With his arm around her waist keeping her pressed to his side, Liv felt his strength and his determination.

Major Tyne glanced at her, then asked, "Should we accompany you?"

Why? Liv wondered. Did they expect hysterics from her? Should she fall apart over a father who hadn't cared, a father who'd willingly walked away from her time and time again? A father who... who...

Damn it, the tears fell, taking her by surprise, closing her throat and making her chin tremble. She sniffled, struggling to stifle the emotional display, knowing it would have disgusted her father.

But she couldn't. And even while it humiliated her, she felt helpless to pull herself together.

Quietly, Hamilton said, "That's not necessary," while gathering Liv close. Warmth and security surrounded her, and pushed her over the edge. Her shoulders shook with her sobs. Damn him, why did her father have to die before they could reconcile? Why hadn't he come to see her just once?

Why hadn't she gone to see him?

With her face tucked against Ham's chest, she heard his quiet conversation with the others. He told them to go ahead and get settled in their rooms.

Captain Nolan put a hand to Ham's shoulder. "If you need me, Howler, give a yell."

"I'll be in touch," he replied. Once the two officers had gone inside, Ham's mouth touched her ear, and he whispered, "I am so sorry, Liv."

She shook her head. He had nothing to be sorry about. Ham, like her father, had gone with his heart. They were both warriors through and through, dedicated to their country, ready, willing and able to defend and protect.

Ham tipped her back and mopped at her face with a snowy-white hanky. "Look at you. You've ruined your makeup," he said with a small sad smile. Then his forehead touched hers. "God, Liv, please don't. Seeing you cry just about kills me."

He wasn't judging her? Her father would have lectured, would have told her to be strong and dignified. To be brave and suck it up.

Ham just cuddled her.

Feeling like a fool, Liv half laughed while taking the hanky and blowing her nose. "So I'm capable of doing what weapons can't, huh? Wow, I feel powerful."

He tugged off his sunglasses, his expression far too serious. "You have no idea how powerful you are when it comes to me."

While she reeled from that cryptic comment, he started them on their way again, across the blacktop lot and toward the brick building.

Tears continued to track down her cheeks. Liv mopped them away and considered what Hamilton might have meant. Surely if she had any real power over him, he'd have been happy to settle with her.

With his long stride shortened to accommodate her, Hamilton glanced at her and frowned. "I'm sorry about the motel. Denton doesn't have much in the way of luxury."

Taking that as an insult to her home, Liv lifted her chin. "It has everything I need and everything I want. It's small and quiet and everyone knows everyone." And then, to ease up on him a little, she said, "It's a place to put down roots. A place to raise a family."

Hamilton paused in the process of opening the glass lobby doors, but only for a moment. His arm went around her waist again and he ushered her down the worn carpeted hallway to the door of his room. The motel was old enough that they still used keys instead of key cards. Hamilton jiggled the lock until the key clicked into place, then held the door open for her to enter.

He must have come straight to the school, Liv thought, noting his unpacked bags and the stuffiness of the air. Automatically she walked to the window to open it, letting in the fresh spring breezes.

Hamilton tossed his hat and sunglasses onto the bureau, leaned back against it and watched her with an intensity that should have been reserved for enemy captives.

Feeling conspicuous, Liv seated herself on the edge of the full-size bed. "Now what?"

Seconds ticked by before he answered, as if he had to give his response serious thought. "Have you eaten?"

"I'm not hungry." Using the hanky, she tried to remove what she could of her ruined mascara. Crying had always been useless, a lesson she'd learned long ago.

Ham's gaze moved over her, from her wind-tossed hair to her sensible teacher-type pumps. Disregarding her words, he asked, "You haven't changed that much, Liv. I know getting upset makes you hungry."

"Everything makes me hungry." Luckily, she had a fast metabolism that kept her from being more than pleasingly plump. "But I can eat at home. Alone."

"You need to talk."

Pushing both hands through her hair, Liv decided to face his arrogance head-on. "No. I need time to think, and I suppose I have to figure out funeral arrangements—"

"The military will take care of it."

She knew that. A military funeral would be what her father had wanted, certainly what he deserved. Nodding, Liv said, "I still have to make plans. I can't do that sitting here and chatting about food and sniveling like a child."

"Showing that you care isn't childish."

She half laughed. "My father would have disagreed with that. I can't tell you how many times I got compared to soldiers. How many times Dad pointed out the differences between my soft bed and a battlefield, my security and the danger in every war."

Hamilton stared at her hard. "He was wrong, Liv. You're one of the strongest women I know."

The compliment warmed something cold deep inside her, but still she said, "Not strong enough to play second fiddle to the air force."

The silence swelled, tinged with anger and frustration. Hamilton pushed away from the bureau to stand directly in front of her, every muscle tensed, his eyes blazing. "I've missed you, Liv."

Oh, God, don't do this, don't do this....

Catching her arms, he pulled her upright and

against his chest. "I'm sorry that I'm here under such awful circumstances. God knows I wish you didn't have to go through this. But it happened and we can't change that."

She started to turn her face away, and he whispered, almost warned, "Don't shut me out, baby. Not now. I *need* to help."

Something in his tone penetrated her sorrow. In so many ways, Hamilton had been closer to her father than she had. They'd had so much more in common, he had to be grief-stricken, too. How could she selfishly add to his hurt?

Fingers splayed against his shoulders, she conceded. "All right."

His hands loosened on her arms, became caressing. He shook off the vulnerability as if it had never been there, adopting instead the confidence and arrogance that better suited him. "I'll take care of the funeral arrangements. All you need to do is tell me where you want him buried, and what you want posted in the local paper."

Her lips began to tremble again. From hurt. From long-buried hope. "I'd like him buried here with my mother." The sad truths of her life intruded. "I know it's not officially my home." How could it be, when her entire life had been spent moving from place to place?

Rather than question her decision, Ham said only, "I think that'd be best."

"Thank you." Again, she felt the emptiness, the loneliness compounded by her most recent loss. Her words sounded sad and shaken to her own ears. "All my mother's relatives are now gone, but I still remember the stories she told of walking to the bakery, riding her bike to the same school where I now teach. I know the playground and the movie theater and…" A deep breath helped to steady her voice. "It's the closest thing I have to roots. Mother is buried here, and so I want Daddy here, too."

Hamilton pressed a kiss to her forehead. "That's what I figured." His gaze searching, concerned, he said, "The body will be here tomorrow. I think it might be possible to have the funeral on Friday. Is that okay with you?"

So soon. Again, her heart clenched, the pain close to crippling. Her daddy was really gone. Between his lack of interest and her own stubbornness, so much time had been wasted. She could have gone to see him, whether he wanted her there or not. She could have insisted he come to her college graduation, or…

This time Hamilton's kiss landed on her lips. A light, barely there kiss, but it obliterated her distressing thoughts, overcoming them with pure sensation.

"Don't do that, Liv," he murmured, his mouth still touching hers. His hands tangled in her hair, angling her face up to his. "Don't beat yourself up with regrets. Nothing was ever your fault."

She'd believed that—until now. "I haven't seen him in so long. I should have—"

"No, baby. *He* should have." Hamilton kissed her again, harder this time, a kiss of resolve and heartache, a kiss that nudged at the grief and curled her toes. "Weston made a damn fine colonel, one of the best. He was brilliant and strong, a natural-born leader." Hamilton swallowed and his jaw worked. "He was an asset to our country, but we both know he could have been a more attentive father."

"He gave everything he had to the military."

Trying to force her to his will, Hamilton held her gaze. "But plenty of guys balance it, their careers, their families. It doesn't have to be one or the other, all or nothing."

"For me it does."

Her statement fell like a sledgehammer, and suddenly new emotion darkened Hamilton's eyes. "This is hard for you. That's why I want to help get you through it. I don't want you worrying about it. It hurts me to see you hurt."

Liv caught her breath—and then his mouth was on hers, devouring, seducing, coaxing. No simple kiss, this. He consumed her, devastating her emotionally and physically. His taste stirred her, his dark, distinctive scent filled her head.

He teased with his tongue, then sank in to make

love to her mouth. Before Liv even realized it, she had her hands on his neck, feeling the muscles there, his short-cropped hair, his heat. Time apart, hurt feelings and resentment all melted away. This was familiar. Necessary. Sadness morphed into desperate aching need.

With a groan, Hamilton slipped one arm around her waist, angling her in close to the hardness of his body. There'd only been a handful of times that he'd ever held her like this, and not at all since she'd become determined to get by without him. Not once, not ever, had she forgotten how wonderful it felt to be in Hamilton's arms.

His strong steady heartbeat reverberated against her breast. His heat wrapped around her, making her light-headed and too warm. Overwhelmed by her own powerful response, she tried to retreat, but he tangled his fingers in her hair with his free hand and held her head still while his mouth ate at hers with voracious hunger.

Too many sensations rioted inside Liv. She couldn't fight them, not now. His tongue stroked, his teeth nibbled, and she wanted him, had always wanted him.

Rising on tiptoes, she aligned her belly with his groin, pressed in against his throbbing erection—

And suddenly Hamilton stepped away from her.

Without his support, Liv would have stumbled back

onto the bed if he hadn't quickly caught her shoulders. Just as quickly, he released her again. He breathed deeply. His nostrils flared, his cheekbones burned. She stood, shaky, devastated.

One look at her face and he swore softly, running a hand over his short dark hair, his other hand curled into a fist. Sexual tension rippled in the air, and heat poured off him.

Giving her his back, he growled, "I'm sorry. I didn't mean to do that."

It sure felt like he'd meant it.

Licking her swollen lips, Liv tried to come up with a coherent response. Her body throbbed and her heart raced, and a sweet ache had invaded her limbs. Given the circumstances, lust should have seemed a disgraceful thing, but she'd never felt shame with Hamilton. He was the only man who could make her forget herself, her surroundings and any sense of propriety.

The fact that he'd lost control, too—a rare event indeed—made her own loss easier to take.

When she said nothing, he glanced over his shoulder at her. Assessing her with a probing look that scanned from her tear-reddened face, her laboring chest, to her unsteady legs, he cursed again. "Stay put. Give me one minute to change and we'll get out of here."

Her chin lifted. "Away from temptation?"

Narrowing his eyes, Ham said, "Don't fool yourself, Liv. You always tempt me, no matter where we are."

Stomach doing a free fall, Liv sucked in needed oxygen. Because leaving on her own seemed unlikely, given she didn't have a car and she looked like hell, she dropped to the edge of the bed. She didn't have to reply to Hamilton one way or the other. He'd already grabbed up his bag and gone into the bathroom. The door closed with a quiet click.

With a feeling of helplessness, Liv covered her face. The next two weeks would try her resolve, but she'd get through it. She'd made a life for herself in Denton, Ohio, and no one, definitely not Lieutenant Colonel Hamilton Wulf, would rob her of the peace she'd found.

CHAPTER TWO

LOVE, TENDERNESS and carnal need still gripped Hamilton as he drove to Liv's house. Calling himself three times a fool, he looked over at her. Eyes swollen from tears and dark from smudged mascara, she kept quiet, her thoughts contained. She held her shoulders stiff and her back straight in true military fashion—thanks to the teaching of her father, *a father she'd just lost*.

And he'd come on to her. One minute more, and he'd have had her stretched out on the bed, his hand in her panties, his mouth on her breast....

His timing couldn't have been worse, but God, it infuriated him whenever she ranked him in the same category as Weston. Hamilton had a load of respect for Weston Amery as a military officer, but very little for him as a father.

How in hell could a man ignore his own daughter as thoroughly as Weston had?

She'd never been a priority in his life, and once Liv's mother had passed away, she'd lost her father, too. Weston had quit any pretense of paternal regard beyond the occasional criticism, and had thrown himself into his field operations. Career military—yeah, that described Weston all the way. Only he'd made career military seem like a nasty thing to Liv, an excuse to disregard family obligations when nothing could be further from the truth.

The military husbands and wives that Hamilton knew were *more* dedicated, *more* caring, because experience had taught them the value of family. They knew exactly what they missed while on assignment. They knew the hardship their partners endured, the number of responsibilities that they carried alone. It was all tough, but for them, separation was by far the greatest trial in serving their country.

Because of what they saw and did during wartime, they lived with a reality that few civilians ever had to face. They understood how easily a loved one could be lost, and they compensated by pouring more attention and affection on their wives, husbands and children. They didn't take their lifestyles for granted, and they couldn't be complacent about the gifts in their lives.

But thanks to Weston and his callous attitude toward his own daughter, Hamilton was stuck trying to work his way past her understandable prejudices against the air force.

He had two weeks. Fourteen lousy days to make her understand that they belonged together.

Hell, they were both of an age that they should have settled down. Hamilton knew why he hadn't. Other women could relieve a temporary ache. He could lose the sexual edginess, but the awful loneliness remained because Liv Amery was the love of his life, a woman who'd taken up residence in his heart.

She was stronger than she realized, too. She had the balance of backbone and empathy necessary to be a lieutenant colonel's wife, to pick up the familial slack when duty took him away from home. She had enough guts to weather the storms of war, and the loyalty to wait, to pray and worry, and accept him when he returned.

But he loved her enough to want to spare her that.

Yet, given that, at twenty-seven, she'd never had a serious relationship, Hamilton had to believe she loved him, too.

His Liv was stubborn; she had that in common with

her dad. She was also beautiful, inside and out, another fact to which she seemed oblivious. Again and again, his gaze was drawn to her. Seeing her seated rigidly as far from him as she could get in his rented car put an ache in his heart, and expanded his determination.

Pale brown hair hung to her rounded shoulders, tangled by the wind and her own frustrated hands. Red highlights glinted beneath the sunshine, though Liv always denied any red in her hair. Her eyes looked bluer than ever after the rush of tears. Her lips were puffy, her cheeks blotchy…and he wanted her so much, restraining himself took Herculean effort. He'd given his body to other women, but never his heart. And until he could give Liv both, he wouldn't feel complete.

Thank God for the aviator sunglasses that hid his innermost thoughts. Liv had always been able to see through him. One look and she'd know what he wanted and how he intended to get it. Ruthless—that could describe his current frame of mind. But damn it, he'd waited long enough. He couldn't wait anymore.

All he needed was some reassurance. Before he spilled his guts and made melodramatic vows of lifetime love and commitment, he wanted her to admit to her own feelings.

He needed that much in exchange for what he intended to give up.

Luckily, she'd paid no attention when he'd dropped his key at the front desk, or when he'd put his bag in the back of the car. He knew she'd assumed he'd stay at the motel, but no way would he keep that much distance between them. He'd missed her so much that he wanted to take advantage of every second of his two weeks' leave.

But he didn't want to take her completely by surprise with his plans. Tightening his hands on the steering wheel, he said, "Liv?"

"Hmm?"

Her disinterest and distraction cut him, and made his words harsher than he'd intended. "When we get to your house, I'm coming in."

Her head turned and she stared at him with a mixture of incredulity, annoyance and…need. "Whether I invite you in or not?"

"That's about it." Needing to touch her, he reached out his hand and left his palm open, waiting, and finally her small hand slipped into his. The sign of acceptance gave him hope and turned his voice gruff. "You shouldn't be alone right now. I want you to eat. Rest." He squeezed her fingers. "I want to be with you."

She hesitated. "I'm surprised an important man like yourself could get two weeks off."

Was that sarcasm in her tone, or did she maybe understand just how much red tape he'd gone through to be with her? As second in command of a squadron, he had plenty of responsibilities on his plate. But Liv always came first in his heart.

Whenever possible, he wanted to be with her. "You know the routine. It's typical to send a commander, a doc and a chaplain. I filled in as commander."

Her gaze still on him, she said, "The doctor and chaplain aren't needed."

"You never know."

She ignored that to say, "But you were closer to Dad than I was, so it makes sense for you to want the duty."

Anger surfaced, and Hamilton corrected her with a growl. "I came for *you*, Liv, not Weston." When she remained quiet, he took his eyes off the road to glare at her. "Damn it, do you honestly think I'd let anyone else tell you? Do you think I'd do that to you?"

Her bottom lip trembled, making him regret his temper. Then she shook her head. "No." Her eyes were huge, accepting but sad, her voice no more than a whisper. "You wouldn't do that."

His damn heart constricted. "Liv, baby, I'd stay longer if I could, but you know that's not possible."

He waited for her to ask him about his duties, about the current assignments that would keep him away. She didn't. He knew she resisted asking because she didn't want to worry.

And she didn't want to further their involvement into intimacy.

"Liv…" Her name emerged as a word of warning, a signal of his frustration.

"I understand, Colonel."

"You don't." He squeezed her fingers again before releasing her. "But before I leave here, you will."

"Is that reassurance, or a threat?"

"Just plain fact."

They made the rest of the short, silent drive along narrow, tree-lined country roads, over a two-lane bridge that spanned a swollen creek, past a family-owned grocery store and a textile plant, until finally Liv directed him down the road to her home.

The houses were small, most of them well-kept but older and situated near to the street. Enormous elms and maples spread leafy branches to form a canopy from sidewalk to sidewalk. Birds darted around and squirrels scurried across phone wires. Ham noticed at least three antique shops, and the post office flew a flag from a towering pole. Farms butted up alongside businesses.

Life, laughter and enthusiasm burst from the area.

And Hamilton felt regret, because this was what Liv had always wanted, and he intended to take her away from it.

"That's my house right there."

Hamilton slowed the car to turn into the narrow gravel driveway as she indicated. The drive wrapped around to the left of the home, leading to an aged one-car detached garage, but Hamilton stopped, still facing the front porch.

Damn.

Surprise left him all but speechless.

"It's…" *Exactly the type of home he would have chosen for them to live in.*

The small, two-story structure could use a little work, but otherwise it looked well loved. Homey, like Liv.

A knot of uncertainty settled in Hamilton's gut.

Knowing all of Liv's hopes and dreams, he'd counted on the lure of a house to help sway her to his plans. But even an idiot could see that Liv had set down roots, and knowing how important that was to her, getting her to move wouldn't be easy. He turned off the car and sat there, staring at the steep roof and its display of loose, damaged shingles, the wraparound porch in need of fresh paint and the tall trees begging for a good trimming.

As a full-time teacher, there were things Liv didn't have time for, things she couldn't afford and things she couldn't do on her own. He'd help her during his visit, and enjoy doing so.

But there were other things, like the sparkling clean

multipaned windows. And wind chimes hanging from
the porch. And a fat, floral wreath on the door. He
hadn't expected…what? That she could truly be content without him?

He'd come here with the staunch belief that he'd finally have her for his own. When he set his mind to
something, he never failed.

Now, failure loomed, and damn it, he didn't like
failing.

Liv turned toward him. "Daddy never saw it. I sent
him a letter, telling him I'd moved. But I never heard
back. I think he was on assignment somewhere." Her
shoulders lifted and fell, and she took a deep breath.
"Now he'll never get to see it—and I'm not even sure
he would have wanted to."

Swallowing damn near hurt because it felt like he
had to swallow some of his own arrogance, his own
confidence. "It's nice, Liv. Real nice."

"Then what's the problem? You look annoyed."

Hamilton shook his head. "You'd accuse me of
being an ass if I told you."

Her smile quirked on one side. It was a smile he recognized, and one he'd missed. "Odds are I'll accuse
you of that even if you don't fess up."

"True." He smiled, too, but when he touched the
side of her face, feeling her warmth, her vitality, his
smile faded away. "I've looked at a few houses lately,

too. It's uncanny how much your home resembles the ones I liked best."

Her beautiful blue eyes widened. "You...you looked at houses?"

"Yeah." He curled his hand around her neck, under the silky fall of her hair. "God knows I want you happy, Liv, but I guess I just hadn't expected to see you so settled in."

Her breath shivered, her eyes closed. And abruptly she turned away, jerking the door open and lurching out of the car. Emotional to the core, she slammed her door and hurried up the walkway to her front door.

Hamilton dropped his head back against the seat with a groan. But he didn't linger in disappointment long. If he did, she might lock him out. He caught her on the first step of her porch. Restraining her with a gentle hold on her arm, he chided, "Stop running from me, Liv."

She whipped around to face him, her eyes no longer sad but filled with fury. "Then stop making me sorry. Stop making me want things I can't have."

His heart skipped a beat. Anticipation tightened his muscles. Holding her gaze with his, he ordered, "Tell me what you want."

She punched him in the shoulder—the equivalent of a fly landing. But what she lacked in physical force she made up for with antagonism. "You know damn good and well what I'm talking about."

He caught her upper arms, overcome with a turbulent combination of fury, hope…desperate need. *"Tell me anyway."*

Going on tiptoe, she said, "Yes, sir, Colonel Wulf."

Her sarcasm pricked his frayed mood and his spine stiffened. "Liv…"

"First and foremost, I want a life free from worry."

Leave it to Liv to want the impossible.

Shaking his head, Hamilton said, "Ain't gonna happen, Liv, no matter how you dodge me. Everyone has worries, about money, about family, about job security. It comes with being alive, with being cognizant of our surroundings and our own mortality." Ham caressed her shoulder. "I know how hard it is. Wives worry about their husbands—and husbands worry about their wives. But the military does the best it can to ensure everyone can at least feel safe from the violence that plagues a lot of other countries."

He didn't mean to preach, but for as long as he could remember, he felt unwavering pride in his country and the armed forces that kept it strong and kept it free. In his younger days, he'd thought about joining the army or the marines. Then, when he was fourteen, he joined the Civil Air Patrol and got his first chance to fly an airplane.

Instantly hooked, he changed his focus to the air force.

When he met Weston, he also met Liv. In time, his love of the air force grew, as did his love for Liv. Now at thirty-seven, nothing had changed. He still wanted them both. He'd never stop wanting them.

With bitterness reeking in her tone, Liv said, "I know all about the military, but my perspective is just a little different from yours. I know about wishing my dad could be home on my birthday, or when I was sick, or when I just missed him and didn't want to be alone."

"He should have been there." But a variety of missions had kept Weston away. Since he often couldn't be there in person, he should have at least been there in spirit. A card, a gift…

He'd never made Liv a priority. He'd never attempted to make his time away easier on her. He'd never let his daughter know that he cared, that he thought of her and worried and wanted what was best for her.

Liv made a rude sound of disagreement. "Air Force Intelligence had more important duties for Dad than placating a whiny little girl." Duties that put him at an awful risk. "Some of the places he went to were terrifying, and he stayed there for so long that there were times when I went to bed at night that I wouldn't know if he was dead or alive."

"That was Weston's choice, honey, not a code of military conduct."

An angry laugh preceded angrier words. "When I asked him about it, when I told him I missed him, he accused me of being selfish." Big tears swam in her eyes and she furiously blinked them away. "He made me feel so...so..." When her voice broke, so did Ham's heart. "I felt guilty for wanting him to spend time with me."

"Shh." Ham desperately wanted to ease her pain. But all he could do was reassure her, as many times as it took. "I'm not him, Liv. I'm not Weston, not OSI, and I would never let you worry if I could help it."

Incredulous, her mouth fell open, then snapped shut. "You wouldn't let me worry? That's rich." She swiped at her cheeks, dashing away the tears. "Do you have any idea what it did to me when you went into Kosovo? Or what about Afghanistan? And oh, God, I can't even think about Iraq without shaking and feeling ill and..." Her loss of control only added to her fury. Hamilton knew how much she hated to be seen crying.

"Liv." He tried to tug her into his arms.

She shoved away. Giving him her back, she spoke quieter, softer. "I can't keep going through that, Ham." And with iron resolve, she added, "I *won't* keep going through that."

Hamilton struggled with himself, but he wouldn't give everything away, not yet. Timing was everything.

"Regardless of how we're involved, it sounds to me like you go through it anyway." He settled his hands on her shoulders and pulled her resisting body back into his chest. "We have a lot of talking to do, Liv."

"Right. Talking about what I want?"

"Yes." They could be together, not here, not where she most wanted to be. But if she truly loved him—

When she pulled away, he let her go, but went with her up the porch steps.

"Here it is in a nutshell, Colonel. I want a home and stability, friends I can keep forever and a community that knows me."

Ham started to describe the possibilities, but she held up a hand. "I have that now, right here. And I'm not about to give it up."

Did she even care about what he wanted? Hamilton stood right behind her, crowding close while she unlocked the front door and stepped into the small foyer. Did she realize that the air force was in his blood?

He felt challenged enough to point out the obvious. "What about a husband and kids, Liv? I remember you used to want them, too."

"I still do," she remarked, giving him a quick glance over her shoulder, "and eventually I'll have both."

Jealousy raged through him, setting his blood on fire. *Only if you marry me,* he silently vowed.

Before he returned to base, Liv Amery would accept that he'd always put her first. She'd admit to her feelings, she'd trust him, and then they'd find a happy compromise in the military—one that would leave them both content, with exactly what each of them wanted. On this mission, he wouldn't fail.

But for now, it'd do him well to back off a little, to show her, rather than tell her, how much she could enjoy life with him.

His plan to give her some space lasted about three seconds, right up until Liv said, "Jack must be sleeping. But you'll get to meet him in just a second."

LIV BECAME AWARE of Hamilton standing frozen behind her, and she turned to face him. Having him in her home left her filled with unmeasured emotions. *He liked her house. He'd looked at some just like it.*

She couldn't, wouldn't, buy into that. What did a lieutenant colonel care about setting down roots? Her father had never cut grass, never voted on school levies or concerned himself with holiday decorations. And Hamilton, for all his assurance otherwise, was as military-minded as her father. "What's wrong, Ham?"

Stony-faced, his brown eyes fierce and hot, he stared at her. In a low, harsh whisper, he demanded, "Who the hell is Jack?"

The question reeked of possessiveness, and Liv

couldn't help feeling just a touch of satisfaction. At least she knew she wasn't the only one uncomfortable with their current nonrelationship. "Jack is the new love of my life. But he must be sleeping. I swear, he sleeps like the dead." Smiling, she called out, "Jack?"

Two seconds later the rush of nails on hardwood floors thundered through the hallway. Jack, her nine-month-old shepherd-rottweiler mix, bounded around the corner in unrestrained joy. He jumped up and his sixty-pound body landed against hers with enough force to take her to the ground, except that she'd learned to prepare for Jack's welcomes, and always braced herself.

More than ever before, she appreciated the unre-strained welcome. Liv put her arms around him, buried her face in his scruff and just held on. She felt emotion-ally ravaged and vulnerable when accepting comfort from Ham, but Jack loved her unconditionally. And she loved him the same.

After accepting a few licks of greeting, Liv eased the dog down. He ran in circles, howling, barking, his tail swatting hard. Touched and oddly proud—just as a parent might be—Liv turned to Hamilton to make the introductions. "Ham, meet Jack. Jack, this is Lieu-tenant Colonel Hamilton Wulf."

With a priceless look on his face, Hamilton knelt down and held out his hand. "Glad to meet you, Jack."

Jack, not in the least discriminating, ignored the extended hand and jumped up against Hamilton's shoulders, almost unseating him. To Liv's surprise, Hamilton laughed and rubbed the dog, patting his sides, stroking his back and just plain enjoying himself.

"Good boy." Then he asked Liv, "How long have you had him?"

Bemused, Liv cleared her throat. "I got him the day I moved in."

"Yeah?" Hamilton looked up at her, handsome, happy, the epitome of a strong man with a big heart. "I remember you always wanted a dog."

True. And her dad had always refused.

Ham gave in to Jack's enthusiasm and sat cross-legged on the floor. The dog crawled right into his lap, still wiggling and turning and exuding elation with every pant and bark.

"You're just a big baby, aren't you?" Hamilton smiled at Liv while rubbing the dog's fur. "You've had the house—what? About six months now? I know you didn't have it when I visited last time."

"That was eight months ago." A short lifetime filled with many sleepless, lonely nights. He'd sent letters since then, and photos and cards. But correspondence wasn't the same as a warm body to hold, and never would be. "I've been moved in for six months now."

"And Jack is still this excited to see you whenever you get home?"

For some reason, that made her heart ache, probably because for as long as she could remember, Jack was the only one to give her such a welcome. "He loves me. I love him. Of course he's happy to see me." Then reality kicked in and she added, "Oops. He always has to go out right away, so I wouldn't keep encouraging his enthusiasm."

At a less distressful time, Ham's expression of alarm would have made her laugh. He quickly stood, distancing himself from the dog and any possible accidents.

Liv went into her living room, crossed through the dining room, and opened the sliding door to the backyard. She was a tidy housekeeper, thank goodness, so her home was in order, presentable to guests. Not that Ham could be considered a mere guest…. "Come, Jack. Let's go out."

The dog raced—which seemed to be the only speed he knew—through the rooms and out the door into the small fenced yard. As usual, he took his time sniffing every bush and several patches of grass before finding a spot that suited him.

Amused by the familiar routine, Liv settled against the doorframe and gazed outside. A brisk spring wind buffeted her face, and she noticed that the sun had slipped behind dark clouds, and a distinct chill now filled the air. A storm was creeping in, and that meant her roof would leak. She hated for Hamilton to see the flaws in her house, but there'd be no avoiding it if he stayed with her—and he did seem intent on staying.

Besides, if she busied herself with preparations for the rain, she wouldn't be able to linger on regrets, and she wouldn't find time to indulge foolish hopes.

Hamilton stepped up behind her, too close for comfort, but then, being around him was never comfortable. Exciting, yes. Turbulent and heated and exhilarating, but far from easy. He drew too many strong emotions from her, most of all love.

"He's a beautiful dog, Liv." While speaking, he took her sweater from her, then stripped off his leather aviator jacket. He laid both over a kitchen chair.

"Thank you." Liv glanced back at him. Before they'd left the hotel, he'd changed into jeans and a white T-shirt that hugged his muscular frame. The cotton shirt appeared soft, urging her to rest her cheek against his chest, to wrap her arms around his waist. He looked almost too good to resist. His biceps bulged and his forearms were twice as thick as hers.

And his hands…

Liv remembered those hands touching her in so many different ways, holding her, hugging her, smoothing her hair and on occasion, exciting her.

Hamilton had strong but gentle hands that could guide a B-2 stealth bomber with precision, or make a woman hot with pleasure.

If she ever made love with him, she knew it would be incredible. And unforgettable. Already, her convictions wavered whenever he got too close. Sharing that much intimacy would rip away her last shred of resistance, and she'd find herself in the same position she'd resented most: alone and lonely, worried, and when the country needed Hamilton, forgotten.

Thinking about the future, about the life she'd always dreamed of, left her empty deep inside, especially when what she'd always wanted most was him.

"Liv?" With the edge of a fist, he tipped up her chin so that she had to look at him. A breeze heavy with humidity washed in through the open door, moving over her skin and sending her hair across her face. With a gentleness that felt decidedly intimate, Hamilton tucked the loose curls behind her ear.

She thought he might kiss her again, and she both wanted him to and feared the possibility.

Instead, his big thumb drifted high on her cheekbone. "Why don't you take a quick shower before the storm hits? I'll get something together for dinner and then we can relax and talk."

She'd missed lunch and hunger made her jittery. Or

maybe it was Hamilton's nearness, his touch, the very warm look in his eyes that kept her on edge.

A hot shower would be heaven, and it'd give her an opportunity to collect herself. "Thank you."

Jack ran in past her legs, still excited, but moderately so. He plopped down beside her and stared up with doggie adoration.

Liv rubbed his ears. "Let me feed him first, and then I'll…"

What? The pain surfaced again. Following her mundane routine seemed somehow disrespectful. She'd just lost her father, and the man she'd loved forever loomed in her kitchen, storming her already lacerated defenses. She didn't quite know *what* to do, or think or feel.

"Go on," Hamilton said. "I'll take care of Jack. It'll give us a chance to get better acquainted."

Crossing her arms under her breasts, Liv said, "Do you think that's a good idea?"

He matched her stance, until they had the appearance of two combatants squaring off. "Why wouldn't it be?"

"When you leave again, like you always do, he might…miss you." *Just as I always miss you.*

Hamilton worked his jaw, his annoyance obvious. "I'll be here two weeks, honey. We're bound to become friends." He held out his hand to Jack and the dog immediately abandoned Liv to go to Ham's side. In a tone that should have warned Liv, Hamilton added, "I told you I'd been thinking about a house recently. Well, I've thought about getting a dog, too."

Animosity rose in Liv, to the point that she trembled. Did he think her a fool? What did he hope to accomplish by mocking the things that gave her satisfaction? "A dog in the air force? I doubt that."

Hamilton didn't look at her, choosing instead to peer around her kitchen. He made note of the colorful drawings held on her refrigerator by magnets. Gifts from her students, signs of affection that she cherished.

His eyes narrowed in speculation. "A lot of people living in base housing have pets, Liv. It's not a problem."

Disbelief rose up. She knew pets were allowed; many of her neighbors in housing had dogs and cats. But her father had discouraged any additional commitments, claiming it wasn't fair to the animal when they never stayed in one place for long. "My dad said—"

Hamilton's gaze locked on hers. "Forget whatever Weston said, okay?" Slowly, he straightened to his full height until he towered over her. Oozing machismo, he stepped so close she inhaled his hot male scent with each deep breath. "Entire families live on and off base and yeah, they have pets and the kids ride bicycles and the men love their wives—" He drew a steadying breath. His voice dropped. "And the wives love their husbands."

Defensively, Liv pointed out, "It's difficult to move with an animal."

"So if you had to move—"

"I won't."

"But if you *did,* you wouldn't take Jack with you?"

"He's mine," she snapped. "Of course I'd take him."

Satisfaction gleamed in Ham's eyes. "Of course."

Feeling cornered, she started to turn away, but Hamilton moved with her, crowding closer still, backing her into a corner of the kitchen. "You're meant to be a mother, Liv. Kids love you, and you love them."

She clasped her hands together to keep them from shaking. "I have an entire classroom of kids. I don't need to birth them to—"

"It's not the same thing and you know it." His nose brushed the delicate hair at her temple. "Why won't you admit it? Why hold on to your old fears?"

"Because I know them to be true."

"No." His lips brushed her ear, sending a shiver down her spine. "You have a unique perspective, but it's not the norm. Marrying into the military isn't a heinous thing, no matter what you want to believe."

Her heart heavy, Liv whispered, "For me, it would be."

His breath came out in a sigh. "Liv, honey, there's always room for compromise."

"Dad said—" Liv caught herself. She winced, then cleared her throat. "There are no compromises in the military. There are rules and regulations, a code of ethics. But no compromise."

For several heartbeats, Hamilton just looked at her, but Liv could feel the force of his frustration and her convictions wavered.

Jack whined, breaking the spell.

Drawing a deep breath, Hamilton stepped back. "To show you how good I am at compromising, I'm going to let that topic go—for now. At the moment, you've got enough to think about without me debating the pros and cons of married life in the air force." He tried a smile that lacked sincerity. "Go take your shower. Jack and I'll be fine."

Taking the opportunity to escape, Liv agreed. "His food is in the pantry. Two cups full. And give him fresh water."

Utilizing a touch of irony, Hamilton saluted her.

If only she could have him forever, her life would be perfect. But perfection aside, she had a job she loved, a house that suited her, a dog for companionship and friends galore. No husband and no children of her own, but she had a classroom full of kids that she truly cared about.

Not the same, but close.

It was a good life, full of consistency and security. She was content.

At least she had been before Lieutenant Colonel Hamilton Wulf had once again invaded her life.

CHAPTER THREE

LIV TOOK ONE LOOK in the mirror and cringed. Tears stained her cheeks, her makeup either gone or where it didn't belong. She could only imagine her father's reaction if he saw her like this.

But Hamilton hadn't seemed to mind. No, he'd kissed her silly. Held her. Supported her.

Why did he have to be so wonderful?

And why did she have to love him so much? Through the years, other men had wanted her attention, but nothing had ever come of it. Liv tried, she really did. She gave each man a chance to wiggle into her heart. But no one compared to Ham.

There were times when she doubted any man ever would.

If she could do things over... No, she wouldn't remove Ham from her memories. Without him, her childhood after her mother's death would have been unbearable. Her moments with Ham made up some of the best of her life. Whether he ever became part of her future, he'd left an indelible mark on her past.

Her most immediate future involved the preparation for her father's burial. She should probably call the funeral home today. Liv rubbed her forehead, knowing that once again, Ham deserved her gratitude. He'd come to help, when this couldn't be easy for him, either.

Taking her time in the shower, Liv let the hot water ease her tension and wash away the remnants of her tears. When she heard the loud rumble of thunder, she turned off the shower and climbed out. In addition to funeral arrangements to make, she also needed to leak-proof her house.

Trouble was, her bones felt useless and her head ached and she had a great, crushing void inside her. She and her father might have been estranged, and true, she'd often been lonely for a caring father. But in her heart, she'd always known he was still there, just a distance away. Now he was gone forever, along with the opportunity to reconcile. She should have gone to her father, she could have *made* him care.

Squeezing her eyes shut and holding her breath, she waited for the wrenching pain to subside. It didn't, but at that moment, Ham tapped on the door.

His deep baritone vibrated through the door. "You okay, honey?"

She had to clear her throat before she could answer. "I'm fine."

He paused before murmuring low, "You don't sound fine."

No, she didn't. She shook her head, swallowed hard and lightened her tone. "I'll be right out. How's Jack holding up? Storms scare him."

"He's right beside me, but he's not fretting about *himself,* so don't insult him that way. He's worrying about *you.*"

That made her smile. Yes, Jack would worry. Whenever she got sad, he crowded close and whined and looked as miserable as she felt.

And talking about sad… Her appearance in the mirror left a lot to be desired. With a red nose, puffy eyes, and still damp hair, poor Jack might disown her. No telling what Hamilton might do….

"Liv?"

Resigned, she pulled on a hooded sweatshirt and flannel pants and opened the door.

Hamilton leaned in the doorframe, staring down at her, solemn and observant. His gaze moved over her before settling on her face. "I ordered some food. It should be here soon."

She was grateful because she had way too much on her mind to ponder what to cook. "I have to—"

"Eat." His hand glided over her hair to her shoulder, then fell away. "You know you get shaky when you go without food."

"True. But I don't have time to worry about it."

Satisfaction brought a small smile to his face. "I know. That's why I took it on myself to order some *Kartoffelsuppe* from *Hofbräuhaus*."

At her wide-eyed surprise, he laughed and tugged on a lock of her hair. "I thought that'd get your attention."

Kartoffelsuppe was a delicious potato soup topped with sour cream and cheese. She'd fallen in love with it the first time Hamilton had taken her to eat at Hofbräuhaus. But the closest restaurant was more than an hour away. "How…?"

"I have a buddy who lives down that way. We were in college together at the Citadel and completed the ROTC program the same year."

Which no doubt made them lifelong brothers. "So you just called him up…?"

"That's one of the calls I made while you were showering. He agreed to send the food here in a taxi." And with deeper meaning, Ham added, "The military is one big family, Liv, always willing to help out when they can."

Unwilling to acknowledge the truth of that, Liv studiously ignored his statement. "It's so much trouble for soup."

"Not just soup. We'll be sharing a *Schmankerlplatte,* too."

The mention of smoked pork chops, roasted chicken and fried cabbage had her mouth watering. "Okay, so maybe I can take time to eat after all."

His smile settled into a frown. "It won't be too much for your stomach, will it? Maybe I should have considered something lighter and blander."

"It's perfect." And so thoughtful—so typical of Ham. "Thank you."

Again, he touched her hair, tunneling his fingers in toward her scalp. For the longest time he said nothing, then with a sigh, he whispered, "Liv," while bending down to take her mouth.

She prepared herself for another explosive kiss, but instead, he kept the touch of his mouth sweet and gentle, exploring, comforting. Before she knew it, he had her cuddled up against his chest, his strong arms around her, and Liv wanted to stay there forever.

Keeping her close, he said, "I made another call, too."

His tone alarmed her. She tried to press back, but he wouldn't let her. "What did you do?"

"I contacted the funeral home. I found there's a real advantage to being in a small town. Everyone can make the time, and make things work, when they know you and care about you. And everyone here cares about you very much."

A little stunned, Liv said only, "You contacted Martin...."

"He sends his condolences, and gave us an appointment for tomorrow morning. He confirmed that Weston can be buried Friday afternoon. If we call within the next hour, they can still get the announcement in the obituaries. I'd have done that, too, but I thought you might have something particular you wanted to say."

For some reason, his autocratic behavior struck Liv as humorous. He'd be here two weeks, so that didn't factor into his rush.

"With the funeral behind you," Ham said, as if he'd read her thoughts, "you can put the grief behind you, too. Then you can start planning for the future."

A future that included him? Is that what he wanted?

Is that what she wanted? She just didn't know, but she did know that Hamilton held himself tense, awaiting her reaction. "You expect me to be angry."

"Well...yeah. I know it was presumptuous of me to sort of take over. But I'm only trying to make things easier on you."

She gave him a fierce hug. "And I appreciate it. We can decide on the announcement together, if that's okay with you."

Ham drew back, his surprise evident, and then he kissed her hard. "We'll get through this, Liv." His mouth still touched hers, his breath warm and fast. *"Together."*

That sounded nice. If only it could always be that way. But the very nature of military service guaranteed that Ham wouldn't always be there—no matter what he promised.

Did she dare to settle for less, to compromise her own convictions…?

More thunder rumbled, closer this time, prompting Liv to hurry. After girding herself, she confessed, "Could we work on the announcement now?"

"If that's what you want."

"It's not that I mean to rush, but…my roof needs work."

He shrugged, confused as to what one had to do with the other. "I noticed."

"You did?" He'd been so openly admiring, she hadn't realized. "The roof's not that old, but it did get hit with some storm damage. A few of the shingles are loose or missing. There are replacement shingles in the garage, but I haven't had time to get to it yet."

"I told you I'd been looking at houses lately,

remember? I've seen more than a few that needed some repairs. As long as it's nothing structural, who cares?"

Liv wanted to ask him *why* he'd been looking at houses if he had no intention of leaving the military. An officer's mobile lifestyle made putting down roots impossible. But before she could find the right words, he added, "That storm is coming in fast. I gather the roof leaks?"

Back in the moment, Liv nodded. "In more than a few places. Luckily, there's no furniture upstairs, and not much in the way of carpet. But I don't want to see the hardwood floors get drenched either, so I need to put some buckets down to catch the worst of it."

Ham pressed another kiss to her mouth, then one to her forehead. His casual touches kept her off balance while at the same time providing the human touch she needed in the face of her loss.

"I'll help." He drew her toward the kitchen. "But first…do you have a pen and paper anywhere?"

It took them over twenty minutes to get together the facts that summed up her father's life. Hamilton called the funeral home to give the information, and Martin assured him he'd be able to get it to the paper on time.

Ham made everything so much easier. With him by her side, she couldn't imagine dealing with her father's death alone.

After he hung up the phone, Hamilton asked, "Are the buckets in the garage?"

"Yes. I'll show you." Everywhere they went, Jack followed. The second they stepped outside to the narrow path connecting her house to her detached garage, the dark sky closed in around them, thick with moisture and static with electricity.

Ham lifted the heavy, warped wooden door with an ease that brought home the contrasts in their physiques. Liv had a replacement garage door on her list of things needed for the house, but like the missing shingles, she hadn't gotten around to it yet.

The dark, dank interior of the concrete-block building smelled musty and Jack, the big baby, pressed into her side. "On the shelf over the lawn mower."

Ham grabbed up three buckets. "Are these enough?"

Half-embarrassed, Liv reached past him and took up two more. "Unfortunately, no."

Ham frowned a little in thought, then urged her back out of the garage. The wind caught his words, rushing them past her as he brought the door back down to close it securely. "If the rain holds off, I'll check out the roof. Maybe I can patch it so the leaks don't damage your ceilings too much."

Unlike her father, who had hated repair work, Ham offered with no hesitation. Such a simple thing; shoot, most men were happiest with a tool in hand. But it was more than that now. She couldn't analyze Ham or the way he made her feel, not now with her emotions so close to the surface. Her independent nature rebelled, but more than anything, she wanted to turn herself over to Lieutenant Colonel Hamilton Wulf's tender care.

Dangerous. Very, very dangerous—most especially to her heart.

They reentered the kitchen just as the rain came in a deluge, washing over the windows and filling the house with noise. Jack whined and tucked himself closer to her legs, nearly causing her to stumble.

"I guess I won't be patching the roof today."

Liv wanted to comfort Jack, but leaks were a major priority. She put a hand to the dog's neck and started for the hallway. "Don't worry about it. I was going to hire someone next week, anyway."

"Fibber."

Affronted, Liv jerked around at the base of the stairs—and saw the gleam in Ham's eyes. He always saw right through her.

She scowled at him.

He smiled crookedly and shook his head. "You can't lie to me, Liv."

"All right," she grouched, stomping up the steps to avoid his astute gaze. "It's a fib. Big deal."

"Why tell it in the first place?"

"Because I don't want to be indebted to you." The second the words left her mouth, she felt the change in the air.

"Don't push it, Liv." At the top of the stairs, he caught her elbow and drew her around to face him. Jack looked between the two of them, alert to the new tension in the air, wary. "There's something between us. It's been there for years." His voice lowered, his expression hard. "It will always be there."

"No."

"Yes." To make his point, he backed her up to the wall, looming, imposing. He still held the buckets in his hands, so he used his chest, pressing in on her, keeping her immobile. His mouth grazed her throat, up the side of her neck to her ear, where his tongue gently explored.

"Ham..." Her protest came out a breathless plea.

"Anything you need, Liv," he whispered, "anything you want, you can always get from me."

Her heartbeat drummed and her mouth went dry. Against the hard muscled wall of his broad chest, her nipples drew tight. Her stomach bottomed out when his thigh pressed against her belly....

And he stepped away, not far, but enough that their bodies no longer touched. "This is a tough time, honey, I know that. Your world has just been turned upside down. And for that reason, as much as any other, I won't let you keep your distance."

Speechless, Liv stared up at him. With every fiber of her being, she wanted him. It didn't matter that she knew firsthand how much heartache resulted from loving an officer. She well remembered her mother's tears and prayers when her father was away. It had been awful then. It'd be ten times more so with Ham.

On the ridiculous hope that by not seeing him, she could distance herself a little from his emotional pull, her eyes sank closed. She sucked in several deep breaths to steady herself, to shore up her wavering resolve.

When she opened her eyes again, Hamilton was halfway down the hallway. As he sauntered away, apparently unaware of her inner turmoil, she stared at the long line of his back, the muscled length of his thighs. His too-tight tush.

Emotionally she wanted him.

Physically she craved him.

Mentally, she knew he could break her heart for good. But the yearning swelled inside her, almost unbearable.

Maybe, just maybe if she indulged her needs—*all her needs*—when he left again, it wouldn't be so bad. She'd have memories to comfort her through the lonely years, memories to cling to if, God forbid, he never returned.

And maybe, if the worst happened, it'd also be a balm to Hamilton in his last moments. He'd always been there for her. He was here for her now. He'd always given to her, and now, she had the opportunity to give back.

The excuses sounded lame even to her, but deep down, she'd known what would eventually happen. And right now, she was just plain too weak to fight his appeal.

HAMILTON FELT HER STARE, her interest. Little by little, he was wearing her down. Soon, with any luck and continued patience, she'd admit to her true feelings. She'd tell him she loved him—and then he could tell her about their future, a future of compromise. A future he'd designed just for her.

A future that he felt sure would keep her content.

He glanced into the first small room, devoid of furniture but with a growing stain on the ceiling and a puddle forming on the floor. "I've got this one," he called back to her, aware of her standing immobile right where he'd left her.

Shaken.

Aroused.

When he spoke, his voice was even, his tone level, but his calm was deceptive. The feel of her warmed skin, her stiffened nipples and fast breath had fired him in return. He had an erection that almost hurt, from months of celibacy and years of wanting. His muscles were stiff, his abdomen rigid with restraint.

Walking away hadn't been easy, but damn it, he had his pride, too, along with his own share of fears.

Even as a child, Liv had been bright and observant, so she knew Weston was the closest thing to a father he'd ever had. His own parents hadn't factored heavily into his life, more prone to ignoring him than caring for him. If it hadn't been for Weston and the air force, Hamilton knew he would have been alone in the world, and probably more in trouble than out of it.

He loved Liv, more than anything life could offer, but the air force had become a vital part of him, harnessing the wildness and refining his leadership instincts. It gave him a purpose that meshed with the most intrinsic part of his personality. And flying fed his soul. It was as simple as that.

If Liv refused to see it… He shook his head, unable to abide the idea of leaving himself open to cold rejection. He knew, deep down inside, that she cared for him, too. But with her refusal to admit it, how could he possibly throw his heart at her feet? How did he know if she loved him enough?

He needed her to confide in him. He needed her trust. And then he could trust her in return.

After placing three buckets beneath drips that left

large, dark wet spots on her ceiling, he reentered the hall. Liv was in the room across from him, another small bedroom with no furnishings.

Seeing her on her knees, mopping up a spill before placing the bucket beneath it, brought out all his protective instincts. Ham rubbed the back of his neck, trying to relieve his tension. "Liv?"

She went still, then glanced up. Eyes wide and watchful, and full of some indefinable emotion, she waited.

"It occurs to me," Ham said, "that you only have one bedroom."

Slowly she came to her feet. A look of expectancy replaced the wariness in her expression. "Yes."

Not yet, Ham cautioned himself. If she wanted him physically, it'd help to ease her into an emotional commitment. "I can camp out on the couch."

She said nothing to that.

"But is it all right if I store my stuff in this room? I don't want to leave it cluttering your foyer."

"All right."

So enigmatic. Ham crossed his arms over his chest. "You sleep downstairs?"

"In the only furnished bedroom, yes."

Close to the couch. But close enough?

She said abruptly, "Jack is spooked." Moving past Ham, she led the dog back toward the stairs. "When I sit with him, he feels better."

But rather than follow her, Jack paused at Ham's side and whined.

"Come on, Jack," Liv said, but still the dog hesitated. Ears back, head low, he whined again.

At least the dog was on his side, Ham decided. "I guess he wants us all together."

Liv opened her mouth, but nothing came out.

Hiding his smile, Ham patted the dog. "Let's go, boy. The lady is waiting."

Jack followed Ham downstairs, then back upstairs again as he stored his things in the spare room. "I should change your name to Shadow," Ham teased the dog. But when he saw Liv standing at the window, watching the pouring rain, his heart went out to her. She appeared so dejected, so…alone, that he felt guilty having her dog's attention.

A loud boom of thunder shook the house, and in a flash, Jack was at her side. Liv's nurturing nature took over and she spent several minutes calming the dog. Ham absorbed the picture she made, gentle and sweet and patient. He could easily see her with a classroom full of kids, relating, guiding, teaching.

He could also see her with a baby in her arms—*his* baby. She would be a phenomenal mother. He imagined the four of them, himself and Liv, Jack and a toddler, settled into the cozy little house in Colorado Springs. She'd be happy there, because he'd make it so.

He'd only seen the house in Internet ads, but as soon as he'd been approached with the offer to be a permanent professor at the academy, he started weighing the pros and cons.

God knew he'd miss being squadron commander, but he'd be promoted to colonel. He'd stay on active duty longer, but they'd never have to move away from the Air Force Academy. The two years it'd take for him to get his Ph.D. would be trying, but he'd stay on full pay during that time, and if Liv knew the end result, that they could be the kind of family she wanted...

Once he convinced Liv, they could check out the house together. She'd enjoy buying new furniture, or planting flowers.

The doorbell rang, announcing the arrival of their food and releasing Ham from visions of a perfect future. He answered the door while Liv got out dishes and drinks. She knew him well enough that she automatically poured him milk with his dinner.

Jack curled up beneath the table, determined to stay close but mannered enough not to beg or make a nuisance of himself. The entire setting felt cozy, especially when the lights flickered and then went out. At the dinner hour, it normally wouldn't have been so dark. But the storm-filled sky, thick with black clouds, lent the sense of midnight.

Liv stilled with her glass of iced tea near her mouth.

"Do you have any candles?"

She swallowed her bite of fried cabbage and nodded. "In the drawer by the sink. Matches are there, too."

Ham located a fat scented candle and set it in the middle of the table. Liv watched him as he lit it. Soft illumination danced across her features, and he felt prompted to say, "Does this remind you of that time in California, when an earthquake took out the electricity?"

Memories surfaced, and she gave a small smile. "Daddy was off somewhere, but you came over to stay with me until the worst of it was over."

Ham remembered that he hadn't wanted to leave at all, even hours later when things were again calm. But she was young then, and he'd had too much respect for her and her father to ever overstep himself.

"You denied being scared." He grinned. "You were what? All of eighteen then—a woman, but still so young. Cute as hell. And so damned independent I thought you were going to throw me out in the middle of the quake just to prove you didn't need me there."

Chagrined, she rubbed away her smile. "I didn't want you to know how nervous I was. Daddy didn't like it when I gave in to fears."

Reaching across the table, Ham took her hand. "Everyone gets afraid sometimes."

"Not you."

He half laughed until he realized she was serious. Then he shook his head. "Hell, honey, I live with fear."

Her somber eyes filled with sympathy. "Because of the danger in what you do?"

"No." Being totally honest, he said, "When I'm in a plane, instincts kick in. There isn't time for fear, because I'm too busy reacting. I'm well trained, the air force has seen to that, and there's a level of arrogance in knowing how qualified I am, sort of a feeling of invulnerability."

She watched his face and her fingers tightened on his. "You love it, don't you?"

Not like he loved her. "It's hard to explain, Liv. What I do… It's a calling to protect and serve my country, a calling I've felt compelled to follow since I was a kid. Just as you feel the need to teach. The air force is me, and I'm the air force."

He felt her need to understand. It was there in her gaze, in the way she clutched at his hand, the sadness in her eyes. "I guess I have enough fear for both of us."

Ham wanted her love and loyalty. Perhaps he should start by giving to her first. "So you want to know what does scare me?"

"What?"

He leaned closer. "You."

"Me?" Her laugh was nervous and self-conscious.

"Yeah, you. You're the most important person in the world to me, Liv, don't you know that? You're my family, and my friend. You're the woman I think about when missiles and antiaircraft fire are thick. I fear leaving you alone. I fear never seeing you again."

Her bottom lip began to quiver, and tears again threatened, breaking his heart. She was so precious to him, and she didn't even realize it.

Damned emotion clogged his throat and he paused to swallow. Deliberately lightening the mood to spare her, he said, "Look at all this good food going to waste. Let's finish up because I have something I want to show you."

She accepted the change in topic gratefully. Pulling her hand away, she bit her lip and nodded. But then she paused, raising her face to his. "Ham?"

His heart pounded. "Yeah, baby?"

The seconds ticked by, and the tension grew.

"Thank you," she whispered, "for being here with me."

"Always." He touched her chin, smoothed her jaw.

Her smile wavered, softened. With reluctance, she gave her attention back to her food.

When their plates were almost empty, she asked, "So. What are you going to show me?"

Another touchy subject, but one that couldn't be avoided. "Before we see the funeral director tomorrow,

I wanted to go over your dad's belongings with you. I took some photos off his desk that might be nice to have at the ceremony, some commendations, too. The photos might be nice to display."

"Daddy would like it to be a big event."

Ham nodded. "Regular military funeral. Bugler, twenty-one gun salute…"

"The works."

"Yeah." He watched her face, and felt her pain. "You've been to military funerals before."

"Too many." She gripped her hands together. Knowing that many military members would attend the service, she said, "Whiteman is an eight-hour trip, at least. Will that cause a problem with the funeral set so soon?"

"A tanker will bring the wing commander and most of the men from your father's office. The word will get around, so there'll be others, too. Those he's served with who are at other bases, and local retired military and their families—they'll all want to pay their respects. Military folks are tight, you know that."

"Yes." She drew a breath. "I've never handled a funeral before."

Hating to see her tension, Ham reached for her hands, drew her up from her seat. "Weston died on active duty, Liv, so the air force will provide funeral benefits and arrange the burial ceremony."

She turned her face up to his, brave and beautiful and his—if only she'd realize it.

"Even now, the air force plays such a big role in his life. But this time, I have to admit that I'm grateful."

More thunder rumbled. Rain lashed the windows and lightning flickered. He cupped her cheek. "I told you, we're one big family." And then he kissed her—and he didn't want to stop.

CHAPTER FOUR

LIV KNEW SHE DIDN'T WANT to sleep alone that night. Ham was right—it didn't matter if she admitted how she felt or not because no one would ever replace him in her heart.

She made up her mind as Ham struggled to rein in his hunger. Not once in the many years she'd known him had he ever shirked what he considered his duty. He was honorable to the core, dedicated to caring for others, driven by a deep and patriotic love of his country.

How could she not love him?

His forehead touching hers, he whispered, "I shouldn't keep doing this."

"This?" Liv stroked her hands over the soft cotton T-shirt he wore, across his chest, up and over his shoulders.

"You aren't thinking straight."

She laughed, feeling lighthearted for the first time since he'd arrived at her classroom. "Does that mean my thinking is bent?"

He squeezed her. "It means I picked a bad time to keep coming on to you."

"I think it's the perfect time." And she went on tiptoes to kiss him again.

Ham groaned, taking control of the kiss, pulling her into the hard lines of his body. Their breathing soughed in the quiet night, vying with the violent storm.

He wrenched away. "Liv, wait…."

"Why?"

He caught her face and held her still. Eyes smoldering with heat, he asked, "Do you love me?"

Liv recoiled from the idea of giving away so much. If she told him her deepest feelings, that she'd loved him forever and probably always would, there'd be no going back. She knew Ham, knew how he thought and how determined he could be.

She licked dry lips. "I want to make love with you."

Something in his expression chilled and became distant. He stepped back. Every bit the officer, he held himself straight and proud—yet somehow wounded.

"Let's sit down and I'll sort your dad's things with you."

"Hamilton…"

"You need time," he insisted. "Time to deal with your loss and to come to grips with your feelings. You need sleep. You need…" Unblinking, he stared at her, then shook his head. "You need me to stop pressing you. Come on." He picked up the candle with one hand and reached out for her with the other.

Given that she had electric heat, the house had quickly begun to cool during the power outage. The spring storm had brought with it chilly temperatures and window-rattling wind. She wore a sweatshirt, but Ham wore only a T-shirt. He didn't look the least bit uncomfortable though.

The moment they left the table, Jack scooted out from underneath and chased after them. Candlelight danced and spread out, leaving dark shadows in her small family room. Once Liv sat on the couch, Jack dropped across her feet with a lusty doggy sigh. It wasn't the most comfortable position, but she enjoyed his nearness as much as he enjoyed being near.

Ham fetched a box that he'd left on the table in the foyer. Sitting beside her, he opened it and pulled out the framed photograph on top.

"This stayed on your dad's desk, in the lefthand corner. It was as much a part of his office as his chair and bookshelf."

Liv recognized the five-by-seven photo as one Ham had taken of her years ago. It was only months after her mother had passed away. She'd been baking, determined to make her father a "welcome home" meal that he'd never forget. Long curls, damp with sweat, hung in her face, and her clothes were limp and disheveled.

"That night, Daddy told me I was as good a cook as my mother." She smiled, remembering one of the good times. "He didn't even complain that the meatloaf was dry or the rolls a little burned."

"He bragged to me that you were one hell of a fine cook."

Laughing, Liv said, "I bet that's exactly how he put it, too."

Ham's arm slid around her shoulders, comfortable and familiar. "Word for word."

Liv challenged him with a teasing look. "Is that why you had it framed for him?"

Caught off guard, Ham stalled, and finally rolled one shoulder with a guilty grin. "He liked the photo. Whenever anyone came to his office, they'd look at that picture and ask about it. Weston would hold it with pride and tell everyone that you were his daughter."

Desperately, Liv clutched at this small proof of affection. "Did he talk about me much?"

"Truthfully? He wanted me to court you."

A surprised laugh bubbled out. "*Court* me?"

"He considered me worthy of his one and only daughter." Ham pulled out another photo. "This one sat on his bookshelf. He'd always point out what a handsome couple we made, and believe me, your dad didn't have an ounce of subtlety."

Skeptical, Liv accepted the smaller, three-by-five shot of her with Hamilton at a military function. She smiled at the camera, but Hamilton stood in profile, his absorbed gaze on Liv's face. Seeing the picture, and his expression, actually made her blush. "I don't recognize this one."

"I have no idea who took it. But it's been in your dad's office for years."

"What did you tell him when he...well, talked about us?"

Stretching out his long legs, Hamilton settled back in the couch and took the picture from her, examining it in minute detail. "I told him the truth. That he'd soured you on the military."

Her mouth fell open. "You didn't."

"Not in so many words. But I explained that you weren't interested in an officer. I told him you wanted a regular nine-to-five kind of husband. One who came home every night instead of being gone months, sometimes years, at a time."

Fascinated, Liv prompted, "And he said…?"

"That you were just like your mother." He tore his attention from the photo and settled it on her instead. "He said that a lot, honey. Always with affection, never complaining. He loved her, just as he loved you."

That left Liv speechless.

Ham smiled. "And then he'd tell me I should damn well work harder at convincing you."

Before Liv could dwell on that too long, Hamilton drew out a variety of medals. "I figured you'd want these."

"They're all his?"

"All the ones I could locate before flying here. He might have more tucked away in his quarters. I'm sure he has more ribbons." Ham pulled out five Meritorious Service Medals, four Air Force Commendation Medals and a Bronze Star.

He gave her a long look. "In all my years in the air force, I've only known two Bronze Star recipients."

New emotions swelled inside her, crowding out the resentment. In a reverent whisper, she quoted, "Given for acts of heroism and meritorious achievement."

Holding up the medal, Ham said, "Weston was definitely a hero." He laid the small badge in Liv's hands, curled her fingers around it. He, too, dropped his tone to one of solemn respect. "Your dad did some pretty impressive things during wartime. He wasn't always there when you and your mother needed him, but a lot of soldiers relied on him and he never let them down."

Liv held the medal to her heart, overwhelmed, touched, forgiving.

Watching her, Ham flattened his mouth. "Plenty of men are willing to risk their necks to save the people they love. But Weston did it for people he didn't even know."

Liv absorbed the enormity of her father's contribution, how important he'd been to so many.

And Hamilton was no different.

He didn't think twice about the risks he took. Instead, he embraced them gladly, determined to serve the country he loved, the people who relied on him, without ever seeing himself as a hero.

Her heart expanded, and with it, her love. She put the medal back in the box and laid a hand on Hamilton's forearm. "I should have understood."

"Maybe," Ham said, "but Weston should have included you as one of his priorities. He didn't make it easy for others to get close to him. He was always reserved, very self-contained. Some men are that way, whether they're career military or not. Some women, too, I imagine."

Liv stared at him with new eyes. He was so selfless, so caring of others, that he didn't realize her new understanding extended to him. "You're right, of course."

"You knew my parents, Liv. They weren't very caring, but neither were they military. I keep telling you, one doesn't have anything to do with the other."

"No, it doesn't."

Her smiling agreement finally registered, and his brows pulled down with suspicion. "What did you say?"

Liv laughed, a little giddy, a lot in love, more at peace than she'd been in years. "I'm sorry. Now I've confused you, haven't I?"

His mouth opened, but then slowly closed. He surveyed her warily. "I would never deliberately hurt you, Liv. You have to believe that."

"I know."

Neck stiff, shoulders rigid and eyes direct, he added, "But I can't leave the air force."

Accepting, Liv nodded. "I know that, too." She lifted the box of medals and photos from his lap and set them on the table.

"Liv…"

Rather than hear whatever he planned to say, she rose to her knees, leaned into him and cupped his face—and kissed him silly. It wasn't often that she took the initiative, but for once, she wanted to put what Ham wanted, what he needed, first.

She'd been incredibly selfish, but no more.

At the prodding of her small tongue, he groaned and

gave in. Gathering her across his lap, he returned her kiss with enthusiastic heat. Until she pulled his T-shirt out of his jeans.

Breathing hard, he rasped, "Hold up, Liv."

"No." Slipping both hands beneath the material, she stroked his hot, hard flesh, the crisp hair on his broad chest, over his impressive pecs. He felt *so* good, so much a man. *Her man.* Being with him felt right. It always had. "Hamilton? What time is it?"

He went blank, a little dazed, then he glanced at his watch. After clearing his throat, he growled, "Nineteen hundred…"

Laughing, Liv caught his wrist and turned it so she could see the dial. "A little after seven o'clock. Hmm." Slanting him a coy look, she said, "Close enough to bedtime."

And truthfully, he had to be tired. God only knew how much running he'd done since the report of her father's death. Knowing Hamilton, he'd probably moved heaven and hell to arrange things to his satisfaction. The emotional toll was tough enough, but he had to be physically exhausted, too.

He held himself very still. "Bedtime?"

"Yes." Working up her nerve, Liv spoke straight from her heart. "Make love to me, Hamilton."

He squeezed his eyes shut—then caught her hands and held her still.

."Ham?"

"You don't know what you're doing to me, do you?"

"I know what I *want* to do to you."

He drew a breath, impaled her with his gaze. "I need everything, Liv."

Her heart beat so hard, it made her tremble. "Everything…meaning?" *Did he want to marry her?*

"Tell me you love me."

Emotions warred against one another, hope and tenderness, disappointment and desire. She wanted to tell him, she really did, but the words strangled in her throat.

"Admit it, Liv." And then, almost desperate he implored, *"Tell me."*

What did it matter? He obviously already knew. In the long run, it wouldn't change anything. As he'd said, he couldn't leave the air force, and she couldn't survive as a military wife, alone and lonely, always filled with worry.

But in the short run…?

They could make memories hot enough to carry them through the endless winter nights to come. At the moment, that's what she wanted most. Tomorrow, next week, next year—every long night that she spent without him—could be dealt with later.

Meeting his fierce gaze, Liv nodded. "Yes. I love you, Lieutenant Colonel Hamilton Wulf."

The change in him was astounding. One moment she was on his lap, and in the next, he'd blown out the candle and stood.

Holding her in his arms as if she weighed nothing at all, he asked, "What about Jack?"

The dog stared up at them anxiously.

Even now, with lust bright in his eyes, Ham had the consideration to think of her pet. Could there be a more big-hearted, strong, compassionate man anywhere?

Liv wanted to melt. She wanted to change the future so she could have him forever. She wanted him over her, inside her, loving her as much as she loved him.

"Jack often sleeps under my bed when it storms. Of course, I've never had a man sleeping with me while he was under there, but—"

Hamilton squeezed her for that admission, his expression wild with possessiveness. "C'mon Jack," he ordered in a voice rich with haste. "Time for bed."

The dog bounded up and loped after them as Ham strode for her bedroom. She'd had several years of buildup to this moment, which left her already primed and anxious and prepared.

Teasing Ham's neck with her fingertips, she asked, "What if he won't settle down with us doing…you know?"

Ham watched her with deep concentration while his

long strides drew them nearer and nearer to her bed. "He might as well get used to me now." And then, after a firm kiss, "I'm not going anywhere."

Liv started to object, to explain that the dog didn't need to get used to him because he'd be heading back to the air force in two weeks—back to his duty, and out of her life.

But Ham took her mouth again, and didn't stop kissing her until he stood beside her bed. He laid her flat on her back, took precious seconds to rid himself of his boots and socks, and then his weight pressed her down and his hand slid inside her sweatshirt, boldly cupping a breast.

Liv forgot whatever she'd wanted to say.

PRESSED BY URGENCY, by the endless fantasy and unrelenting desire to make her his own, Ham covered her breast…and groaned. *God, she felt good.* His thumb found her nipple, already peaked, achingly tight, and he gently stroked, aware of the ripple of pleasure that ran through her. He felt almost violent in his need.

He deepened his kiss, savoring the taste of her on his mouth, the moist silky heat of her curious tongue. His hips pressed down and in and she gave a high, female moan of pleasure.

"Open your legs."

She did, anxiously spreading them wide so that his

hips settled between and he could feel her heat cradling him. She lifted up, increasing the pressure, moving, stroking him.

"God almighty, it's too much." Eyes closed, he strained his upper body away from her, wedging his lower body closer.

"Ham," she said on a near wail, her fingers knotted in the coverlet, her head tipping back.

He loved seeing her like this. Hot for him. Nearly out of control. Rocking his hips in a rhythm that complemented her own, he watched her face and reveled in the heightened signs of desire and pleasure. Heat flushed her cheeks, and another moan broke past her parted lips.

He wanted to strip them both naked right now. But if he did, if he saw her bare and open to him, accepting him, he'd be inside her in seconds. She wasn't ready, no matter how far gone she looked. Their first time deserved special care.

Liv deserved special care.

Coming back down over her, he nibbled on her ear, kissed his way to where her neck met her shoulder. Sucking the delicate skin of her throat in against his teeth, he marked her with satisfaction, primal in his need to lay claim.

Her spicy scent—not perfume, but Liv, all woman and now all his—filled his head.

The storm outside abated, softening to a steady rain.

Jack did indeed crawl beneath the bed and apparently, he slept, because he made no objection to Ham's presence.

Shifting his hold, Ham slid one arm beneath her, raising her back. With his other hand, he shoved up her sweatshirt. "I want to kiss you everywhere, Liv."

She held herself still, watching him, her breath suspended.

In the dim room, her pale breasts gleamed opalescent, shimmering with her nervousness and excitement. Seeing her taut nipples made his erection ache and throb. "I'll start here," he rasped, and closed his mouth around one small nipple.

The second his tongue touched her, Liv arched up, groaning raggedly. Ham sucked, not hard, but languid and easy, curling his tongue around her, suckling her with gentle deliberation.

Frustrated, she tried to pull off her sweatshirt while panting and gasping. Ham jerked it up and over her head and tossed it to the foot of the bed.

When he started to return to her, she fended him off with both hands flattened to his chest. "Now you."

Blood thundered through his veins. His testicles were tight, his cock full and heavy. She wanted him. Finally. He nearly ripped his T-shirt getting it off. And still she held him back, her hands now moving over him, exploring him.

"I've dreamed of this," she murmured, her eyes a little dazed, her voice thick with need. "You have the most perfect body, and there've been so many nights when I've imagined getting to touch you, to kiss you."

She came up on one elbow, and put her soft, damp mouth to his shoulder. Her tongue came out, tasting his flesh. Her open mouth administered a soft, wet love bite.

"You taste—" her nose brushed up the side of his throat to his ear "—and smell even better than I'd ever imagined. All hot. All man." She licked his ear, along his jaw to his mouth. "Delicious."

The sexual connotation of that one word stole his breath. Hamilton prided himself on his control, on his iron resolve to do everything the very best that he could. He *would* make this good for Liv. But in order to ensure that, he had to take charge before she obliterated his already fractured patience.

The flannel pants she wore had a loose elastic waistband that made it easy for his hand to get underneath, onto her silken belly. "Let me enjoy you, honey."

Her eyes darkened. Stroking her skin, he teased his way lower and lower, and with a deep breath, she settled back onto the mattress.

"Are you wet yet, Liv?"

Her breathing stilled. Eyes wide with shock locked

on his. Ham knew she'd be blushing, but he couldn't see it in the dim interior of the room.

"I—"

"Let me see." Touching her, sliding one long finger over her pubic curls, and farther down between her swollen lips, Ham whispered, "Yeah. You are."

As his finger moved, stroking, sliding, her eyelids grew heavy and she bit her bottom lip. Breathing fast and hard, she watched him, their gazes a connection beyond the physical. Ham felt it deep into his soul, just as he'd always known he would. He was the man who'd have Liv. Period.

"How's this feel, honey?" He pressed in, not far, just deep enough that her innermost muscles clamped around him.

"Ham…" she said raggedly, trying to lift her hips to take more of him, but he held back.

"Getting wetter, Liv. And hotter." He kissed her shoulder, her chest, and drew her other nipple into his mouth. Forcing himself to remain slow and steady, he suckled her, fingered her, licked and stroked, alternating his attention from her breasts to the slick, swollen flesh between her thighs, gradually gaining urgency, driving her closer to the edge.

When she cried out in dissatisfaction, Ham pulled out his finger, only to stroke two back in, fast and deep.

Her nails bit into his shoulders. Her head tipped back, her neck straining, her hips lifting.

"That's it," he encouraged against her wet nipple, feeling the start of her contractions, and so damn excited he wanted to shout. He found her clitoris with his thumb and carefully manipulated her, pressing, fondling in a steady rhythm, pushing her—and with a deep, raw groan her entire body bowed, damp in sweat and fragrant with lust, she came.

Ham wanted to savor the moment, to hold her and ease her, but he couldn't. Violent need shook his body. He'd wanted her too long—all his life it seemed. Waiting now would be impossible.

He knotted a hand in her hair, turning her toward him. Her mouth opened under the force of his. When he sank his tongue in, she sucked on it.

He needed out of his jeans—*now.*

Thrusting himself away, he went onto his back and raised his hips. Jerking open the snap of his jeans, easing the zipper down the bulge of his hardened cock, he freed himself.

Sated and limp beside him, Liv whispered, "Finally."

Damn it, she didn't help with her verbal prodding. It felt like he'd explode if he didn't get inside her soon. He had enough sense left to grab a condom out of his jeans pocket before tossing the pants, with his underwear, aside.

While he tried to ready himself, she kept touching him, and she said, "I wish the electricity hadn't gone out."

Hands shaking, Hamilton rolled on the rubber and turned to her. "Me, too. I want to see you."

"And I want to see you."

"We've got forever, baby. A million more nights, just like this one. I promise." He settled over her soft, warm body. She automatically adjusted her legs to allow the closeness, and put her arms around him.

"I love you, Ham." Her hips undulated under his, the slow, wanton movements firing his blood more, heating his flesh and causing all his muscles to clench.

He reached between their bodies, used his fingertips to spread her delicate vulva. She was very wet now, slick with her own orgasm, still tender and sensitive and he felt ready to shatter when he wedged the head of his cock against her.

Restraining himself, he rasped, "Tell me again."

"I love you."

A fine trembling invaded his limbs, making it impossible to ease into her. Through his teeth, he said, "Again."

She hugged him fiercely. "I love you, Lieutenant Colonel Hamilton Wulf—"

Her words ended on a harsh gasp as he plunged into her, burying himself despite the tightness of her body, clamping his arms around her to keep her immobile.

He could feel her stretching to accommodate him, felt her small shivers as she tried to adjust.

He buried his face in her neck. Raw, unfamiliar emotions rose to the surface, bombarding him. He felt vulnerable. And he felt powerful.

In a voice unrecognizable to his own ears, he rasped, "You're mine, Liv."

"Yes." Her small hands moved over his back, both soothing and inciting him.

He drew back, pushed in again, deeper this time. *"Mine."*

Her warm tears tracked his shoulder; a small kiss seared his skin. She drew a shuddering breath. "I love you, Ham."

It was enough. It was too much. He began thrusting fast and hard, unmindful of anything but Liv and the fact that she'd finally accepted him, all of him. Their heavy breathing filled the room as they strained together. Her arms hugged him. Her legs hugged him. She gasped, writhed, clasped around him—and Ham felt himself ready to come.

Wanting to see her, he stiffened his arms to rise above her. Her face twisted with her pleasure. Her cries were sharp and throaty and *real.*

Looking at her, loving her, Ham let himself go. The turbulent release washed through him, wave after wave, each one stronger, more acute than the other. He groaned, kept himself pressed deep within her until finally, utterly drained, he lowered himself into her arms.

MINUTES WENT BY. His heartbeat slowed. His breathing evened out and his overheated skin began to cool. Ham decided that Liv was far too silent, almost withdrawn.

He didn't like it, but he felt so replete, so happy with her, so damned in love, he couldn't work up the energy for more than a smile. Rubbing his nose against her ear, he whispered, "Hey. What's wrong?"

With a deep sigh, she ran her fingers over his military haircut. "Nothing."

Why did women always say *nothing* when they meant *something?* "Tell me, Liv."

Her rounded shoulder lifted, nudged against him. She sighed again. "I just wish this moment could last forever."

Because he still had to do two years of study for his Ph.D., two years that'd keep him on active duty, which would involve compromise on her end, he didn't get into his plans yet.

Hoping for some middle ground that wouldn't spoil the moment or his mellow mood, he promised, "I'll make you happy, baby." He rose up to see her face. Her hair was wild, and he smoothed it, tucked it behind her ears. A slight whisker burn marred her smooth cheek, and he touched it with his thumb. Her breath caught.

Smiling into her smoldering eyes, aware of her nipples stiffening again, Ham continued to touch her softly and asked, "For now, can you just trust in that?"

"But—"

He put a finger to her mouth. "No buts, Liv. You love me. I love you. I'm not about to ruin that by doing anything that'll make you unhappy."

Still she hesitated, and Ham gave a partial admission. "I've made some plans, changed some things. It'll be all right, Liv. You have my word."

She searched his face, her eyes suddenly filled with hope. "I do trust you, Ham."

Thank God. She didn't yet know what his plans would be, but he knew she couldn't possibly get the wrong idea. He'd been too clear on his position in the air force. He wouldn't give it up. Her acceptance showed her willingness to compromise—just as he'd hoped.

He put a firm kiss on her mouth and left the bed to stand on shaky legs.

Their eyes had adjusted to the darkness, and she visually devoured his naked body with interest. It was a good thing, to please the woman you loved, the woman who would be your partner for life.

Staring at his lap, she asked, "Just where are you going?"

Stifling his grin with an effort, Ham explained, "I have a box of rubbers in my bag upstairs."

"A whole box, huh?" Looking sassy and sweet, Liv raised herself onto one elbow. "You must have been feeling pretty hopeful when you came here."

"Honey, I've lived off hope since you turned twenty-one." He put a hand on her bare hip, trailed his fingers down to her knee, relishing her warmth, the silkiness of her bare skin. "Now I have you right where I want you, and I don't intend to let you sleep anytime soon."

Since she didn't object to that plan, Ham left to get the protection. And when he returned, she smiled and opened her arms to him. Finally, he had what he wanted.

He had it all.

CHAPTER FIVE

SOMETHING WOKE LIV, some strange pounding that barely penetrated her subconscious. Lethargy pulled at her, the results of a long, wonderful, sleepless night.

The pounding continued, and finally she stirred. Just as she'd done throughout the long humid night, she automatically smiled. Time and time again, Ham had curled her close, petting her, kissing her. They'd made love three times and each time had been as exciting as the first. After that third time, her mighty warrior had slept. Liv hadn't. She didn't want to waste a single second of their time together, so she'd watched him, listened to his breathing, and loved him more with each passing second.

The excess of pleasure threatened to burst her heart. She felt physically languorous and mentally relaxed, peaceful in a way that had eluded her until Lieutenant Colonel Hamilton Wulf had shown her how special lovemaking could be with the man of her heart.

And he had said he was changing things. *For her.*

Without opening her eyes, smiling in satisfaction, Liv stretched out an arm to the side of the bed he'd occupied.

Her hand encountered only cool rumpled sheets.

She bolted upright and surveyed the room. No sign of his clothes, but the drapes were open. The gray sky, still dark with storm clouds, gave no indication of the time, but it had stopped raining.

The humming of the house let her know the electricity was back on. Her battery-operated bedside clock told her she'd slept much later than usual. Her class would be on their first recess by now!

When Liv slid her naked legs out of the bed, she became aware of the chill in the air, and of all the places that now suffered a tantalizing ache. Another smile, sappier than the first, curled her mouth.

And then she heard the rapping of a hammer, the very sound that had awakened her.

Taking the sheet off the bed and going to her window, she looked out at the backyard. Jack ran along the side of the house, barking and looking up…at the roof.

It took Liv all of two minutes to pull on another pair of flannel pants and a sweatshirt. The loose, comfortable clothes were her favorite "at home" wear. She gave a brief glance in the mirror at her hair, finger-combed it back and secured it with a cloth-coated rubber band, then headed for the kitchen.

The scent of fresh coffee made her pause to pour a cup. After two fortifying sips, she opened the kitchen door and stepped outside. The soggy ground froze her feet. Jack spotted her right off and came tearing toward her. Since his feet were muddy, she fended him off, and made do with a lot of petting on his scruff.

Going to the edge of the house, she looked up and found Ham on the roof, replacing her lost shingles. The chilly morning air cut through her sweatshirt, but Ham wore only a black T-shirt, jeans and boots. It was gloomy enough that he didn't need his sunglasses.

His squatting position showed off thick thigh muscles and the obvious strength in his back and upper arms.

She had experienced that strength firsthand.

With a rush of yearning, she called up, "Good morning."

He paused with his hammer raised, a few nails in his teeth. The moment he spied her, his gaze warmed and grew intimate. After removing the nails and scooting to the edge of the roof, he said, "Good morning yourself, sleepyhead."

Everything had changed, Liv realized. The way he smiled at her, the way he held himself in her presence. It was as if mammoth barriers had been ripped away. Even with him on the roof and her on the ground, a new closeness existed between them.

Her heart started thudding in fast, hard beats. He'd said she would be happy with him, and since he knew her feelings on the military, that could only mean one thing.

Breathless, filled with hopefulness and expectation, she stared up at him.

"Liv? Yoo-hoo. Did you go into a trance?"

His smile touched her heart, encouraging her own smile. Because the previous night had been so wonderful, she didn't question the change, just accepted it as her dream coming true.

"You should have awakened me earlier."

"I thought about it. You looked so damned enticing, all warm and sleepy and…naked." He cocked one eyebrow, his expression wolfish. "Then the electricity came back on and I heard the weather report. More violent storms predicted." He indicated the pile of shingles with a tilt of his head. "As tempting as you are, I figured you'd appreciate a dry house."

Normally, she'd have been resistant to his assistance, but that, too, had changed. His promise to her had radically altered her outlook on life, because life now included Hamilton.

She smiled brightly, full of love. Sated with security. Content with their future.

Very softly, she said, "Thank you." Her gratitude visibly warmed him, made him appear more relaxed and more confident than ever. "How about I make some breakfast?"

"Perfect. I'm starved. I only need another twenty minutes to finish."

"Pancakes?"

"You know me too well."

Yes, she did. Better than she knew anyone else, especially after last night. She took great satisfaction in that fact. "You be careful up there. Everything is wet and slick."

Ham saluted her and returned to work.

Humming to herself, Liv went back inside and, while finishing her coffee and thinking pleasant thoughts, began breakfast preparations. Jack tired of watching the activity on the house and scratched at the door a few minutes later. Liv grabbed up an old towel to dry his feet before letting him in. When she started to fill his dish, she noted that Ham had already taken care of it.

So thoughtful.

He'd be great with kids, too, she mused. His attentiveness extended beyond his military duties; that was clear to her now. The community would love him as much as she did.

A few minutes later when Ham came in, she was at the table, setting out syrup and butter. Ham put his arms around her from behind and kissed the nape of her neck.

"I could just have you for breakfast," he murmured.

Oh, if only there were time. "I'm sure I'd love it," Liv admitted, leaning into him and sighing. Sadness intruded, and she pointed out, "But we need to eat, and I still need to shower and put on my makeup before I face the public."

Saying, "You don't need makeup," Hamilton effectively swept away her melancholy.

Liv rolled her eyes. "Don't overdo it, okay? There are mirrors in the house, and I've already seen one." She turned to kiss his chin.

His hand moved down her back to her bottom. Fingers spread, breath warm in her ear, Ham said, "I think you're beautiful."

The compliment, coupled with his touch, nearly took her knees out. "Well, thank you. But we still don't have much time, and I'm still going to put on my makeup."

Giving her backside a pat, he said, "Tonight, then."

Yes, tonight. And then she'd ask him about his intentions, when his obligation to the military ended and when they could marry. But that could wait until they finished the burial arrangements.

While Ham washed up at the sink, she said, "I want to swing by the school to pick up my car while we're out."

"Sure." He knelt down to pet Jack, who lifted his furry head with delight. "I was thinking—will Jack be okay here by himself while we're gone? If that storm hits again, is he going to be scared?"

"We're in Ohio. It storms here all the time, remember? I just need to put him in the bathroom with a radio playing. It helps drown out the thunder and with no windows in there, he can't see the lightning. He'll probably sleep until we get home."

Ham continued to stroke the dog, who wallowed in the attention. "I had this awful image of him hiding under the bed, trembling in fear." Ham shook his head. "Not a pretty picture."

He never failed to please her with his consideration. "You're something else, you know that?"

His gaze met hers, warm with insinuation. "As long as I'm yours, that's all I care about."

The words were almost too wonderful to believe. "You're mine all right," she said with mock warning. "And I'm never letting you go, so don't get any ideas."

He'd been teasing, but now he grew solemn, pushing back to his feet, standing close to her. "That's something we need to talk about, isn't it? The future, how we're going to work this all out."

That sounded too serious by half. Liv bit her bottom lip, and nodded. "Yes."

He searched her face, glanced at his watch and scowled. "I suppose now isn't the time." He wrapped his hands around her upper arms, caressing. "How are you holding up? I know today isn't going to be easy."

Liv touched his face. "Actually, I'm fine. Sad, of course. And a little hollow with the knowledge that I'll never see Dad again, that opportunities are lost. But thanks to you, I have good memories now, too, memories that had been buried beneath resentment. That was wrong of me, but from what you told me, Dad didn't have any grudges."

"No. Weston loved you a lot, he just wasn't a very demonstrative man."

"Unlike you, Howler?"

His crooked grin looked boyish and reeked of charm. "You've never called me that."

"But everyone else does." She turned to seat herself at the table, and Hamilton did the same. "I listened last night, you know."

Swallowing a mouthful of pancakes, Hamilton cocked an eyebrow.

"I kept thinking you'd…well, howl."

He almost choked on his food, then burst out laughing. "You're kidding, right?"

"Nope. What else would Howler mean? Howling during sex. Howling out your pleasure. I naturally assumed it was something like that."

"Well, smart-ass, for your information, I never howl."

"Not during sex, anyway." She carefully forked a bite of buttery pancake. "It's more like a growl. Or a groan."

He fought a grin. "What I do is roar. And only when I'm really pissed. But guys being guys, and pilots being bigger jackasses than most, they took a perfectly acceptable roar and starting labeling it a howl." He shrugged. "It stuck."

Liv let out an exasperated breath. "Well. I'm almost disappointed." Her lips twitched. "After all, it's something you and Jack could have had in common."

Displaying an enormous appetite, Hamilton shoveled down the last of his pancakes, then stood. "You wanna hear me howl, I can howl." He pulled out her chair and lifted her to her feet. "Let's shower together. If we hurry, we'll have enough time before we have to leave. Plenty of time for—"

"Howling?"

He lifted her into his arms. "Exactly."

IT TOOK HOURS BEFORE all the arrangements were complete. Watching Liv, how she dealt with it all while keeping her emotions in check, putting up a brave, proud front, made Hamilton want to bust with pride. He interjected where necessary, supplying information about the air force's contribution to the service, and by the time they left the funeral home, they had everything in order.

His arm around Liv's shoulders, his thoughts focused on her and her turmoil, Ham walked her outside to the rental car. As predicted, the storm loomed overhead again. Low-hanging clouds, bloated with rain, scuttled across the sky. Hamilton and Liv got into the car just as the sky opened up and the storm attacked with a vengeance, this time supplying large hail and tree-bending winds. Against the roof of the car, the hail sounded like gunshot. Debris rolled over the ground and already the streets were awash with runoff.

Wide-eyed, Liv snapped on her seat belt. "Talk about Mother Nature's fury."

Ham stared out the windshield. He didn't like the looks of this storm. Something about it, something beyond the obvious, put him on edge. Making up his mind, he said, "I'd wait for it to let up, but I hate the thought of Jack home alone." He started the car and eased out of the lot into the street. "The sooner we get home, the better."

Watching the storm through the passenger-door window, she said, "I'm sure Jack will appreciate your concern." Then she glanced at him and added, "Don't forget, I want to get my car."

Incredulous, Ham tightened his hold on the wheel. "In this downpour?" He gave a grunt of disbelief. "No, I don't think so, babe. Those hailstones are the size of marbles."

Slowly, her head turned toward him. "I'm not one of your men, Lieutenant Colonel. You don't dictate to me."

Uh-oh. Maybe he'd worded that wrong. Ham worked his jaw and tried for an olive branch. "We can go back later and get it."

"It might rain all day, Hamilton, so don't go caveman on me. I want to go now while we're already out, and with the school day over, I don't have to worry about running into anyone. Not that I don't appreciate their concern, but… I'd rather not face a lot of sympathy and condolences right now." Her hands laced together in her lap. "Not after just making the arrangements. I need some time."

"Liv…"

"I've driven in rainstorms before, and I'll drive in them again. Since I'm usually alone, I don't have much choice."

She sounded entirely reasonable—but it grated on

him that she'd ever been alone, without backup or support. He was with her now, and if he had his way, she would spend very little time alone in the future. "I'll have Doc bring it over tonight."

"I don't want to impose on her."

"She's a friend. She won't mind."

"*I mind.*" When Hamilton didn't reply, she rolled her eyes. "For heaven's sake, rain hasn't gotten the best of me yet. Besides, I think we've driven out of the worst of it."

Hamilton didn't want to, but he had to agree. The sky had suddenly calmed, the rain fading to a mere drizzle.

"All right. But my agreement is under duress."

Grinning, she quipped, "Duly noted."

Because it was on the way, they reached the school in a matter of minutes. By the time Ham pulled into the mostly deserted school lot, the rain had completely stopped.

"Look at that," Liv said, pointing out the sight of the clear, sunlit skies moving in behind the storm. "You were worried about nothing."

Hamilton narrowed his eyes at the calm, greenish sky. He couldn't recall ever seeing anything like it.

Since Liv got out of the rental car, he did the same. She circled the hood to reach him and twined her arms around him in a bear hug.

Pleased with her open show of affection, Ham returned her embrace. "I like this new side of you. Kissing me and hugging me. I can get used to it."

"You better." She hugged him again before stepping away. "I intend to do it a lot over the next fifty years or so."

With that awesome promise, Hamilton forgot all about the oddly colored sky and walked with her to her car. "You know, this'll sound corny, and don't take it wrong, but I was hoping that sex would put us on better terms. I wanted to wait until you admitted that you cared about me. I figured sex would help seal the bond between us." A bond she had denied until recently.

Liv faced him with chagrin. "That's why you held out so long? Why you wouldn't sleep with me before? You needed me to commit verbally first?"

He trailed his fingertips over her jaw and chin. "Hey, I'm only human."

Her eyes widened. "You're admitting it? And here I thought you considered yourself superhuman," she teased.

"Yeah, well, if I had realized that sex would have such a profound effect on you," he said with a grin, "you can bet I would have gotten you naked years ago."

Feigning disdain, Liv lifted her chin. "I'll have you know it wasn't your skill in bed that did the trick." She unlocked and opened her car door, then faced Ham.

She was so damn cute, Ham thought. "It wasn't, huh?"

"No, it wasn't." She smiled up at him. "It was your promise to leave the military."

Those words struck Ham with the force of a missile blast. He went rigid. "I'm not leaving the air force, Liv. I've been clear on that."

The color leeched from her face. "But you told me—"

He knew exactly what he'd told her, and apparently she hadn't been listening. "I said I'd make you happy. And I will." He caught her arms, feeling the tension vibrating from her. *"With compromise."*

An awful expression stole over her features—disappointment, betrayal, pain. In a barely audible rasp, she said, "I told you I couldn't."

Damn it, he didn't want to have this conversation in an elementary school parking lot. He didn't want to have it at all. He'd thought, hoped, that they were already beyond it, well on their way to those fifty years she'd mentioned earlier. "We can make this work, Liv. Just hear me out."

She swung away, more wounded than she'd been over her father's death. Her stance, her expression, her tone, all reeked of accusation. "You told me to trust you. You said you loved me."

Jaw tight, eyes burning, Ham leaned his face down

to hers and forced out the words he'd thought would save him. "You told me the same."

Liv flinched away from him, not denying her love, but not reaffirming it, either. Without looking at him, she whispered, "I...I need to think about this." She got into her car and started the ignition.

Ham leaned on her door. Fury, hurt and something more, something almost desperate, churned inside him. "Don't do this, Liv." He'd given her so many chances, and he'd made so many plans....

Big tears hung from her lashes. Her mouth moved, but nothing came out. Then compressing her lips, she closed her door, forcing Ham to step away.

And she drove out of the lot.

Without caring that he stood there, watching her go.

Christ, it hurt. His heart felt trampled. His lungs burned as he sucked in needed oxygen, trying to fend off the awful pain.

How could she claim to love him, and then not even hear him out? So many emotions conflicted inside him, leaving him lost, furious and desolate.

Then he heard it.

A low roar that gained in cadence by the second. The hair on the back of his neck stood on end. A gust of wind blasted across the lot, buffeting his back, almost knocking him off his feet.

Ham jerked around, seeing that eerie green sky with

new understanding. Tornado sirens began screeching throughout the small town of Denton. Off in the distance, roiling with fury, an enormous black cloud churned, spitting off spectacular shards of lightning, sucking at the ground. He stood transfixed as, a good distance from the school, the funnel scrambled from spot to spot, licking here and there with destructive negligence—hurdling toward the path Liv had taken.

No. Disagreements and disappointments ceased to exist. He had to get to Liv, had to protect her. The rental car tore out of the parking lot while Ham frantically searched the wet road for the taillights of Liv's car. As he drove into the path of the tornado, the roar grew, louder and louder. Fierce winds fought the vehicle. Debris lashed the windshield, diminishing visibility. Hamilton registered it all, but wasn't swayed from his purpose.

His heart beat in time to his panic, his hands locked on the steering wheel, his gaze unblinking.

Finally, he spied Liv's car, stopped in front of the two-lane bridge. The river surged out of its banks, rising high, grabbing trees and rocks with the same ferocity as the tornado did.

His foot hard on the gas pedal, praying to reach her in time, Hamilton watched in horror as a gusting wind spun her car, throwing it hard against the guardrails. Metal ripped away, leaving a gaping hole on the side of the bridge. As if in slow motion, her car kept turning until finally, it dropped into the muddy, fast-churning water below.

Ham hit the brakes, bringing his car to a jarring halt. Too far away.

Too damn far away.

He exploded from the vehicle in a dead run. Fear drummed in his ears, louder and more insistent than the destructive force of nature. Prayers tripped silently from his mouth, adrenaline pumped through his veins.

With survival instincts honed by air-force training, he absorbed the destruction around him without letting it slow him down. Beyond the bridge, houses came apart, their roofs flying away, the walls pulling apart. Downed utility poles left live wires snapping and dancing.

Even as Ham pushed forward against the powerful wind, a huge elm split in half and crashed into the water close to where Liv should be.

He roared out his anger, refusing to believe she could be hurt. Something struck his face, knocking him back two steps, bringing him to his knees. He was back up in the same second, swiping away the warm trickle in his eyes, ignoring the sudden pain in his right arm and leg.

Jolting to a halt on the entrance to the bridge, he saw Liv's car stuck half in, half out of the fast-rising water, a few feet from the fallen tree.

There was no hesitation.

Gripping what remained of the guardrail, Ham bolted over the side, close to the shore, and landed hard in the slippery slope of muddy grass, sliding and stumbling to her car. He saw Liv's face, pale with fear, in her driver's door window.

She screamed, but Ham couldn't hear her words over the storm and sirens and his own clamoring terror.

Slogging in a rush through the water, he reached her in seconds. She pulled frantically at the door handle, but the car had buckled with the impact, jamming it shut. The trickling into his eyes threatened to blind him, but he again swiped it away.

Unwilling to wait seconds, much less any longer for rescue workers to reach her, Ham located a heavy rock. When Liv saw him lift it, she scampered back against the passenger's side door.

The window shattered into gravel-size pieces of glass. "Are you okay?" Ham yelled, and she nodded, crawling back toward him, her hands frantically brushing his face, her sobs loud and undisciplined, bordering on hysteria.

"It's okay," he yelled. "I've got you." And he hauled her out and into his arms.

For reasons Ham couldn't understand, Liv fought him, cursing and crying.

He tossed her over his shoulder, pinning her legs down with one arm, holding her backside still with the other. He plodded to the shore with difficulty, each step a strain as the air around them sucked and pushed and pulled.

The deafening roar seemed all around them, and the rain struck with bruising force.

Dropping with Liv in his arms, Ham covered her. He sunk his strong fingers deep into the soggy ground to anchor her. His lungs compressed, and he felt light-headed—but no way in hell would he ever let her go.

At the worst of it, he feared they'd both be torn away and his mind rebelled at such an awful thought. His muscles cramped and trembled with his efforts. Raw determination gripped him. He prayed.

And then the air calmed, the roar drifting away. Gasping for air, trying to protect her from harm with his body, Ham couldn't manage to loosen his hold. If anything happened to her…

"Shh." Liv touched him, stroking his hair, his neck, with shaking fingers. "It's over, Ham. It's okay. I'm okay."

Despite her reassurances, he couldn't unclench. Hell, he could barely draw air.

"Ham, it's okay. Let me see your head."

His head? Who gave a shit about his head? He found he couldn't speak so he just pressed in closer to her.

Her lips grazed his cheek. "Ham, please." Tears sounded in her voice. "You need to go to the doctor. Your head is bleeding."

By small degrees, with mammoth effort, he regained control of his body. The loud rushing of water mixed with the sirens—but the awful, animal roar of the tornado was gone. Hamilton pulled his face from her neck.

With his heart in his throat, he looked at her beautiful, bruised and dirty face. "You're really okay?"

Her lips were bluish with cold, trembling with an excess of emotion. She blinked hard, sobbed again, and said, "I love you so much." And then, with a surge of anger, "How could you *do that?* How could you go over that bridge—"

"You went over."

"And *risk yourself* and—"

Ham swallowed hard. "I love you."

Another sob, louder and more irate, and she said, "Damn you, *I love you, too!* I don't want you hurt."

His left eye twitched. "Then don't hurt me."

Gasping, she stared at him, touched him again, so gently. "Look at your head."

"That'd be a little hard for me to do."

And she smiled. "Look at what's happened to you. You're bleeding and you're going to need stitches and…and…" Openly sobbing again, she clutched at him. "Oh, God, Hamilton. I'm so sorry. I love you. All of you."

Finally, he could breathe again.

"Please," she whispered against his neck, "can you forgive me?"

"Yes." He didn't have any choice. He could never stay angry at her, not for anything. And then, with caution and a heavy heart, "Will you marry me?"

"Yes," she said, with an equal lack of hesitation, almost shouting that one, wonderful word. "Yes, yes, yes."

Ham heard the approach of a siren, not the tornado warning, but an emergency vehicle. Soon, they'd be rescued. He cupped her cheek, turned her face up to his.

His blood had gotten in her hair, mixed with mud and leaves. Her nose was red with cold, her lips pale. "I'm not going to let you change your mind."

"I'm not going to stop loving you."

"I'm still in the air force."

She gave a small nod. "I know."

"It's who I am, Liv."

"I know." She touched his lips. "I've been so afraid of losing you that I've wasted precious time."

"Yes." She needed to hear the truth. There could be no more misunderstandings.

"I'm so sorry."

He kissed her. The sirens drew nearer, then suddenly ceased, leaving a hushed vibration in the air. "Those plans I told you about? I can be a permanent professor at the academy in Colorado Springs. We can't live here, I'm sorry. But we wouldn't have to keep moving."

Her lips parted. "But...wouldn't that mean you'd have to give up the squadron commander position?"

"For you, yes."

A firefighter yelled down from the bridge. "Hey! You two okay?"

Ham turned and lifted one hand. "We're fine."

"Stay put and don't move. We'll come to you." The man moved away, shouting orders.

Ham turned back to Liv. "So. Will you marry me, Liv Amery? You'd be a colonel's wife, because the position comes with a promotion. And before you answer—"

"Yes."

"You should know that I'll be on active duty even longer—"

"Yes."

"And it'll take me two years to get my Ph.D. before we can move to the academy."

"Yes."

His heart lightened. "I'll still get full pay and—"

She pressed a hand to his mouth. "Yes, Ham. Yes

to everything. Yes, no matter what you decide to do. Yes, because I love you. Yes, yes, yes."

That awesome emotion had him in its grip again. Then the firefighters were there, toting blankets and water and first-aid kits.

As Ham rolled off Liv, the man closest to him said, "That's a nasty gash you've got."

"I'm fine."

The firefighter gave him a dubious look. "Let me get a stretcher down here."

"No need. I can stand."

Frowning, the firefighter asked, "Are you sure?"

Ham turned to Liv. "Tell me again."

She smiled, paying little mind to the man who wrapped her in a blanket and began cleaning the mud from her face, checking for wounds. "I love you, Lieutenant Colonel Hamilton Wulf."

Hamilton smiled. "Yeah, I can stand." He pushed to his feet and offered Liv a hand.

"Lieutenant Colonel?" the firefighter repeated. "I'm impressed."

Liv laughed, wrapping her arms around Ham. "Yep, me, too."

The firefighter grinned. "Sir, if you'll come this way, we'll have you both checked out in no time."

And minutes later, they were on their way to the hospital—and on their way to a very bright future.

EPILOGUE

GIVEN THE DESTRUCTION caused by the tornado, the funeral for Liv's father took place later than planned. Parts of Denton were devastated, and Hamilton and Liv pitched in with the cleanup and repair. Luckily, despite the crippling damage to structures, there were no lives lost.

The sun brightened the clear blue sky the day they laid Colonel Weston Amery to rest. Several people spoke at the service, including Hamilton. Their words gave proof of the incredible man her father had been— not an overly loving dad, but a leader who had selflessly given to his nation.

With full military honors, the ceremony included a flag-draped casket, pallbearers in dress uniform and a highly impressive twenty-one gun salute. As the flag lowered to half-mast, "Taps" played, giving respect for a fallen comrade.

In military fashion, step by step, the pallbearers folded the flag into a neat triangle. Hamilton held Liv's hand, giving her his support, his love, during the very moving moment when the men knelt before her, their heads bowed.

They handed her the flag. "Our deepest regrets, with the thanks of a grateful nation."

Warm tears slid down her cheeks, and an invisible fist squeezed her heart. Yes, regret clouded her past. But her future was with Ham. He was her hero, and he was the hero for a vast number of unknown citizens, in America and around the world. They were the people he'd sworn to protect. The people for whom he'd willingly endangered his life.

No finer man existed, and she wouldn't regret one single second of being his wife, no matter what risks the future brought.

As he'd said, life was always uncertain.

But Hamilton's love and loyalty weren't. She had him, she loved him—and that meant she had it all.

Dear Reader,

Ever since the first time I saw *The Wizard of Oz*, twisters have fascinated me. As I grew older and learned more about them, I was also fascinated by the men (and women!) who actually go out and chase those monsters. So I was thrilled to finally get to write a story about one of my passions. Cooper Harrison and Marty McKenna have a passions for twister chasing, too. And each other!

It was exciting to take these former lovers and drop them right smack-dab into the middle of a dangerous storm, with twisters coming down right and left. What better way to force them to deal with each other and expose their innermost wants and desires than to trap them in the middle of one of the wild and volatile storms they love to hunt? They might be chasing a storm, but what they want to catch is each other's heart!

Happy reading,

Donna Kauffman

BLOWN AWAY
Donna Kauffman

CHAPTER ONE

MARTY MCKENNA was having a very bad day.

"I should never have left the goddamn airport. For that matter, I should have stayed in freaking Kansas." It wasn't the first time she'd had that thought since leaving Detroit in the wee hours of the morning, after a storm there had grounded her connecting flight to Cincinnati. She just hoped it wasn't the last thought she'd ever have.

Teeth gritted, she wrapped both hands on the wheel of her rental car, and fought desperately to keep the little compact on the road. If you could call the dirt and gravel cow path she was on a road. But staying on that cow path was preferable to landing in the flood-filled ditch that separated the road from the field that ran parallel to it.

The ditch she was rapidly swerving toward.   .

Fighting the muddy, branch-strewn road *and* the blown-out tire turned out to be more than Marty or the little compact could handle. Every second felt like a slow-motion movie, and yet barely a blink later her compact had left the road, spewing gravel, before tipping over sideways as it careered off the embankment, down into the gully.

Marty's seat belt was the only thing that kept her from being flung downward against the passenger side door. She hadn't struck anything, so her airbag remained intact, but escaping possible facial burns was of little comfort at the moment. The instant her heart slowed down enough so she could hear anything past the thumping beat of it, she heard the slurping, sucking sound of her car sinking into the muck. Muddy water was rushing around either side of her car. The narrow gully was probably nothing more than a dusty ravine most of the time, but the heavy storm had turned it into a raging miniriver that was pummeling her car and rapidly seeping inside of it.

Of course, if it hadn't been for the water filling the ditch, she'd have likely flipped over completely. Only now she had another set of problems to worry about. Namely getting out of the car while she still could.

She reached downward, straining against the seat belt to get to her backpack, which was lying against the passenger window. She had no idea where her cell phone was. She'd pitched it in the general direction of her backpack when the tire had blown, needing both hands to grip the wheel. Hopefully Ryan had assumed they'd lost connection. She didn't want him worrying about her.

She was doing enough worrying for both of them at the moment.

After all but dislocating her shoulder, she finally managed to snag the backpack's strap, then awkwardly wrapped it around her fist. The seat belt was cutting into her body, choking off her breath. She needed to get out. As the rain had gotten heavier, the sky had grown swiftly darker, despite that it wasn't even noon yet. And the wind was picking up speed, which, considering it had been buffeting her little car all over the road for over an hour now, was saying something.

Hanging as she was, she couldn't see over the edge of her side window to what was on the other side of her door, but it was her only avenue of escape. Rain was beating against the glass, and from the tiny tapping sounds she heard, she realized it was mixing with bits of hail. Not a good sign during tornado season. Like she needed more bad ones.

This was supposed to be a beautiful June day. The

kind where you watched an old friend get married, threw rice, then danced under the stars while drinking too much champagne. "So much for my compatriots at the local National Weather Service," she muttered. At least *she* wouldn't be getting the letters and phone calls complaining that the forecast was wrong. This wasn't her district. Hell, it wasn't even her state.

Using the center armrest for leverage, she opened her door and levered it straight up, sticking her foot out to keep it propped open against the wind. "See," she grunted, "this is why you should join a gym. If you'd done a few leg presses in your life, this wouldn't be killing you." As it was, by the time she got a good grip on the slick edge of the doorframe, her muscles were screaming against the constant force the wind was putting against the thinly made door. She levered herself as close to the open door as she could, hoping she could bail out when she released the seat belt. The car tipped more upright with every shift of her body weight, causing it to sink even more rapidly.

She was already getting wet and now hail bits were pricking at her skin. Water and muck were oozing into the passenger side and filling up the foot well. "Time to get the hell out of here," she muttered, then hauled herself up as best she could while simultaneously popping her seat belt off. The buckle caught her hard in the cheek as it whipped past, but she could do no more than swear, as she was now fighting gravity all by herself. It took everything she had to heave her body up and out onto the edge of the car doorframe. The car began to flip the rest of the way over as she quickly reached for the open door. Pushing it against the wind, she levered herself against it. Wobbling badly, she shoved herself upright.

Without time to so much as glance downward to gauge the distance needed, she made her leap. The car went the rest of the way over as she shoved off, reducing her leverage just enough to send her sprawling a foot short of the other side of the water-filled gully.

Water and muck smacked her in the face, filled her mouth, making her sputter and choke. She flung her backpack toward the road, then literally clawed her way out of the water. Gasping, she lay on the side of the road, heedless for the moment of the rain and hail pounding her now completely sodden frame. The adrenaline that had pumped so swiftly into her system, allowing her to focus energy on saving herself, was rapidly turning into a queasy ball of nausea in the pit of her stomach.

She finally found the energy to push to a sitting position. All that showed of her car were the wheels and the bottom half of the driver side door. She began to shiver hard then, knowing she could only partly contribute the reaction to her soaking-wet condition.

Now that she was safe, looking at the rapidly swelling gully and her water-filled car, she realized how close she'd come to being in a far worse situation. Well, at least now she wasn't as mad at the airline people who'd refused to take her luggage off the plane in Detroit when she'd opted out of waiting for the runways to open back up. She might look like the creature from the black lagoon, but her clothes would make it the rest of the way to Ohio safe and dry.

"Rah, rah," she muttered, scraping mucked-up strands of hair from her face and shifting enough to look up and down the narrow country road. Wincing as the hail continued to sting her skin, she wasn't surprised to find nary a sign of a car or truck headed in her direction. Given the kicking winds, hail and rain, not to mention the fact that probably few cars used the road on any kind of normal basis, she doubted that was going to change. "No, only an idiot weather researcher would be out in conditions like this."

She'd had Ryan's local reports from late last night to go on, and she thought she'd read the signs pretty well. Obviously the storm had shifted position, though, which not only didn't bode well for her, but didn't bode well for her friend Ryan, or his wedding, either. Cell service sucked out here, so she'd been unable to get any kind of regular reports. In fact, she'd been amazed she'd gotten through to him at all.

Wait—her phone! Galvanized, she scooted forward and grabbed her backpack, dragging it into her lap. She fished around inside of it, hoping against hope her phone had somehow landed inside when she'd tossed it earlier. But no such luck. *Because why should my luck change now?* she thought morosely, giving in to an uncustomary and hopefully brief bout of self-pity. She stared at her submerged rental, but quickly disabused herself of any notion of wading back in to look for it.

Instead she struggled to a stand and took stock of the situation. She'd told Ryan where she was, at least she hoped he'd heard her before the tire had blown. Maybe he'd send someone out after her. "Like he doesn't have anything more important to do," she reminded herself. Besides, the way her luck was running, he'd probably send Cooper Harrison of all people.

Oh, yeah, that would just cap off her day completely.

Of all the possible scenarios she'd come up with if she ever ran into Cooper Harrison again, both of the personal, and recently the more professional variety—okay, who was she kidding? Every time she thought of seeing Cooper again it turned personal in her mind pretty much instantly. Anyway, none of those dream sequences had centered around any kind of rescue fantasy. Well, fantasy, yes. But she didn't want him to rescue her. Far from it.

If and when she saw Cooper again, she would present herself as nothing less than his equal. Maybe not in professional achievement, but certainly in attitude and maturity. She was no longer a lovesick college coed, enthralled with the campus wunderkind.

"No," she muttered, scraping at the muck and gravel clinging to her muddy, wet pants, "you're stranded in the middle of a supercell thunderstorm mooning about him instead." She sighed and gave up any attempt at salvaging her clothes. Yeah, she'd certainly come up in the world.

Disgusted with both her clothes and her attitude, she shoved thoughts of both from her mud-caked brain and started doing something helpful, like looking for shelter. She was perfectly capable of handling this. Hadn't she just rescued herself from a sinking car? Proof right there she didn't need saving by the Cooper Harrisons of the world.

Forcing the accompanying rescue fantasies aside, she turned her focus back to where it should be. And that's when she spotted the barn. It was on the far side of a wide cow field, tucked up against a narrow stand of soaring pine trees. The barn was huge, like the ones they used in the South to dry tobacco. It was also old, weathered, and from all appearances, abandoned. There weren't any other outbuildings in the vicinity, much less any kind of working farm. But it was the only structure in sight. It would provide shelter and give her a chance to dry out, wait out the storm.

The downside was that the only way to get to the barn was to hike across a few hundred yards of flooded, rutted, overgrown cow field. She tried not to be discouraged, to be thankful instead that she had any shelter. While doing one last scan of the sky, judging the cloud formation, gauging wind direction and speed as best as she could, she noted the first of a series of lightning strikes in the distance. "Perfect."

Rain, high wind, hail…and now lightning storms. Pretty much every ingredient necessary for tornado activity. And what was she going to do? *Right. Run toward a rickety old barn.* But she had no other options at the moment. Another closer strike ended her indecision and had her slinging her tote on her back and heading in a very undignified stumbling trot to the other side of the field.

It felt like hours, but what was more likely about twenty minutes and a very disgusting trek later, she was in an open and, thankfully, cow poop-free area around the barn. Up close, the weather-beaten structure was in even worse condition than it had appeared from the road. Slats were missing or rotted, and it was a pretty good bet that the lion's share of the inside was as wet and muddy as the outside. She couldn't see if the entire roof was intact, and after a moment of indecision, decided against circling the barn to check it out first. The hail was getting larger and what little adrenaline she had left in her system was rapidly disappearing. She was exhausted enough by this point that she could hardly fight the wind gusts to remain standing.

She forged her way to the huge double barn doors, only to discover that against all logic, they'd been chained and padlocked shut. Given the rusted condition of both chain and lock, it had to have been years since anyone had bothered to check on security. Flinching as the hail started coming down harder—and with the wind behind the icy pellets hitting her hard enough now to leave marks—she struggled to squeeze herself through one of the missing slats. Her shirt and the strap of her bag caught on the rough planks on either side, snagging and ripping at her, but with a final shove she stumbled inside. Which, given that half the roof was missing, she soon discovered wasn't much different from the outside. But as she was presently under the remaining half, most of the hail and rain were finally, blessedly, being deflected.

She slumped back against the rough planks, eyes shut, chest heaving now more from relief than exertion, and tried to marshal her strength and what was left of her determination. She wasn't out of the woods yet. This storm was just gearing up. And she was hiding in a wide open field, in a crumbling building that might not withstand the heavy winds, much less anything more dramatic.

Forcing her eyes open, she scanned the gloomy interior of the barn. It was a huge structure, with a loft running across one half of the upper area. The rest was wide open from dirt floor to the apex of the roof, which was a good two-plus stories up. There were no stalls, just a few pieces of rusted plow attachments and soggy, decaying bales of hay.

The missing section of roof was exactly that—missing. As in gone completely. She'd half expected to find it collapsed or caved in, but it was simply gone. Probably ripped off during a previous storm.

"There's a comforting thought," she said, rubbing her arms and shivering at the sound of the wind howling through the exposed beams and gaps in the walls. The force of the wind was so strong, some of the boards were literally groaning under the pressure. It felt like the whole thing could collapse at any moment. And part of her was definitely tempted to flee. But the part that was wet, tired and sore wanted to stay put, minimal shelter being preferable to playing hail target.

The only completely dry area of the barn was the corner underneath the loft, which had no missing planks nearby, and both the loft and the roof to keep out the elements. It was also the least safe as it would put her squarely in the one part of the barn with the heaviest load of lumber over her head. All of which could come tumbling down, or be snatched away—her along with it—if indeed this supercell spawned the tornadoes it had every appearance of being capable of.

But that was where she headed anyway. She was shivering hard now, her teeth chattering. She just needed to sit out of the rain for a few minutes and gather her strength. Formulate a plan. Besides, she told herself, there must be something stable about that section of the barn. It had held up this long, hadn't it?

It wasn't much of a reassurance, but it was the best she could do for herself at the moment. Falling apart wasn't an option. She was scared, she admitted it, but more than likely this would end up just being another interesting storm story to add to her repertoire. Only one she'd just as soon not relive or recount as she did the others.

One in particular came to mind. But she quickly squashed any temptation to allow her mind to stray in that particular direction. Thinking about Cooper Harrison wasn't conducive to the clear-headed, rational mindset she needed at the moment. How in the hell she thought she was going to work anywhere in the vicinity of the man, she hadn't a clue. But now was not the time to dwell on that problem, either.

She scraped her wet hair off her neck and wrung out as much of the water as she could. The melting hail pellets had created icy rivulets of water that were streaming down her back. She slipped off her backpack and plucked her sodden shirt away from her skin. She was tempted to pull it off and wring it out, but dragging it back on again would probably just feel worse. And leaving it off wasn't an option. It was wet, but it did provide some protection. Even if it was only in her mind.

There wasn't much she could do about her mud-and-muck-splattered pants and she didn't even want to consider what was caked into her shoes. She thought about taking them off and leaving them in the opposite corner. Or outside. But she had no idea what the next few hours would bring. And if she had to move quickly, she couldn't afford to be shoeless. She walked back and scraped as much of the muck off as she could on the nearest rusted piece of metal equipment, then removed the rest by rubbing the soles and sides on the wet hay bale. At least she didn't smell now, she thought, as she headed for the dry corner. If only drying her clothes were that simple.

Rubbing her arms, she crossed in front of one of the many missing planks...and stopped dead in her tracks. So did her heart.

In the far distance, probably a good mile or so away, the eerily dark sky was topped by a ceiling of dark clouds. But it was the four tiny funnels pulling down from that black cauldron that riveted her to the spot.

As she watched in dread, two funnels joined together, pulling farther down from the cloud ceiling to-

ward the ground. Then the remaining three funnels became two. And as her heart kicked back in, thumping
in double time, those two funnels become one.

CHAPTER TWO

IT WAS CRAZY, REALLY, to still be thinking about her like this. It had been six years and a lifetime ago since he'd seen Marty McKenna. Of course, she'd been naked at the time, and they'd just had sex in the back of his chase truck after witnessing the mother of all tornadoes. Something like that tended to burn certain indelible images into a man's brain.

But now they were simply two professionals in the same field of study, colleagues whose paths had never managed to cross since that fateful day. He'd gone his way, she'd gone hers. It was a stupid waste of time wondering about the what-ifs and might-have-beens.

He'd tried telling himself that his recent preoccupation was completely normal, considering he was up for a promotion, and her name had surfaced as the leading candidate to fill the position he'd be vacating.

Except this wasn't the first time he'd thought about what it had been like between them, both of them all charged up, sweaty and wild for each other. Her sweet naked body, writhing beneath him, shuddering around him.

Cooper Harrison jerked his thoughts back to the road. Christ, he really had to get a better grip. He'd be seeing her again in a mere couple of hours. And starting off their reunion with an obvious, throbbing hard-on wasn't exactly going to set the professional tone he hoped for.

He hadn't expected to deal with seeing her again for another six weeks, which was when she was slated to come in for her final interview before the board of directors. He'd told himself he'd be so swamped with his new duties by then, he'd be relieved to have anyone fill the vacancy on his crew. He'd told himself she'd probably long since forgotten all about him anyway. Not that that had helped any.

Then Ryan's wedding invitation had arrived. And during a follow-up call to his old college buddy, Coop had found out that most of their old chase crew had been invited as well. Marty being one of them. Cooper had had every intention of begging off. He'd just been offered the new director position at that point, and wasn't sure about taking it. Truth be told, he still hadn't completely reconciled himself to taking it.

When he'd heard that Marty would be attending, he'd rationalized that taking a few days' vacation time to get away from work would help him come to terms with this new direction his professional life was taking. And that maybe it would be best to see Marty before she came to Oklahoma. That way they could clear up any potential hazards that might be better averted in a social situation, rather than a business setting.

Yeah. That was why he'd rearranged his entire life, taken vacation days for the first time in his five-year tenure at the National Severe Weather Center, and at the worst possible time, too. So he could attend the wedding of an old friend he hadn't seen in years.

Cooper steered his truck through the steady traffic on Route 75, glad to be past Cincinnati, heading north again. He kept half an ear tuned to the chatter on his weather radio as he scanned the horizon ahead. The late June sky was a gorgeous clear blue, not a cloud in sight, but he knew that a massive severe weather system from Canada had moved in far more rapidly than they'd thought, and was currently targeting western Ohio. He'd been tracking it closely, along with another system shaking things up across the Texas panhandle, and a third developing along the mid-Atlantic. To look at the national weather map, you'd never know tornado season was almost over.

His NSWC team back in Oklahoma had their hands full. He'd felt bad for leaving them like that, but it was just as well they got used to Cooper not being around. His tenure as team leader was due to expire at the end of the month. Which was how long he had to change his mind about accepting the job in the first place.

The green exit sign for Denton flashed overhead. The small southern Ohio town had already been hammered hard this spring. The residents were still dealing with the damage left behind by the sudden flooding from the most recent system that had torn through their small, bucolic township. In fact, listening to the news coverage, he'd been half expecting Ryan to call and tell him the wedding had been postponed.

Given that the groom had been on his storm chase crew longer than anyone back when they'd both been at Oklahoma University, Cooper should have known that as long as the church was still standing, the ceremony would go on as planned. Coop smiled, remembering the recognizable buzz in his friend's voice when he'd called Ryan after the recent weather disturbance to make sure everyone was okay. These days Ryan was a forecaster for a local news affiliate out of Cincinnati, but they both knew that once chasing got in your blood, it never went away.

Staring out across the open pastures and small rural towns dotting his path north, he couldn't deny the charge was still there in his blood. He still wanted to be the one out there. The one leading the hunt.

He, better than most, understood just how rapidly that blue sky out there could turn gray. Then a sickly green. Then a sudden roiling black—a cauldron of thick clouds, downdrafts and convection currents that could quickly combine to create creek-swelling downpours, hail the size of golf balls, winds capable of ripping the siding from houses, constant lightning strikes and, quite possibly, a twisting vortex that could flatten an entire town in less than sixty seconds.

He knew he was more fortunate than most, having carved a career out of studying severe weather in a field that was very narrow when it came to full-time, self-supporting work. He had no right to feel even a twinge of self-pity over giving up the hands-on work that had been his focus for so long. He'd gotten way more out of it than most. And he'd still be a contributor to his field of study. He just wouldn't be in the field himself.

He ignored the sudden increase in chatter on his radio, letting it fade to white noise as his thoughts came full circle. Back to another late spring day, much like this one, the day that had ended up launching his career. The day that had put Marty McKenna in his path, as volatile and unpredictable, it turned out, as the tornado they'd been lucky enough to record that day.

Graduation day. It hadn't even been his graduation. It had been Marty's. She'd just turned twenty-two, and was mere hours away from getting her hands on the diploma she'd worked so hard for. Coop had been a twenty-five-year-old grad student, far more interested in studying the mysterious and complex relationship between supercell thunderstorms and the formation of tornadoes than the similarly mysterious and complex relationships between men and women.

Not that he didn't enjoy occasional personal time with the opposite sex, as long as it didn't distract him for any length of time from what was most important to him: his research. He'd been so close to developing new diagnostic tools that would help demystify some of the many questions scientists had about tornado formation and development. He was certain he'd eventually get the attention his ideas deserved, that he'd be a force in his chosen field. Any serious, long-term relationship was out of the question for him, so he didn't even consider it, an attitude that had admittedly narrowed his dating options dramatically.

Marty had been part of his chase crew that semester, having just transferred in from Kansas, specifically to work in his department. Smart, funny and a hard worker. That had been the total sum of his thoughts about her at the time. Gender didn't really matter much to him when it came to manning his crews. Functionality and dedication was what he looked for. But that fateful afternoon, what became a career-making event had turned, for a few short hours, into an unforgettable personal one. Marty McKenna was the only woman ever to cause his focus to veer so dramatically off course. Before or since. And where she was concerned, it had never fully gotten back on track.

While the rest of the campus had been in the throes of spontaneous bursts of celebration and general graduation chaos, Coop had been locked in the weather lab, tracking the mother of all storm systems. The way things were shaping up, it had looked like he had an excellent chance of seeing some major action. He had felt both excited and frustrated. Excited, because this supercell could provide him with a wealth of very timely data that would enable him to test and tweak some of his latest innovations. Frustrated because a chunk of his team had already graduated early, and the remainder of his crew was currently donning cap and gown, more interested in diplomas than twisters.

And then Marty had burst into the lab, breathlessly demanding to know if what she'd heard on the weather radio was accurate. She'd tossed her tasseled cap on the bench and peeled out of her robe. He remembered smiling at the discovery that instead of some fancy dress, she'd worn jeans and a faded Butler County Girls Volleyball T-shirt beneath her gown. Maybe it was the act of seeing her strip that had drawn his attention to her body for the first time. Both her faded T-shirt and her jeans had been soft and snug, cupping a nicely rounded backside and pert breasts in a way he had no business noticing.

Coop flipped his turn signal and made the Denton exit, unable to keep from smiling as thoughts of that afternoon continued to play out in his mind. Apparently even the promise of the mother of all severe weather systems hadn't been enough to completely stomp out his newly awakened libido. At the time, that had been irritating to him. He'd had far more important things to worry about than how soft Marty McKenna's breasts would feel if he peeled both their shirts off and pulled her against his chest.

It was a good thing he hadn't known then that Mother Nature intended to teach him several lessons that afternoon, or he'd have never let Marty McKenna inside his truck, no matter how desperate he'd been for a navigator.

"And what a perfect waste of a life-altering moment that would have been," he said, his smile turning to a grin. Scientist or not, he was a man.

Just then the stream of radio chatter was interrupted by a string of warning beeps. A moment later his cell phone rang. He tuned in the radio to listen to the weather alert even as he flipped open his phone. His pulse was already thrumming even before Ryan began rapidly talking in his ear.

"Where are you, Cooper?" Ryan demanded without preamble. "I mean, specifically."

"I'm close, about an hour south of you," Cooper told him, not questioning the abruptness of the call. "Why?" He struggled to listen to both Ryan and the weather alert at the same time. "What's coming?"

"Front moved in faster from the south. Wind shear is awesome. There are multiple supercells, but the biggest is west of here, about twenty miles."

"Moving?"

"South."

"So you all are safe?"

"Not sure. It's going to cut a wide swath. I'm calling because I just heard from Marty McKenna. She flew in from Kansas City, and since she couldn't manage to book a nonstop flight, she had a layover in Detroit."

Screwy flight plans had been partly the reason Cooper had chosen to drive up, rather than fly. That and the impending weather system had convinced him to keep his truck and gear with him.

Just in case.

"The airport had shut down from the northern sector of this same weather system, so I told her to stay put."

Despite the worry that was rapidly escalating, Cooper was smiling as he said, "I'm guessing she didn't heed your request."

Ryan snorted. "Should have saved my breath. She rented a car, reassured me she wouldn't do anything stupid, and asked me the best route to take to circumvent the storm. It was moving east then, and we didn't think the jet stream would meet up so early. So I sent her south."

Cooper's smile vanished. "You just told me—"

"I know," Ryan said, sounding as upset as Cooper felt. "I sent her right into it."

"Have you contacted her? She's no fool, she'll read the signs. I mean, she works for the NWS."

"Yeah, but there're only a few routes she can take out that way. It's all rural. I've had the guys tracking for me and there's hail, flooding, lightning strikes, trees and power lines down."

"Have you contacted her?"

"I've been trying for hours. Cell service is spotty at best out there and right now, probably from the storms, it's been nonexistent. But she managed to get through briefly just a few minutes ago. It was a really bad connection, but I got the gist of where she was. Then we got cut off and I haven't been able to get her back."

Ryan paused then, and in the silence that followed

a sick feeling began to pull at Cooper's gut. "What aren't you telling me?"

"She, uh, right before we got cut off, well, she was swearing, and it's probably nothing but—"

"But what?" He'd heard Marty swear before. Of course, her nails had been tracking marks down his naked back at the time. He shook off the memory. "Did she say what was happening?"

"No. Like I said, the connection was horrible. But, Cooper, I think she screamed."

Marty? Screaming? The woman he remembered was high octane when it came to getting things done, but not the type to be given to overreaction or dramatics. Now the adrenaline was kicking into overdrive. "Where did she say she was?"

"Route 192, just outside of Greenville."

Horns blew as Cooper swiftly changed lanes and pulled to the side of the road. He had maps spread on the seat beside him a moment later. "Okay, I've got it. I can cut across 17 and be there in that area in about forty-five minutes."

"Cooper—"

He heard the fear in his friend's voice and intentionally lightened his own. "Hey, I know you're jealous that I might get to see something interesting out there, but if I'm not mistaken, tonight is your wedding night, so I'm not feeling too sorry for you."

There was a pause, then a sigh of relief. "Thanks. I don't know how to tell you how much this means to all of us. Everyone else has made it in but you two, and we're just really worried that she might be in some kind of trouble. I'd never forgive myself if—"

"Hey now, don't go there. Marty might be hard-headed, but she can also take care of herself." He knew that better than most. She'd proven what a capable woman she was when, on their way back to the university, not an hour after having been sweaty and naked with him deep inside her, she'd been all business. She'd been more concerned about what they'd seen and the impact it could have on his career than about what they'd just done with one another and the impact it might have on them personally.

He'd been still somewhat shocked by the sudden turn of events and very mixed up about all the new feelings and dangerous thoughts she'd started racing around inside his head. That, on top of what they'd witnessed, well, he hadn't wanted to trust any of it, much less put it into words. So he'd followed her cues. Being all business, after all, was his comfort zone. Talking about his feelings was not.

They'd hit the campus and within hours their film had been released to major news organizations and wire services. By the time the hubbub had subsided, Marty had quietly grabbed her diploma and taken off for a job offer in Kansas. She'd sent him a letter shortly there-after, thanking him for including her name in his pub-lished reports and congratulating him on the profes-sional success his footage was bringing him. And he hadn't seen or heard from her since.

But that was about to change. And leave it to Mother Nature to make their reunion as dramatic as their part-ing.

"You've got enough to deal with," he told Ryan. "Go focus on marrying that beautiful fiancée of yours. I'm sorry I'm going to miss it, but if all goes well, we'll be there by the reception."

"Be careful," Ryan told him. "From the reports I'm getting, it's getting volatile out there. Anything can hap-pen."

Cooper thought about the last time he'd seen Marty, and how she might react when he found her this after-noon. And he'd find her all right. "Yeah," he said, the corners of his mouth kicking up despite the knot in his gut. "That's just what I'm hoping for."

CHAPTER THREE

"DAMMIT!" COOPER SMACKED the steering wheel with open palms. He'd finally made it to the rural route number Marty had given Ryan, though the road was hardly more than a farm trail. And, as was the case in a lot of the rural areas he'd chased storms through, there weren't many connector roads or alternate routes to choose from. He'd already made it through several swollen creeks, detoured around downed telephone wires, and rolled over more than one busted tree branch just to get this far.

But he wasn't getting over or around the massive pine tree presently slumped across the road. Ripped up by the wind, exposing a massive root system with little left to cling to after a season of heavy rains, hail had quickly piled up alongside it, as well as all along the sides of the roads. He was just thankful it had finally stopped. His truck had been taking quite a beating for the past twenty or so minutes. He supposed he should just be thankful it hadn't cracked his windshield. The rain had dwindled now as well, but lightning strikes were still frequent and the wind was near constant. Due to lack of signal or downed towers, he'd been out of cell-phone range for some time now, but he didn't need a weather update to tell him what he could see for himself.

The cloud ceiling in front of him was circulating, with a rear downdraft pulling down the occasional tiny funnel. So far, none had formed strongly enough to come close to touching down. But the system was moving toward him, and he knew that at any time, another one could form. All of the conditions were ripe for a rare supertwister, and he wouldn't be at all surprised if one formed right in front of his very eyes.

At any other time he'd be cursing his current lack of equipment. He had his personal gear, but right about now he'd kill for one of his Severe Weather Center vans, complete with its own mini Doppler radar. He'd chased many a supercell, but it was still difficult to pinpoint the right place at the exact right time to witness a tornado forming and touching down. Which was why scientists like himself were still struggling to answer some of the most basic questions about twister formation. Actually witnessing the birth of a twister of F4 or F5 proportions—a supertwister—was even rarer. In fact, he'd only done it once.

He and Marty had covered hundreds of miles that June afternoon, charting and mapping their way across the Plains, linking up with various weather centers as they'd tracked the storm. Even though the conditions were all but screaming for a supertwister, they'd never expected to see what they saw. And though Cooper had seen other big tornadoes since, none had been as massive, as dangerous or as destructive as the one he and Marty had all but smacked into that day.

He'd seen the footage he'd taken that day replayed a hundred times over. And yet the video was so far removed from the intensity of the actual moment. There were no words to describe what he and Marty had witnessed. No strip of film or spool of video could adequately convey the crushing, thundering power of that F5 as it had railroaded its way across open fields, stampeding through small rural towns, tossing homes around like dollhouses, flattening offices and strip malls as easily as an angry toddler having a foot-stomping tantrum.

Cars, trees, tractors, even boats had been flung about

like Frisbees at a Sunday picnic. Some had landed dozens of miles away, some had never been found. Aluminum siding had been driven like steel railroad spikes through tree trunks. People had been sucked out from under overpasses, or worse, plucked right from their homes.

What he remembered most was the sound. People often said it sounded like a freight train. And they were exactly right. What they weren't able to convey was that it sounded like a freight train...if you were tied to the tracks and it was rumbling right over you. It changed the rhythm of your heart.

He and Marty had chased and recorded the twister as intelligently as they could, given the circumstances. But once they'd both realized the magnitude of what they were recording, they'd gotten a bit reckless. And in the end, they'd been trapped right in the path of the beast, with nowhere else to run. It had been Marty's quick thinking then that had saved their hides...and the precious reel of film. She'd been the one to spy the narrow drainage tunnel that ran beneath the road. Muddy water, muck, tree branches and God knew what else had been clogged inside the corrugated tube, but it had been their only hope. Lying flat in the muck, bodies pressed together, with his video camera tucked hard between them, they'd ridden out the twister as it literally roared directly over them, shaking the ground around them, sounding as if the demons of hell were snapping at their feet.

They'd hidden behind the mass of debris that had collected from the heavy rains, then watched in nerve-racking terror as the tornado had plucked the entire twisted mass out of the tube as if it were nothing more than a bouquet of pansies. The two of them had been left miraculously untouched.

Later, after they'd staggered out of the drainage pipe, clinging to one another, the shock of their close call had turned to an almost giddy feeling of joyous triumph. His truck had been shoved almost a hundred yards down the road and was angled off the pavement, half in a ditch, but otherwise unharmed. They'd both worked to push it out and back on the road, then Cooper had discovered a stream running parallel to the road. Nothing more than a ditch normally, but now filled to overflowing with rainwater. Without hesitation, they'd stripped off their sodden, muck-covered clothes and splashed about like two giddy schoolkids on the first day of summer break.

Only after laying their garments across the hood and windshield of his truck to dry out did they climb in the back seat…where their almost drunken relief at still being alive had led to a decidedly more adult form of entertainment.

Cooper shoved those thoughts away and climbed

out of his truck. Right now his only focus was on finding Marty. He'd already come up with a dozen plausible explanations for that scream Ryan had heard, but that hadn't stopped the instinctive knot tugging his gut. The one that told him she was in trouble. Maybe the kind of trouble even someone as sharp as Marty couldn't get herself out of.

He levered himself up on the front grill so he could see beyond the downed tree. What he found was disheartening. Even if he somehow found a way around this one, there were several more just like it strewn across the road ahead. For the umpteenth time he wished he'd packed all of his stuff—including his chain saw and other survival gear. He hadn't come to Ohio to chase storms, however, so he'd limited himself to his usual set of maps, a weather radio, his camera and laptop. None of which were going to help him cut that tree into movable pieces.

Just past the stand of trees lining this section of the dirt-and-gravel road, the landscape opened up to vast, largely empty cow fields on both sides. In the distance he saw some forest growth, but from his restricted vantage point, that was all he got. The road ahead, for as far as he could see, was absent of any kind of vehicle.

"Where the hell are you?" Since turning on this route, he'd stopped in several hole-in-the-wall towns, scoping out the handful of cars in every lot to see if any sported a rental sticker. He'd stopped in a handful of tiny general stores to ask if anyone had seen a woman fitting Marty's description. But he'd come up empty. There was only one way she could have been traveling to Denton after turning on 192.

Of course, it was possible she was stuck farther ahead somewhere, just as he was at this end, but given the rapidly deteriorating conditions, he doubted she'd leave what was already a rural road for one in even worse condition. Besides, there simply weren't that many roads out here in the western part of the county. According to his map, there weren't any detours she could have taken.

What troubled him most was that, by his estimations, he should have come across her already. There had been next to no traffic on the roads. He'd passed a few pickup trucks, but nothing matching her description of a little compact.

And he only knew that much because she'd groused to Ryan about there not being any "real vehicles" left to rent at the airport. Marty had definitely been the type of woman who valued substance over style. Some things, he was glad to know, hadn't changed. If he wasn't feeling so helpless, he would have smiled at that.

At the moment, however, he was too busy realizing what a fool he'd been, racing down the road without planning anything first, thinking he'd do, what? Just ride out here on his four-wheel drive white steed and rescue the fair damsel in distress? Okay, that did make him snort. If Marty thought for one second he'd considered her a distressed damsel, she'd be the first to remind him about who'd saved whose ass the last time around. And rightfully so.

"So where the hell's my white knight when I need her?" Raking his hand through his hair, his amusement faded as tiny seeds of panic began to take root. He stared down the empty road, then at the sky, and knew he was running out of time. "You've got to be down there somewhere," he murmured.

A lightning strike punched down in the distance, lighting up the sky…and flashing off of something shiny on the side of the road, about two hundred yards down to his right. It had probably been a trick of the light, but there had definitely been a glint of something. And with nothing but grass, mud and gravel clogging the sides of the road, there shouldn't be anything flashy down there at all.

Where he was standing now, the right side of the road was a swollen gully, rolling over and through the extended branches of the downed tree. The left side was more passable, but that was the root end of the tree. Which meant he had a messy, slippery climb ahead of him. He looked at the roiling clouds, then at the road behind him. There was no place to move his truck that would be any safer, but it wasn't like any other traffic was going to be moving through here anyway. The only real question was could he make it down the road and back and still have enough time to haul ass out of there before the oncoming storm front hit?

But he was already looking for a foothold on the rain-slicked bark, and swearing under his breath. "Yeah, let's risk life and limb to go chase after a bright, shiny object," he grumbled, clawing his way up and over the mud-covered, sap-sticky bark. "Because you haven't done enough stupid stuff today already." Like purposely positioning himself alone and on foot in a wide open field, with the only nearby ditch presently filled to over-flowing with water.

But he'd seen something, dammit.

After scrambling down the other side, he immediately jogged to the next downed tree and started the process all over again. Thunder rumbled overhead and lightning strikes continued in the distance. Wind slapped fistfuls of dried pine needles at his face and body as the storm cell crawled closer. But he was too focused on climbing over the gargantuan tree trunk to do much of anything but find his next handhold. A good fifteen minutes passed before he was free and clear. He didn't waste any more time, but headed down the dirt lane at a fast jog, scanning the gully for any sign of what the lightning might have flashed on. He'd only gone about fifty yards when he spotted the source up ahead.

Hubcaps. Four of them, sticking straight up in the air. The car they were attached to was submerged in the rushing water.

No! He was running flat out before he'd even completed the thought. *It can't be her.* Sending up one prayer after another, he closed in rapidly on the flipped car. He saw that one tire had blown out, and even with all the rain that had come down, the marks the skidding tires had made in the dirt and the churned-up gravel they'd left behind were still obvious. But what grabbed his full attention was the upside-down rental sticker on the exposed bumper.

A blown tire. Marty's scream.

He was already sliding down the embankment into the thigh-high, swiftly running waters streaming through and around the car. Then he saw the open door. "Oh, thank God. Thank God." The car was full of water, but it looked like the driver had gotten out. Still, he crouched down and shoved his arms shoulder-deep into the muddy water. Groping around, all he felt was the steering wheel, dashboard and windshield.

No arms. No legs.

Relief churned through him so hard and fast, he felt sick with it. Climbing back to the road, he looked up and down the muddy lane, wondering if she'd managed to hitch a ride to the nearest town. For her sake he hoped so. Still, he had no idea if she was badly hurt, or if she was safe and dry somewhere. The idea of her out here alone, dealing with God only knew what kind of possible injuries…

He blew out a shaky breath, knowing there was nothing else he could do now. There was nothing in front of him close enough to walk to. Depending on when the pine trees had come down, it was also possible she'd been a passenger in any one of the pickup trucks he'd already passed. For all he knew, she could be back in Denton by now.

"Damn," he murmured. "Damn, damn, damn." He didn't like leaving without knowing for certain what had happened to her. His instincts were still jumping, or perhaps that was just the fear that had clutched at his belly when he'd spied that rental sticker.

It was funny, all the thoughts that had raced through his mind as he'd run, hell-bent, toward her submerged car.

Flashes of that afternoon in the back seat of his truck. Memory clips of the other hunts they'd gone on. Of Marty laughing and joking with the guys on the chase crew. Marty, her sunstreaked brown hair in a messy knot on top of her head, wire rims propped on her nose, a dry-erase marker clenched in her teeth as she'd pored over maps and weather printouts, trying to gauge the

best route around a storm. Marty, anticipation making
her fidget in her seat as she directed him down one
route, then across another, as they closed in on another
storm cell.

Marty, staring at him with eyes so blue, so huge, bit-
ing the corner of her trembling bottom lip…right before he'd yanked her into his lap and devoured her
mouth. Devoured her. Whole.

Why in the hell had it taken almost killing themselves that afternoon for him to notice her as a woman
and not just a crew member?

His heart still beating a tattoo inside his chest, he
asked himself why in the hell, after he had figured it out,
he'd let her walk away? Why had he let her pretend that
the tornado had been the only important event that had
happened between them that day? Or why, despite all
those times he'd thought about her since then, he'd
never once bothered to contact her? And he was almost
physically sick at the thought that now…now maybe it
was too late.

He scraped a hand over his face, swearing beneath
his breath, hating how absolutely useless and impotent
he felt at that moment. It wasn't until he turned back
toward his truck, that he looked across the field on the
opposite side of the road…and noticed two things. First,
there was an old barn on the far side of the field. And
second, funnels were dipping down from the black ceil-

ing of clouds that had moved far closer, far faster, than he'd realized.

He'd been so caught up in worrying about Marty he hadn't paid any attention to the shift in the developing storm.

He stood, riveted, watching as the funnels grew longer, stronger, then began to join up. He swore under his breath, gauging the distance back to his truck and the distance to the barn. Neither were smart choices in a tornado, but he might be able to outrun the thing in his truck, or at least get to a place where the roadside gully wasn't full of rushing water. As to the barn, well, there was no other shelter, but he wasn't going to trust it to hold up.

Then he saw it. The zigzag pattern of tramped down grass leading from the opposite side of the road, across the field, directly toward the barn. *Marty!*

He took off running, stumbling over the rutted ground, staggering through the waist-high grass and weeds, as he made his way across the field toward the barn. All he kept thinking was *Marty's in there.* Possibly hurt. Or worse.

He beat at the tall grass with his hands, using his arms like machetes, trying to clear a path. But the sky was darkening by the minute, making it harder and harder to see what he was running through. Several times he hit divots that almost face-planted him in God-knows-what kind of muck and mire. But he kept moving forward.

The wind picked up, making forward progress even harder. It was so loud now, shouting for her would be a useless endeavor. He was about twenty yards away when he noticed the burned-out ruins of a farmhouse about fifty yards past the barn. There was little more than a charred foundation left, overgrown with weeds to the point that it was barely noticeable. He immediately slowed down, though, squinting through the growing gloom.

One thing he knew was that farmhouses out on the plains usually came equipped with underground storm shelters. He stumbled closer, angling himself between the barn and the charred ruins, until… There! Another ten or so yards back behind the remaining foundation was a raised cement box, only noticeable now because the wind was flattening the overgrowth around it. *Hallelujah! A storm shelter.*

He looked back at the barn, at the trample pattern in the grass. She must not have seen the shelter. Maybe she hadn't thought she'd need it. A quick glance over his shoulder had him stumbling momentarily to a complete halt. Four funnels were now one. "Holy mother of—" He stood transfixed by the display, as he always was when confronted with one of Mother Nature's twisters. His first instinctive thought was that he'd left his camera, all his equipment in his car.

And then he snapped out of it, swinging his attention back to the trail to the barn, then over, past the ruined farmhouse, toward the shelter. He probably wouldn't have time to make it to both. But no way was he leaving her in that weather-beaten barn.

Another glance at the twister showed it pulling down and making landfall. "Christ almighty," he swore, then took off toward the barn. He spied the chain and lock on the wide double doors and veered toward a gap in the barn wall. The wind gusts were almost too much to withstand, and he was forced to grip the planks on either side of the gap, just to keep upright. He was too big to squeeze through, but there wasn't time to find a bigger opening. He stuck his head in and wedged his shoulder and upper body into the open space for leverage.

The sky was almost black now, so despite that half the roof was gone, it was still too dim to see much of anything. "Marty!" He had to shout at the top of his lungs just to be heard over the noise of the wind. "Marty, are you in here?"

He heard a scrambling sound from the near corner, then a shout. "Cooper?"

Hearing her voice gave him a moment of almost light-headed relief, but they weren't out of this yet. "Are you hurt?"

An instant later she popped out of the gloom in front

of him. She was muddy, her face and arms were all scraped up and her hair was a plastered mess against her skull. He hardly recognized her. But he recognized those wide blue eyes. He'd never forgotten those.

"Come on," he shouted, reaching his hand in for her. "It's coming right at us. We have to get out of here."

"For where? The ditches are full of water and the ruts in the field—"

"There's a storm shelter about fifty yards west of the barn. Behind the burned-out remains of a house."

"What? I didn't see—"

"Don't worry about it. Come on." She got close enough for him to grab her wrist. He didn't waste any time and tugged her through the narrow gap in the planks.

The rough wood caught at her wet clothes and scraped off more of her skin, but she didn't say anything, just worked as fast as she could to get herself free. "Where is it?" she shouted, the wind making conversation almost impossible, even though they were less than a foot apart.

He kept his grip on her forearm as she finally freed herself and pointed with his free hand. "That way. Run!"

And yet instead of taking off, they both turned, almost in unison, still clinging to one another as they fought the wind, but needing to take a look at what was bearing down on them.

"My God," Marty mouthed.

"I know," Cooper said, more in awe than anything else.

Then Marty turned to him, her bruised face and wide eyes lit with a wild excitement that only someone who chased down these bastards could understand. "You know, we really have to stop meeting like this."

Cooper found himself grinning. This was the Marty McKenna he knew. "Yeah, I'm beginning to detect a pattern."

The wind was picking up hail and gravel from the ground, along with stray tree branches. Marty put her arm up to deflect the debris from her face as she looked back one last time. "Don't suppose you've got a camera on you."

"Back in the truck. I got a little preoccupied when I saw your car belly-up in the ditch."

"You've gotten rusty on me."

It struck him then, standing in the middle of a cow field, being pummeled with debris, with what looked like a solid F4 gunning straight for them…that she'd summed up with one word exactly what it was he'd been feeling lately, but hadn't been able to define. Rusty. Huge chunks of his life had been put on hold for the sake of advancing the cause of severe weather research. And with neglect and disuse comes dormancy.

The wind slammed them both back against the barn

wall. With a shared glance, he knew she'd heard what he had. The wood planks were making a new groaning sound as the air pressure inside the structure and out increased and shifted. An instant later, still gripping each other's arms, they were racing hell-bent for the shelter. One glance at her as they stumbled and fought the wind showed her expression to be anything but tense. In fact, she was grinning. Come to think of it, so was he.

And suddenly life didn't feel so dormant anymore. Of course, that was probably a normal reaction given the potentially deadly situation they were in at the moment. But he'd faced down Mother Nature before. More than once he'd felt just like this, heart pounding its way out of his chest, adrenaline spiking off the chart.

But as they skidded to a stop in front of the shelter entrance, grabbing each other around the waist for balance as they slid in the mud puddles and piled-up hail, he knew it was more than the danger making him feel so alive. Maybe it was the mix of danger and Marty McKenna that did strange things to him. God knows it had the last time he'd mixed himself up with that combination. And looking at the grin on her face, he couldn't help but wonder if she was thinking the same thing.

That might explain why they were laughing like lunatics as they disentangled themselves and began tugging open the flat double doors. They struggled against the wind to open the doors, barely getting them open enough to shove themselves inside, plunging headlong into the total darkness of the shelter, using gravity and the weight of their bodies to pull the doors closed behind them.

But not before seeing the remainder of the barn roof fly overhead like it was nothing more than a child's kite.

CHAPTER FOUR

THE WIND SCREAMED AND GROANED through the wooden doors of the shelter. Marty literally hung from the handles, feet dangling over the cement steps leading down into the shelter, barely managing to keep the doors shut as Cooper grappled with the metal beam that slid through the braces put on the doors to keep them from being ripped off. The ground above them shuddered as the barn roof landed somewhere close by.

It wasn't until Cooper gripped her by the waist and ordered her to let go that she realized she was no longer laughing. In fact, she was shaking. Hard.

He tugged her down the stairs and turned her into his

arms. As if it were the most natural thing in the world, she clung to him. He pulled her farther into the shelter, away from the doors and they both stumbled over something on the floor, unable to see what it was in the pitch blackness. They managed to stay upright, barely, but didn't let go of each other.

"Are you okay?"

Even though his mouth was near her ear, she could just hear him over the noise generated by the tornado. She managed a nod, though it was far from the truth. She was anything but okay. And she was afraid if she allowed herself to think on it for more than a moment, she'd realize it was more than the storm shaking her up.

She'd known she was going to see Cooper again. Hell, she was going to be working for him if the interview went well. But even with the wedding looming, knowing he was going to be a guest there, too, she'd never imagined their reunion would be like this.

She'd thought more than once of what it had been like to be in his arms, but never let herself dream she'd get that chance again. Okay, okay, so she'd spent maybe a night or two (or twenty) with sheets twisting around her feverish body, dreaming about that afternoon in the back of his truck. But hell, what red-blooded female wouldn't?

She could recall with crystal clarity how he'd taken her. How she'd given herself to him so completely.

She'd been so in love with him by then, having fallen hard for the sexy grad student shortly after getting the chance to work with him. But his focus had been so exclusively on his work, he'd had no clue, never noticed her in any way but as a crew member. He hadn't seemed to notice women, period, his focus was so intense. But that hadn't cooled her desire for him. Hardly. She'd been young and hungry to learn and she'd so admired his dedication and his genius.

She'd contented herself with working with him, being around him, telling herself it was enough. He hadn't given her a single signal he'd even noticed her that way, and no way, at twenty-two, did she have enough moxie to come out and tell him how she felt. And then that fateful afternoon had happened. Hours away from graduating and leaving him forever to take a job back home in Kansas, the storm of the century had sprung to life. Even then she'd been thrilled just to spend her last day with him. Never in her wildest dreams could she have predicted what they were about to see. Much less what they were about to do.

A large dose of fear and adrenaline had driven them into each other's arms, a fantasy come true for her. Beyond a fantasy. It had been so much more than she could have ever hoped for. And, afterward, with her departure imminent, and knowing what had happened had been a matter of circumstance and couldn't have meant anything to him, she'd made the decision to keep her feelings to herself. What purpose would it have served to blurt out she loved him? Other than to very possibly ruin what had been a stunningly perfect end to her first serious—if one-sided—love affair.

So she'd chickened out—telling herself she was being mature—and pretended that it was nothing more to her than a spontaneous explosion of frenzied, raw sex.

In the weeks, months and years that had followed, she'd thought of him often, wondered what might have changed if she'd laid her heart bare with the rest of her body. She'd told herself she'd done the right thing. She'd been an hour away from leaving, what purpose could it have served?

As time had passed, she'd convinced herself it hadn't been that perfect. That explosive. Couldn't have been. Her wild infatuation with him had simply combined with the fury and power of Mother Nature at her most severe, so of course their coupling had felt cataclysmic.

But here he was, miracle of miracles, in her arms once more. And it was as if nothing had changed. Including her heart beating a thousand times a minute…and a raging Mother Nature, venting her wrath above.

She had to let him go, to regroup. Too much had happened to her today for her to be able to trust her judgment. But it sounded like the fury of hell was being un-leashed over their heads, and his hands felt too damn good on her. Steadying her, calming her. His body was a welcome shield to her battered defenses, and she couldn't seem to make her hands unfist themselves from their death grip on his shirt. It was much, much easier to stay right where she was, no matter that she sensed the bigger danger to her wasn't the storm over her head, but the one stirring up right here between them.

As if he sensed her thoughts, she felt his fingers dig-ging into the flesh of her back. She should simply be grateful, comforted he was letting her know that she wouldn't have to face this ordeal alone any longer, which was most likely his only intent. And she *was* grateful, she *was* comforted.

But she was also aroused.

It was impossible not to remember this wasn't the first time she'd felt him tighten his grip on her. Impos-sible not to remember exactly what they'd been doing, the ferocity of his expression, which had matched the tension and strength of his arms around her.

She swallowed against the moan rising in her throat and forced her eyes open, shoving away visions of the past. But the dark was absolute. Though she could hear the rain, dirt and debris trickling in through the slats of the wooden shelter doors as they rattled fiercely against the wind, no light penetrated the black depths of the shelter. She had no idea how big the place was, or what else might have been stored down here.

"Are you okay?" he asked again, shifting his mouth next to her ear so his lips just brushed against the tender skin.

She shuddered in pure pleasure, but he misread the reaction and loosened his hold. "I'm sorry, am I hurting you? What happened with your car? Are you sure you didn't seriously injure yourself?"

She shook her head, forgetting he couldn't see her. "The only thing I banged up was my ego," she assured him, fighting the need to do something foolish, like clutch him back against her. But she was the one who'd been in love, not him. God, he'd probably be mortified if he knew what she was thinking. "My tire blew and I hit the mud on the side of the road and couldn't get it back on track. The car didn't flip entirely until I pushed off the doorframe to leap clear of it."

He smoothed his hands up and down her arms, his touch gentle in a way he'd never been with her before. Of course the only time he'd ever touched her at all was when they'd been buck naked and going at each other like animals. Not a time that was exactly conducive to gentle caresses and soft whispers.

And now was not a time to be reliving that moment,

either. Had she been able to, she'd have laughed at herself, at just how foolish she'd let herself become with her memories of him. If she got the job with NSWC, her career would definitely progress more smoothly if she could put their shared moment in history firmly in its place. Once and for all.

But then he was tipping up her chin, making her heart trip anew as she wondered how he'd found her face so unerringly in the utter darkness.

"I think you knocked a few years off my lifespan when I saw that rental car in the ditch," he told her.

"How did you even know it was me? How on earth did you find me?" She sounded breathless, and hoped he attributed it to the storm…and not the effect he was having on her.

"It wasn't easy," he said, still stroking her arms.

A fanciful woman would believe that he was just as incapable of not touching her as she was of him. But she was a practical, career-minded woman. The kind of woman who didn't swoon. Not even when the proverbial man of her dreams ran his hands over her.

Psh. Yeah. If only.

She took a steadying breath, willed herself to step away from his touch. Because the fact of the matter was, she did want the job with NSWC. Badly. Maybe not as much as she wanted Cooper Harrison right at this very moment, but that was a fleeting need. The career move was long-term. And most assuredly, sleeping with the boss, while tantalizing personally, was a death wish professionally.

She swallowed a sigh as she stepped out of the protective circle he'd created around them. "They might revoke my feminist membership card for saying so, but I'm glad you found me." She rubbed her arms, and her knees trembled a little as she pictured the roof of the barn flipping away like it weighed nothing more than a pancake. "A few minutes later and—" She couldn't finish.

As a chaser she'd seen plenty of severe weather and the oftentimes massive destruction left in its wake. Smart chasers moved around storm cells, not through them. Even that afternoon she and Cooper had seen the supertwister, they'd never intended to put themselves in direct, life-threatening danger, as they had again today. She shook her head. "I could go a long time without ever being that close again."

"Why were you still in the barn? Didn't you see it coming?"

"It didn't form until after I'd taken shelter. I thought I was pretty clear-headed, but I guess the accident rattled me more than I thought because I didn't see any alternate shelter. And I didn't realize the shift in the circulation and downdraft. I should have paid closer attention, but at the time I just wanted to get out of the drilling hail. I spotted it right before you stuck your head in that other opening. I owe you." Which was the understatement of the century.

Cooper surprised her by letting out a laugh. "I'd say we're even. If you hadn't found that drainage tube that last time, we wouldn't be standing here right now. Maybe it's our karma, coming full circle."

Marty smiled at that. "You were always the ultimate pragmatic scientist. Since when did you believe in spiritual things like karma?"

There was a long pause. She thought maybe she'd just missed his response due to the clattering noise of the wind pummeling the shelter doors. But there was a sudden and distinct shift in the air around her. A moment later, he touched her face with the tips of his fingers, and she knew that was why. She stilled at his touch, every one of her senses already on high alert, but now in a different way.

"You must have acute night vision," she blurted, wanting almost desperately to keep this encounter in some kind of rational perspective. Which was difficult, even without them risking their lives, as the mere thought of him had always caused a reaction in her that was anything but rational.

"I can just sense you," he said, sounding almost awed. "All those months, almost a whole year, we were working together in the lab and on the road, and I have no idea how I missed it. How I tuned it out. But from the instant I locked on to you, I haven't quite been able to figure out how to switch it back off."

She was either more injured than she realized and officially hallucinating now, or he was telling her he still thought about her. And not just the sex part. But what with the wind and noise, she couldn't tell if he thought that was a good thing or a bad thing.

"We haven't seen each other in six years," she responded carefully, when she wanted to be anything but careful. He did that to her, too. Still. Made her feel reckless. Made her want to do things that were uncivilized.

She'd always thought it was the rather uncivilized nature of their studies that made her feel that way. Considering what was going on over their very heads at the moment, perhaps she'd never know the truth of her visceral attraction to him.

"Surely you gave up wondering about that a long time ago." She made it a statement, as if it didn't matter whether or not he'd given her a second thought. But her heart was beating way too fast. And hope was rapidly moving in. Foolish, really. Even if he had thought about her over the years, it was highly unlikely that he held that afternoon they'd shared in the same sort of unmitigated, yearning awe that she did.

"You'd think so, wouldn't you?" There was amusement now in that deep, gravelly voice of his. Self-deprecating rather than condescending. And endearing as all hell.

The need to touch him as he'd touched her shivered along her skin, skittered down her spine. She curled her fingers inward to keep from reaching for him.

He shifted closer then, ostensibly, she was sure, to make it easier for her to hear him. But his hand was still on her shoulder, the tips of his fingers lightly brushing the back of her neck. All he'd have to do was exert the slightest pressure with his fingertips, urge her the least bit closer, and she'd be full up against him. Their mouths would collide; their lips would connect.

And, as if she'd willed it, she felt that sweet pressure, that blatant invitation to move closer. No longer clinging to one another in the adrenaline-charged aftermath of racing for their lives, if she moved now, it would be deliberate. And would put her directly in the path of a different sort of peril altogether. She should have been thinking about the job opening, about her career, about the professional chance of a lifetime.

But it was a completely different chance of a lifetime she was focused on at the moment. A chance once and for all to put the fantasy to rest…or prove her memories weren't romanticized after all. And she was shifting forward before she could think clearly about all the reasons why she shouldn't.

"Do you?" he asked, and she could feel his breath, the heat of him, warming the sensitive skin at the corner of her lips.

"Do I what?" she asked, feeling as if she were standing on the brink of something very precarious.

"Still think about it. That day. Us." The amused tone was gone. In its place was a tension she couldn't quite define.

"Yes," she said, the confession at once harder and easier than she thought it would be. "Yes, I do."

"Six years later?" he asked, tossing the same question back at her. There might have been a hint of amusement, a thread of challenge. But mostly she thought he sounded, well...sincere. Like he really needed to know.

She turned her head then, looking to where she knew his eyes would be. "Yes." Just the one word. Simply stated. And yet with so much more riding on it than either of them likely comprehended.

"Well, that makes this decision much easier," he told her.

Her entire body quivered—hard—at the possibilities. "Which decision is that?"

"This one." And the gently urging pressure at the back of her neck vanished. His palm slid to cup her neck fully. He held her there, for an interminable breath of time before his mouth found hers. Found her, claimed her with the same unerring precision as before. The same precision that had guided Cooper Harrison to his prominent place in their profession. After all, no one was better than Cooper at being able to pinpoint, with absolute accuracy, the exact, most dangerous place to be.

CHAPTER FIVE

THIS WASN'T LIKE LAST TIME. Yes, they'd once again cheated death. Together. But everything else had changed. They weren't reeling like adrenaline junkies, drunk on a prolonged rush, giddy from shooting history-making film footage. He wasn't an idealist, still dreaming about making his mark. Marty wasn't a bright-eyed coed, fresh diploma almost in hand.

This time she was soaking wet, her skin damp and gritty. Her hair hung in ropes, snagging his fingers. She'd been battered and banged up, even before they'd come close to being sucked directly into the vortex of a twister. She still had a smart mouth and a sharp mind.

He was older now, supposedly wiser. And yet he'd never felt so confused. Conflicted about his future, conflicted about taking what he wanted, instead of doing what he was supposed to. He'd learned to master his impulses, but she'd undone all that. He understood actions had consequences, which meant he had no business pushing her like this.

But the body pressed up against his was all woman. And her lips were shockingly warm. The instant his mouth brushed hers, what common sense he possessed was ripped clean away, just like the roof off that barn. He'd often wondered if he'd idealized the way they fit together, if his reaction to her had simply been the adrenaline talking. But six years fell away in a blink when she returned his kiss. No more wondering. Bedraggled and muddy, yet she tasted even sweeter than he remembered. No more wasting time wishing he'd handled things differently. She was in his arms again, her lips so soft, pliant under his. Now was his chance to pursue what could be. He might not know what he wanted to do with his life, but he definitely knew what he wanted to do with Marty McKenna.

She sighed against his mouth, her body sinking into his as she returned his kiss. She clutched at his shirt, her body trembling hard. He wasn't sure if it was from the dank air, their wet clothes or the kiss. And he couldn't manage to tear his mouth away from hers long enough to ask. Instead he wrapped his arms around her, pulling her into the relative warmth of his body. But his hands refused to stay still. The tease of her curves as he slid his arms around her beckoned him to explore her body just as he was exploring her mouth. He smoothed wide palms up and down her back, making her shudder harder as she huddled even closer to him, her fists still full of his shirt.

"Cold?" he managed to say against her jaw, as he drew his mouth along the soft contour of her cheek, ending with his teeth sinking into the soft flesh of her earlobes.

She shook her head, but his face was pressed to hers and he could feel her teeth chattering.

He didn't know whether to laugh or swear. Here he was, mauling her like an animal, mistaking her clutching response for an admission of similar need, when all she was doing was trying to get warm. Keeping her wrapped in his arms, he shifted them both around, then put out one hand, searching blindly, hoping to brush against shelves or something stocked with survival supplies.

He stumbled over the handle to something, swearing, even as he tightened his hold on her to keep her from stumbling, too.

"Cooper," she began, struggling for him to let go.

"You're cold," he told her. "I'm sure they have some blankets down here somewhere."

"It'll pass soon," she told him, her speech halting as her teeth continued to chatter. "We won't be down here long. I'll be fine. Just—"

"Just, what?" he asked, pausing in his blind man's search to nudge her face back to his. "Let you go?" He brushed his lips across her earlobe. "I don't want to." This time when she shivered, he didn't think it was from the chill. And he was talking before he could convince himself otherwise. "I didn't want to six years ago, either."

She stilled for a second, and he felt her shift in his arms, felt her gaze on his, even though he couldn't see it. "Then why did you?"

"You made that decision for me. I knew you were leaving for that job in Kansas, and I still had another semester to go. And, afterward, you didn't seem…" He lifted his shoulder, let the sentence trail off unfinished.

"I didn't know how to handle it," she confessed. "I didn't want to feel foolish by saying something I'd regret later."

"Like what?" He slid his hand to her face, tilting it to his, wishing like hell he could see her eyes. "What did you want to say to me, Marty?"

She said nothing, but the trembling returned.

He braced her shoulders. "Stand here. Don't move."

"Still issuing orders, I see," she managed to say, sounding amused despite that her teeth were chattering.

His tone was wry in response. "I've been told I'm quite good at it." He made sure she was steady, then turned with both hands out, edging his toes forward as he moved to what he hoped was one wall. If he had to, he'd shuffle around the entire perimeter until he found something useful. Most families stocked canned goods, bottled water and dry blankets or clothes. He supposed this particular family could have taken their supplies with them after they'd lost their home in the fire, but if he was lucky they'd left something behind.

His outstretched fingers finally smacked against a shelf, rattling what sounded like canned food. When he gripped the rack to steady it, his fingers brushed against a pile of something soft and cottony. But his "eureka" of discovery was lost when a thundering crash shook the earth around them, rattling both doors of the shelter so hard he thought they might disintegrate.

He instinctively leaped toward Marty, who'd let out a shriek—and who was still standing close to the stairs leading out of the shelter. Too close.

Water droplets, forced through the sliver of air between the wood planks, flew in every direction as the doors groaned beneath the impact.

"What happened?" Marty yelled.

Her voice echoed loudly inside the small underground chamber and Cooper realized that when the shuddering vibration of the impact had died out, so had the roaring sound of wind. The twister had passed right over them. And as was often the case, the roiling black clouds should have moved on as well, and probably had. But the density of the darkness ensconcing them remained unrelieved. Not so much as a sliver of light seeped through the wood planking. Which meant that whatever had landed on the doors had blocked them completely.

The storm might have passed, but the danger to them had just gotten worse.

"What in the hell just landed on top of us?" she asked.

"Sounded like the entire barn," he muttered, moving slowly toward the stairs leading up to the double doors.

She must have heard his shuffling. "Cooper, don't go near them. For all we know, you're right and the whole barn is lying on top of them. We don't know if the doors will hold up. We should move back as far as we can, in case they cave in."

What Marty didn't say, but what Cooper knew they were both thinking was that they'd better hope that whatever did land on the doors caved them in, because the alternative was they were probably blocked in permanently. He tried not to think about the fact that the storm shelter, barely visible before, was now likely completely hidden from view. Other than their cars out on the road—if they were still there—and trampled field grass, which could all be flattened by now, the storm had likely left nothing behind to indicate where they could be found.

When Marty didn't say anything else, he suspected her thoughts had traveled in the same direction. It wouldn't do any good for either of them to panic. They'd deal with the situation. But first things first. "I think I found some blankets or something," he told her, returning to the shelves and groping along until he found the soft pile of fabric again.

"Good. Because I'm thinking I'll take you up on that offer of keeping warm now." Her voice still sounded a bit shaky, but her determination shone through.

That made him smile. "Let me see what else I can find while I'm over here." He heard her shuffling now. "Why don't you just stay—"

"I realize that finding my car upside down in a ditch might indicate otherwise, but I'm generally not all that helpless," she informed him. "I can find my way around down here same as you."

"Probably better than me," he told her. "After all, you were the navigator."

"And a damn good one."

He picked up the stack of blankets. "I haven't forgotten." In fact, it seemed all he could do was remember. Memories, bits and pieces of their past, were crowding more and more of his brain. He remembered why he'd liked having her along on his chase crew. She got just as caught up as he did in the excitement of it all, but she never stopped working. Always checking maps, calculating data, even as she excitedly pointed him in this direction or that, she was competence personified. Why he thought she'd need him now, he had no idea.

Judging from the sounds, she was shuffling away from him toward the opposite wall. "Jackpot," she shouted a moment later. "A lantern and a flashlight."

He heard clicking sounds, but no light came on.

"A flashlight with dead batteries. Oh, well. Hopefully…" She trailed off for a second and he could hear her foraging around. "Excellent," she breathed a moment later. There was a scratching sound, then a small flame popped into brilliance, creating a glowing circle of light in their black cave. "It's flickering," she said approvingly, as she jockeyed the lantern so she could light the wick.

He knew why the flickering was a good sign. It meant that whatever the hell had landed on the door hadn't sealed it completely. Air was getting in.

The small space glowed to life, forcing him to shield his eyes momentarily until they adjusted to the sudden light after prolonged exposure to absolute darkness. However, when he lowered his arm, instead of immediately taking in and gauging their surroundings, plotting their escape…he looked at Marty.

Her hair was still a wild mass of snarled tangles, her

clothes clung to her skin, muck and other gunk clung to her clothes. "I know this is going to sound like such a line," he told her with a smile as he held out a blanket, "but you know, maybe you should get out of those wet things."

She walked toward the open center of the shelter, setting the lantern down on a five-gallon bucket. She gave him a considering look, but didn't say anything as she accepted his offering.

For the first time in as long as he could remember, he didn't know exactly how to handle the situation. She had him completely turned upside down. Words, thoughts, needs, desires were all tangled up inside him. So he forced himself to look away, hoping he'd quickly regroup. After sitting the remaining stack of blankets down in the middle of the floor, he took note of the room for the first time. The whole space was maybe twelve-by-twelve-foot square. Two walls were lined with metal and wood shelves. The back wall was blocked by a clutter of junk—shovels, rakes and, inexplicably, an upright vacuum cleaner—that had all been shoved in front of it. The remaining wall was angled and comprised the stairs and the huge overhead double-door panels.

He turned his back to her and folded his arms, giving them both a much needed moment of privacy. "I promise I won't peek," he told her.

She just snorted.

"You think I would?" he asked, honestly surprised by the reaction.

"It just seemed an unnecessary offer, considering. I mean, it's not like you haven't seen, well, everything."

"Once. A long time ago," he told her.

"You're saying I'm forgettable then?" she asked with a laugh. "Or is there a statute of limitations on something like that?"

"I'm just trying to be a gentleman here."

"Why start now?"

Gaping at that comment, he barely resisted the urge to turn around. "What is that supposed to mean?"

"It means you weren't all that gentlemanly in the back seat of your truck six years ago," she said, quite calmly, sounding almost amused, in fact. "And I don't recall complaining then. In fact, I don't think I was complaining six minutes ago, either."

His body leaped at the mere suggestion that she might be coming on to him. "Meaning?"

He was startled when she came up behind him and touched him on the shoulder. Turning around, he found her smiling. Gritty, pale skin, snarled hair and sparkling eyes, as it turned out, packed quite a punch.

"Meaning that sometimes being a gentleman is highly overrated."

He couldn't stop himself from touching her then. He stroked the side of his thumb along the curve of her cheek, along her jaw, then across her lips, making her tremble again. Only now he could see the look in her eyes, and he knew it wasn't the wet clothes making her shiver.

It was him.

"You've been through a lot today," he choked out through a suddenly tight throat. "I didn't think a little TLC was out of place." Her lips quirked and he couldn't keep from rolling his eyes. "Why is that so hard to believe? I'm a pretty decent guy. We worked together for a long time. It was one wild afternoon, yes, but on a day-to-day basis, didn't I always treat you fairly?"

"You did. You treated me well that afternoon, too. In fact, you took very good care of me."

She'd said it matter-of-factly, but tell that to his body, which was hard as a rock and basically throbbing for some direct attention at this point. And he was pretty damn sure he could take very good care of both of them again right now if she'd let him. He struggled to keep his hands where they were, stay focused on the conversation. "So why the look just now?"

"You're just not a TLC kind of guy, that's all. Well, you've got the 'C' part down, it was those other two letters that gave me pause." When he scowled, she quickly went on to explain, but that hint of a wry smile still crooked the corner of her mouth. "I know you cared about us, about the team," she clarified. "But tender? That's not a word I'd associate with you. Dedicated, driven? Definitely. And a great motivator by example. And, don't take this wrong, but the only thing you ever really showed love for was your work, your research."

He opened his mouth to reject her assessment, then closed it again. She was right. About the man he'd been then. And the man he was now, too. He wasn't sure how he felt about that, but the gut reaction wasn't a good one.

"I'm not complaining, mind you. You were a very focused, very intense man," she went on. "So far, I'm thinking that hasn't changed, either." She paused then, and that half smile faltered a bit. Her eyes darkened and her voice was softer when she went on. "Those qualities were very seductive to the enthusiastic, driven, like-minded college student I was then. I'd always been a little in awe of you. You probably never even noticed my unstinting worship."

"No," he said, honestly, "I didn't. I never considered myself a role model, just someone—"

"Interested in making an impact, and happy to have people around willing to help him make one," she finished for him. "I know. That was part of why I respected you so much. I wanted to be like that."

"What makes you think you aren't?"

She didn't answer right away, maybe a little surprised by the question. *Well, fair was fair,* he thought.

"You've made the most of your opportunities," she

went on finally. "I haven't done as well with reaching my goals."

"Like what?"

"I spent two years in that lab-assistant job I took in Kansas, with the hope of getting into their research lab as a full-fledged researcher."

"I remember."

"Well, as you probably know, the funds for the program were yanked. Seeing as I'd yet to make the team, I was offered a spot in the National Weather Service's field offices, working with the other meteorologists, doing general weather-tracking work." He saw the flicker of a dry smile. "Not exactly my dream job."

"So why did you stay?"

She shrugged. "I still had school loans hanging over my head, and without any other real opportunities, I chose to keep the steady paycheck, remain close to family."

He grinned. "Dorothy back in Kansas."

Marty had been raised in the Plains. Growing up on a farm, she'd been fascinated with storms pretty much since birth. From the day she'd transferred from Kansas State University to Oklahoma, his crew had teased her, nicknaming her Dorothy, constantly reminding her "she wasn't in Kansas anymore."

She smiled a little, too. "Yeah. You still have family in Virginia?"

Cooper had grown up south of Richmond, but every

summer his parents had sent him to stay with his grandfather on his farm in Oklahoma. He'd seen his first twister at age eight. His grandfather had been an amateur storm chaser and by the time Cooper was twelve, he'd been on more than a dozen hunts. "No. My folks took over my grandfather's farm when he passed away. Turned it into a bed-and-breakfast, believe it or not." He smiled. "More often than not, they rent out rooms to chase crews and college students."

"So now you're in D.C. and they're in the Midwest. You guys switched places."

"Yeah. But we manage to see each other often enough." Mostly when they came to see him, or when he had speaking engagements out west.

"I'm sure they're very proud of you, of what you've accomplished. And they should be." She smiled a little when he raised his eyebrows in question. "I've followed your career. Just a little."

He grinned at that, wondering if her interest had been personal or strictly professional. "I'm sure your parents feel the same."

She just snorted. "Oh, they're happy I've got a good job and pay my bills on time. But they know I'd hoped for more. I think I know, deep down, I could have pushed harder. I didn't. Because it was safer not to." She looked at him. "You would never do that. That's the difference between us."

"Don't be so sure," he told her. "I've played it safer than you know." More, even, than he himself had realized. He'd always been driven, yes, and he loved his work, but when was the last time he'd even considered doing anything that wasn't in the best interests of his job, his research? Even taking this promotion wasn't for himself, but for the good of the job, of the people working for him. When had he taken his own needs out of the equation? he wondered. When had he let his work define him to the point that there was nothing else?

"I've never been a risk taker," she told him.

Me, either, he realized. In fact, giving in to his sudden desire for her during that explosive afternoon they'd shared might well be the last time he'd put his needs first. But he hadn't been willing to risk reaching for more. Rather than go after her, he'd played it safe, too. "There are different kinds of risk," he said, more to himself than to her.

"True," she said, her smile self-deprecating now. "Funny how easy it is to chase Mother Nature's finest fury around the countryside, with hardly a thought about the danger to life and limb. Hell, I even got buck naked in the back of your truck with hardly a blink. But boy, put me in a situation where I might have to bare my soul and I'm scared spitless." Her lips quirked. "Why was it I could share my body with you, but not my feelings?"

And just like that he wanted to touch her again. He framed her face, drew his fingertips along her jaw before tilting her chin up so her gaze met his head-on. "What feelings were those?" he asked her in a quiet demand. "Tell me now."

If she was surprised by his sudden intensity, she didn't show it. Instead he felt her jaw firm as she gathered her resolve. She swallowed hard, but held his gaze. "That afternoon was a culmination of two of my biggest dreams. One professional. One very personal."

Now it was his throat working.

"Because, you see, in addition to a little hero-worship, I was also head over heels in love with you." Her mouth trembled into a dry twist of a smile. "I'm surprised you didn't notice the drool."

He rubbed the pad of his thumb over her lips. "I was a blind man. And a very dumb one."

Once again she trembled beneath his touch and it was all he could do not to take that mouth again.

But before he could put action to thought, she went on, haltingly, but determinedly, "That afternoon was the ultimate fulfillment for me. I knew you hadn't noticed me in that way, that I was simply in the right place at the right time. For you, it could have been anyone. But for me…" She shook her head. "I have no idea what you thought of me after that, of how easily I did, well, what we did." She broke off, sighed. "It might have been a reaction to adrenaline overload or whatever for you, but for me…it was all about you. I wouldn't have done that with anyone else."

"Marty—" he began, but she spoke before he could say anything else. Though, to be honest, he had no idea what he would have said to her. He'd had no idea how she'd felt. Before or after. Or now.

"I was afraid if I said anything, I'd blabber every last moony-eyed thought I'd ever had about you," she told him. "Then you'd have had to pretend to be nice about the whole thing, and well…" She lifted a shoulder. "Back to the risk thing."

Her confession floored him. And, as much as he wanted to believe that if she'd told him how she'd felt that day, he'd have jumped at the chance to pursue things with her, the truth was she might have been right. It wouldn't have changed the fact that she'd graduated and was taking that job in Kansas.

At the moment, however, she wasn't going anywhere.

Forcing thoughts of their current predicament from his mind, he moved closer, tipping her chin farther back. He slid the blanket from her arms, flipped it around her back, then used his grip on the corners to tug her close.

Her gaze dropped to his mouth, then lifted back to his eyes. There was no masking the very adult desire he saw there.

His fists tightened on the blanket and he fought the need to drag her to the floor right then and there. She'd claimed he hadn't been tender, that he'd been too focused on work to know what it was to love. She didn't know how right she was. And not much had changed in the ensuing years. He wasn't particularly tender, or loving. But the one thing about Marty that hadn't changed either was that she made him want to try.

A bit shakier than he wanted to admit, he brushed his lips across hers, swallowing a groan at her soft response. "Part of me wishes you'd told me how you felt," he admitted, his voice rougher now. "I may have been too wrapped up in my work to notice your attraction to me. You pegged me right when you said I didn't notice much of anything that wasn't work-related back then. But you got my attention in a way no one ever had before." He held her face in his hands, looked into her eyes, and put it out there. "Or since."

She stilled under his touch, and he heard her breath catch. "And the other part of you?"

"The other part of me thinks that maybe that old saying is true, that everything happens as it does for a reason. You were leaving that day, graduating and moving back home. I was preoccupied with my research. You were just stepping out into the world. I'm not sure where it would have gone then."

She searched his face. "Have things changed?"

His grip tightened. "I don't know. But this time I don't seem to care so much about the what-if's and how-can-we's. All I know is I feel like I've been given a second chance. Maybe there's a reason for that, too." He could hear the edge in his tone, but was unable to soften it. He couldn't shake the sudden sense that it was imperative he make her understand.

"What are you asking me?"

"Do you feel like it's a second chance, too?" He crowded her closer, knowing he was pushing, unable to stop. "Maybe it will be easier if we take the leap together this time."

She tipped up on her toes and whispered, "I think maybe we already have."

CHAPTER SIX

THEN MARTY WOVE HER FINGERS through his dark hair and pulled his mouth hard to hers. But even as she sank into the kiss, and felt him respond, the little voice in her head was telling her she had to stop it, and right now.

What she hated most was that the little voice was right.

She should have spoken up, about the whole job thing, before ever letting things escalate like this. She'd meant to earlier, when they were talking about her job history, and then they'd gotten sidetracked. And now they were really sidetracked. But then, they'd never been good about putting words before deeds. Or after for that matter.

Of course, it was the national board who made the final decision about the job. But as the open slot was on his former team, he probably had some say in the matter. And as the new director of the entire program, having a personal relationship with one of the research team might be frowned upon, something neither of them could afford. Worse, what if he thought she'd intentionally encouraged his attentions as a means of securing the job?

He slid his hands to her waist, gripping the edge of her shirt as his mouth found its way along her jaw, down the curve of her neck. *Step back right now.* But the blanket was in a tangle around her feet. Her breath caught as she felt his fingers skim beneath the hem of her sodden shirt and skate across the sensitive skin at the small of her back.

"We really need to get you out of those wet clothes," he murmured against her ear.

As he began to tug her shirt up her torso, she gripped his forearms, stopping him, then sighed as she leaned away from him, ending the lovely contact of his nice, warm lips on her cold, damp skin. "I need to tell you something." Even to her ears, the words came out sounding ominous.

He took a second to regroup, then said, "Are you involved with someone?"

She gaped at him for a moment, then snapped her mouth shut. "Are you?" she countered.

"Of course not," he said immediately. "I would never—" He broke off when she merely stared at him. To his credit, his ensuing grin was sheepish, and his tone when he spoke was sincerely contrite. "I'm sorry. You're right. I shouldn't have made that particular leap. It was just the first thing that came to mind when you said what you did."

"The reason I stopped you wasn't a personal one," she told him. "It's professional."

He frowned. "What are you talking about?" Then his expression cleared. "I know you're up for the position at NSWC. In fact, when they asked for my input on the final two candidates, I recommended you."

That stopped her. "You knew? I mean, this whole time? Why didn't you say something?"

"I assumed you'd know that I would be aware of it."

It took her a second to regroup. Okay, she needed more than a second. "So…you don't have a problem with me…with us—" At a loss, she just made a swirly motion with her hand. "You know."

"I honestly haven't thought it through." He held her gaze, his own was starkly sincere. "For once I was just doing what I wanted. For me."

"There's nothing wrong with that," she told him. "I just didn't want you to think I was doing this to influence—"

"Please," he said easily, which relieved her more than it should have.

Perhaps she was the one not giving him due credit when it came to personal ethics.

"You weren't worried about working with me, were you?" he asked. "Because of our history."

"No. Well, yes, but that didn't keep me from applying."

"So why didn't you contact me directly then? You had to know I'd put in a good word for you."

"If you'd been anyone else, I would have. But I felt like I'd be trading on our past. Our personal past." Now *her* smile was a bit sheepish. "Or maybe I was just afraid I'd contact you to ask for help, and you'd have forgotten who I was altogether. I wasn't sure I wanted to face that prospect, either."

He laughed. "Did you honestly think that was possible?"

She shrugged. "How was I to know?"

"If you got the job, you were going to have to face me eventually."

"I know. If or when you found out I'd applied, I figured you could contact me privately if you had a problem. You didn't. So I just went with the assumption that if I got the job, it was because I'd earned it. As to working with you, well…" She smiled. "I figured I'd cross that bridge when I got to it."

"You're more than qualified to be on our research team," he told her. "NSWC is lucky to have you and they know it."

She flushed, flattered despite that she hadn't sorted all this out yet. "Thank you. You didn't have to say that."

He shrugged. "I was just being honest. And you're right, you didn't need my recommendation. You would have gotten it anyway."

What was he saying? Did that mean she'd definitely gotten the job? But he was already talking before she could ask.

"When you got Ryan's invitation, did you know I'd be here?"

"I knew. Did you?"

He nodded. "It was part of the reason I took the time off to come."

The admission sent a little thrill of joy through her. "I was hoping I'd hear one way or the other about the job before leaving Kansas. Then, if I got it, we could resolve any possible issues we might have away from the workplace. I got the call for the final interview, but that's not for another six weeks."

"But you came to the wedding anyway."

She nodded. "Partly for Ryan. And in part because, job or no job, I couldn't pass up the chance to see you again. Depending on if you came with someone, or who knows what else, I didn't know if I'd even talk to you…but I wanted the chance to, if the opportunity presented itself." She gave him a shy smile. "Of course, none of my imagined scenarios included the present situation."

Now Cooper's smile curved into a deeper grin, making his eyes gleam. And he stepped closer to her again. "But here we are. Again. And things are still as complicated as ever."

"Maybe that's our karma, too."

"Is that a bad thing?"

That look in his eyes made her want to strip naked on the spot and the hell with being responsible. "No. If I'm being completely honest, this is better than anything I dared hope for."

He reached for her then, and damn if she wasn't strong enough to stop him from taking her into his arms. "You hoped for this?"

"I'd be lying if I said I wasn't curious to know what might have been. Or how things would be if…you know, I ever had another chance. I just never thought I'd get to act on it."

His blue eyes darkened, and she saw his jaw work despite the wicked grin he gave her. "Why stop now that we're just getting to the good part?"

"Because as much as I want to find out what's going on between us, I also want to take that step in my career. I waited a long time for this chance, too. I finally found the courage to go after what I want, and I don't want to do anything to jeopardize that."

He ran his hands down her arms, making her shiver with need, damp clothes long forgotten now as her body rapidly heated up. "Once we get out of here—"

She'd been steadily trying not to think about that little problem they'd yet to deal with. Much easier, in this case, to focus on other things. Like him. "You mean *if* we get out of here." She tried for a dry laugh, but it sounded a bit shaky.

"When," he reiterated, and with such confidence, she let herself believe him, at least for now. "If we decide to see where this goes—what's the worse that could happen?"

She was surprised at the intensity of the question, but it was that very intensity that drew her to him. "I—I get the job. We're together. People start to talk."

"So? You're good at what you do. You earned the job. Let your work speak for you."

"Okay," she said, knowing they both understood that it really wasn't as simple as that. "For argument's sake, let's say everyone is thrilled we're a couple. What if we leap into the flame only to burn out a week later, a month. A year. Then what?"

"Then we worry about it then."

She huffed out a sigh. "Cooper."

"Marty," he mimicked, making a face.

She smacked his arm for making her laugh. "I'm serious. We've both worked hard to make strides professionally. You've gone far, I feel like I'm finally starting. I don't think either of us wants to chance ruining that for—"

"Exactly," he cut her off. "For what?" His hold on her tightened. "For doing something that's human? Something that, for once in my life, isn't about my job? For wanting something more than reaching another professional milestone? Especially when I don't even know if the milestone I've reached is one I want?"

That stopped her. "What? What do you mean?" Certain she hadn't heard him correctly, she shook her head and said, "Of course you want the job. You're the perfect guy for it. You have all the background in the world—no one understands the cutting-edge technology we're embarking on better than you. Hell, you developed most of it. You're passionate about the importance of the research you're doing and I know you'll finally bring real attention to severe weather study, not to mention scads of donor money. You're like the hero of every severe weather researcher I know. Not that that's a huge fraternity, but—" She broke off, aware she was rambling, and also aware that his expression had grown even more shuttered. She squeezed his arm. "Cooper?" When he still didn't look at her, she framed his face with her hands. "You're serious, aren't you? You don't want the job? I don't understand."

"Trust me, I know we need the funding. And I realize I'm in the best position to get that for us. I know what this means in terms of exposure for our field." He stopped, sighed, but didn't continue.

Now it was her turn to cup his cheek as realization sunk in. "But it also means you step out of the lab, doesn't it?" she asked softly, already knowing the answer. "Away from the R & D end of things. Away from the hands-on part that you really love." She could kick herself for her gushing tribute to all he could do for the job...and for so completely missing that maybe for once it should be about what he could do for himself. "I'm so sorry," she said softly.

"Don't be. I know I'm fortunate just to be working in the field, making a career of it. I understand I've got the best platform and reputation to get the notice we need. And if I don't take this on, it might severely damage our chances of continuing the work that the rest of the team is doing. I feel like I really don't have a choice."

She saw the resignation in his eyes and hated it. She ran her hand along his cheek. "Why is it we can't have everything we want in life?"

"Doesn't seem fair, does it?" he murmured, sliding his palms up to cap her shoulders.

"No," she said, her breath hitching as he pulled her closer. "No, it doesn't."

"I want you," he told her, his mouth dropping closer to hers.

Her heart tripped. "A shame it's so complicated." *Too complicated.* More than she'd ever realized.

"Yeah," he said, his gaze drifting to her mouth, then ever so slowly back to her eyes. "A damn shame."

"Otherwise, we could do anything we wanted," she managed to say, barely, her throat having gone completely dry.

"Anything." His jaw was taut, the single word rough.

Images pounded through her brain, her body aching to act on them. She curled her fingers inward to keep from yanking him to her. "It's a good thing we stopped before we lost control."

"Yeah." He wove his fingers beneath the hair at the nape of her neck, was already tilting her head back. "Losing control would be very bad."

"Very," she echoed. "Bad." So dry, so parched. Parched for him. She wet her lips.

"Aw, hell," he swore, right before he crushed his mouth to hers.

CHAPTER SEVEN

SHE WAS RIGHT. It was complicated. At the very least, they shouldn't be rushing in to anything. Then that wet tongue had darted out, moistened lips he'd become all but obsessed with tasting again. And his mouth was on hers all over again.

So let her go now, he lectured himself. *Don't part her lips like that. Don't push inside the warm, sweet recesses of her mouth. Don't shudder and grow harder than stone when she sighs into your mouth, sinks against your body. Definitely stop before you tug her shirt up over her head, before you touch even another inch of her skin, before it's...*

…too late.

Her shirt fell to the floor, and by lantern light her skin was a burnished gold, every dip and curve highlighted in the flickering shadows. Logic no longer played a part in what he was doing. If he was sane or even remotely capable of rational thought, he'd be finding a way out of the damn shelter. Instead he was sliding her bra straps over her shoulders, skating his palms downward, until her silk-covered breasts filled his palms. After all, whatever was blocking the doors would still be there later. Whenever he was done—he lost track of the rest of that thought when she dropped her head back and shivered beneath his touch, baring the perfect column of skin at her throat to his still-questing mouth.

The only element of survival that concerned him at the moment was not having a heart attack before he could finish tasting her, getting his fill of her. With that in mind, and only that, he ran the edge of his teeth along the side of her neck, down along her now-bared collarbone. His fingers curled into the damp lace edging the cups of her bra. He pulled downward, freeing her from the wet chill, and, as he sank to his knees, into the warmth of his mouth.

She groaned and her legs buckled. He wrapped an arm around the back of her thighs to steady her, then shoved at the tangle of blankets on the floor around his knees. She slumped forward, gripping his head, and when he turned back to her, he found his face buried between her thighs. He couldn't stop himself from nuzzling her there, despite the barrier presented by her pants. She cried out, her nails raking his scalp as she clutched at him.

His arm tightened around the back of her thighs as he pulled the snap open and yanked the zipper down. He had only one goal now, and there was little that would stop him from reaching it. He shoved her pants down, tugged at her panties, until both were past her hips. Her fingers had long since fisted in his hair as she struggled for balance, but she didn't yank his head away. That was all the invitation he needed.

She was wet for him, he could smell the heady musk of her. He jerked with the need to bury himself there, his body screaming to be released from the confines of his clothes, so he could tumble her to the floor and sink every aching rigid inch of himself deep inside her waiting body. It would be like before, only better. He knew this with a certainty he didn't question.

Which, perversely, was what gave him the strength and patience to slow down. He didn't know what the hell would happen when they got out of here, so he was going to savor every last second of what was happening right now. And so, if he had anything to say about it, would she.

With the tip of his tongue, he ran a wet trail from her

navel downward. He slid his hands to her hips, then shoved her pants and panties all the way down to her ankles. She shuddered hard, bucked against him, fists so tight in his hair now he was surprised it hadn't come out in clumps. That only served to jack him up higher, punch more adrenaline into his system. Her need ate at his already ragged control. So he fought that much harder to contain it.

He smoothed his palms down the outside of her thighs, then slid his fingers around behind them, nudging her legs apart, so he could reach what he so badly wanted to taste.

She was trapped by the tangle of clothes, unable to shift her thighs apart. With a grunt of impatience, she levered out of her shoes, then stumbled and kicked her way out of the clothes pooled at her feet. The instant she was free she spread her legs wider. And an instant later, he'd speared her with his tongue.

The shelter filled with her long, keening moan, matched only by his growl of triumph. Sweet, perfect. Ready. And all his. He slid his tongue free, shifting his hands around the backs of her thighs far enough now so that he could replace his tongue with the smooth length of his finger. She cried out, clenched around him, wet and hot and so tight he thought he might come before he got his pants off. Undeterred, he shifted his attentions higher, flicking the tip of his tongue over her until moans turned to gasps, gasps to whimpers.

This was insanity. The more he had, the more he wanted. And when she climaxed, her nails digging half-moon welts into his scalp as she convulsed again and again, he knew the time of savoring was over.

But his plans to pull her down to the blankets and get out of his pants as fast as possible only went half-accomplished. She sank down into his arms as if she were melting over him. He could feel the aftershocks of her orgasm still shuddering through her. The limp weight of her forced him backward, and they landed in the heap of blankets with her naked and half sprawled across his lap and chest.

But before he could recover his balance, she rolled him to his back and straddled his thighs, shoving his shoulders to the floor when he tried to sit up. Her hair was a snarled tangle around her face, her eyes, so big and full of determination, gleamed in the lantern light. But it was the wicked grin that curved her lips that had his body jerking to full attention. As if it wasn't already there. He hadn't known he could be this hard.

But given the very intent look on her face, he was thinking that might not be such a bad predicament.

"Fair is fair," she informed him, then quite deliberately undid the buckle of his belt and flipped open the button of his pants.

He twitched hard, a certain part of his anatomy in complete agreement with her assessment. Her eyes widened at his involuntary movement, and her grin spread wider.

"I seem to recall last time we didn't allow ourselves the luxury of exploration," she told him, toying with the zipper tab.

"We were a little impatient," he agreed, completely unable to dredge up a single image of their first time together. He was too fixated on all the new ones they were rapidly piling up. Her nimble fingers were carefully easing open the strained zipper of his pants. And he was having no problems whatsoever coming up with quite detailed images of what was likely to follow.

She left his pants unzipped, but instead of pulling them down and mercifully freeing him to, God, do anything she damn well wanted, she scooted up a bit, so the apex of her thighs snugged just below his zipper, cupping him so perfectly he groaned and bucked helplessly against her.

"I could take my pants off if you'd like," he offered, thinking it might have sounded more like begging. He was beyond caring.

She merely smiled. "I seem to recall you took off my shirt before my pants. I got a bit ahead of myself."

"I don't mind."

She said nothing, but scooted up just a bit more,

tucking her body around every rigid, constrained inch, making him swallow a long, deep growl of half frustration, half absolute pleasure, before she lifted up on her knees and bent over him. She yanked his shirt from his pants, letting him press between her spread thighs when he lifted up his hips so she could untuck the back. His body shuddered at the too-brief contact, but he was rewarded with her soft little moan.

She pushed up his shirt, but batted his hands away when he tried to expedite the mission. "I can handle this."

"I know," he bit off. "That's what I'm both praying for, and half-afraid of."

She laughed. "I'm making you nervous?"

"You're a little more aggressive than I remember."

"I'm not a dewy-eyed coed any longer. Does that bother you?"

He glanced down at the very obvious bulge in his pants, then grinned back up at her. "Apparently not."

"Good. Then you'll have to get used to sharing control."

It was a little punch of reality, the idea of doing this again with her. And again. Learning more about her, her likes, her dislikes. And maybe learning about himself in the process, as well. Sharing, she'd said. Sharing her, sharing himself. It hit him with surprising force just how excited he was by the mere prospect.

For the first time he let himself consider that maybe this promotion was actually a gift in disguise. He'd been bitching about not doing for himself. As a director, he'd be out of the lab, yes. But that had the added benefit of giving him the luxury of time to focus on other more personal, intimate avenues in his life.

Maybe he hadn't thought about it that way before because up until about an hour ago, he'd had no intimate personal life.

He'd always enjoyed the process of focusing his analytical mind on solving the mysteries of storm development. Now there was another mysterious force of nature developing on the horizon, capturing his attention. And he couldn't imagine a more seductive mystery begging to be unraveled than the whirlwind that was Marty McKenna.

Any further analysis of that little epiphany was lost as she leaned over him far enough to push his shirt up past his shoulders and over his head, forcing his arms upward while the tips of her breasts grazed along his now-bared chest.

If he hadn't been hamstrung by the straitjacket she'd made out of his shirt, he'd have grabbed her and rolled her under him before taking so much as another breath. But, once again, control of the situation was not his to claim. He wasn't as upset by that as he might have been.

His arms remained where they were. Mostly because she was presently drawing the tip of her tongue in a lazy trail down the center of his chest. She casually drifted her clever little tongue over to circle first one nipple, before shifting quickly to flick the now rigid tip of the other. He gasped at the shock of pleasure that zipped through him, bucked a little, but otherwise did absolutely nothing to stop her.

He couldn't remember the last time he'd been the subject of foreplay. But as Marty continued to play with his nipples—something no one had ever done—while she drew her ever-questing tongue lower and lower, he began to wonder what he might have been missing out on. For a guy with a scientific mind and an endless curiosity about things, how had he managed to entirely bypass this field of study?

When she gently freed him, then shoved his pants down, he raised his hips to help her, thereby thrusting himself quite neatly into her waiting mouth. He actually shouted a rough groan of deep satisfaction. And decided right then and there that he could devote a great deal of time and attention to rectifying the serious lapse in his education.

Marty was definitely no fresh-faced coed. And hallelujah for that, he thought, as she very enthusiastically circled him with her hand and drew her tongue in wickedly pleasurable circles around the head. In fact, he could think of no better instructor for his newfound interest. God knows he would be a very willing, enthusiastic student.

Occasionally she'd take him deep in her mouth, get him groaning, make his hips start to piston uncontrollably, then go back to circling him, teasing him, until he thought he'd go mad. Much more of this and this was all they would do. And while a large part of him—a large throbbing part—thought that was a most excellent idea, the rest of him had long since decided this was only going to end one way—with every one of those aching, throbbing inches buried fully inside what he already knew was a very wet, hot, tight sanctuary, ready and waiting to accommodate him.

He started to struggle with the sleeves of his shirt, trying to push it down off his arms, even as he continued to jerk beneath her decidedly skilled manipulations. But she surprised him by taking him deep into her mouth and keeping him there. Squeezing and stroking. And he was already so damn close—

"Marty," he choked out. "I'm not—I can't—"

But she didn't stop, gave no indication she was planning to, either. And then he felt the pull, the sweet, sweet building of pressure, and he was arching his back, his eyes shut as it punched through him with a force so intense it was like his own personal supercell, taking him over in an abrupt, exquisite, powerful rush that had him shouting and bucking, unable to stop or control himself.

He might have seen stars. Or blacked out momentarily. Either or both were entirely possible. *Damn.*

Try as he might, he couldn't make his eyes open. Nor, it seemed, could he muster even the slight amount of energy it would take to move so much as a pinky finger. A groaned "My God" was pretty much all he could manage.

After pressing a very soft, sweet kiss beneath his navel, Marty rolled off of him, slid to her side and scooted up just enough so she could press her cheek to his chest. She didn't say anything.

Leaving that momentous task to him.

Last time she'd been the one to talk, almost eager to shift the conversation back to the amazing spectacle they'd witnessed…and away from the amazing spectacle that had just occurred in the back seat of his truck. Only now he knew she'd done that out of nerves, and fear. So what was she thinking now? What did she want him to say? Or do?

He managed to get his shirt off, with every intention of pulling her more fully into his arms. He wanted to erase any chance of her pulling away from him physically, and then go to work on making it impossible for her to shift away emotionally, too. He wanted to make her desire what he desired, fill her with the same goal he'd already decided to pursue.

Yes, it would be complicated, meshing his life with hers, dealing with the potential fallout of office politics. Handling the frustration of leaving lab work behind. But what goal worth having wasn't? He wanted to unravel every secret she'd ever harbored. He wanted to understand every how and why of his complete and absolute attraction to her.

But the way she was tucked against him, her face angled away from him, made him pause. And once again he was faced with the confusion of not automatically knowing how to go about getting what he wanted.

"You didn't have to—" he began, only to stop when she gave her head one little shake.

"I wanted to," she said, her voice hoarse. "Really wanted to," she added, and he could have sworn he heard a thread of smug satisfaction.

It made him smile. And relax. A little anyway. He propped one hand behind his neck, and let the other come to rest on her hair. He stroked it gently, toyed with it, as he toyed with exactly what he should say to her. How he handled the next few minutes could decide everything. Just thinking about it should have given him pause, made him question everything about this sudden decision. Logic would tell him it was the orgasm talking, and the desire for more just like it. But all he had to do was glance down, feel the warmth of her body curled into his, enjoy the pleasure that filled him as she drew aimless patterns on his chest with those clever, determined fingers of hers, and he knew the grin that spread across his face had little to do with mind-blowing sex. Okay, it had something to do with it. He was human. And male.

Yet, he realized there was more anticipation, more excitement, in simply waiting for her to look up at him, smile, make some smart-ass comment, do or say something completely unpredictable, than there was a desire simply to come again.

When the board had asked him for his input on hiring her, he'd spoken easily and at length about her qualifications, about what a wonderful woman she was, what a valuable addition she'd be. And he'd meant every word. He should have realized then just how thoroughly she'd captivated him, how deep his feelings still ran.

If he'd been able to be at all objective that afternoon of her graduation, maybe he'd have understood it six years ago. And in the weeks, months, years that had followed, when he realized he'd never been able to get her completely out of his mind, he should have known it then.

Now, there was no denying it.

CHAPTER EIGHT

SHE WAS HIDING. She knew that. And, like before, she felt like the worst kind of chicken. But that didn't make it any easier to look up at him. Much less tell him what she was thinking. Feeling. Wanting.

Last time she'd purposely guided the conversation away from the personal, and he'd allowed her the escape. She wondered if he'd let her escape again.

Part of her didn't want him to let her off so easily. The same part of her that hoped he wanted what she did. So she was waiting for him to say something. Anything. To give her some insight into what he was thinking. After all, why was it up to *her* to make the first move?

She'd been worried about what would happen if they started something, only to have it flame out, thereby making working together awkward, or downright untenable. Now? Now they'd already started something, hadn't they? The risk had been taken. And the alternative—not even trying to make it work—was untenable. Because, when it came right down to it, she really hated being a chicken.

So they hadn't had sex this time. Technically. That didn't matter. It was the way being with him made her feel. He'd been just as confident a lover now as before. And then, when she'd taken over, he'd looked uncertain, almost vulnerable. Which had both surprised and encouraged her. He'd done what felt right and natural to him while making love to her, so it was only right she do the same. This time was about not being a chicken, about not having regrets.

Of course, at the time, taking charge hadn't seemed so risky. He'd been every bit as caught up in her as she'd been in him. She'd trusted he'd enjoy her attention as much as she'd enjoyed his. Why not trust herself—and him, now?

Her thoughts in a jumble, she became increasingly aware of his touch as he slowly stroked her hair. And she gladly let her focus shift outward, until she became aware of the exact pressure and placement of each of his fingers, of even the slightest brush of his fingertips along the nape of her neck, of every beat of his heart, steady and strong beneath her cheek.

She was also aware of her own heartbeat as it began to pick up speed. Did she want to spend the next six years as she'd spent the last six? Wondering what could have been if only she'd just up and told him how she felt? She took a breath of courage and lifted her head so she could look at him. "Cooper, I—"

At the same moment, his chest rose as he took a deep breath and blurted, "Marty, I have something I need to say."

"Go ahead," she told him, relieved to be momentarily released from taking the next step, yet frozen with fear at what it was he suddenly had to tell her.

"No, that's okay," he said quickly. Too quickly. "Ladies first."

He sounded almost…nervous. Could it be they'd both been wrestling with the same thing? There was only one way to find out. She pushed her hair from her face and scooted up a bit more so she could really see him clearly.

His expression was both intent and wary. But more telling was that as she'd shifted her body, he'd immediately—instinctively?—reached for her, holding her as if he had every intention of keeping her close.

She had to find a way to make sure that didn't change.

Watching him closely—although truthfully she was unable to tear her gaze from his, anyway—she said, "I know we talked about what we face ahead, in our respective careers. You're not sure about this new direction you're taking and—"

"I'm keeping the job," he said flatly. "As director. It's the right step." There was absolute certainty in his voice.

"You're sure?"

He cupped her cheek then, drew his fingers along her hairline. And the look in his eyes made her forget her own name, much less whatever it was she'd been worried about.

"I am the right man for this job. I know that."

"But what about the lab time? Your research?"

"I'll miss it. There's no way around that. I can hope that I'll find a way to keep my hand in, but I know that realistically, with my new responsibilities, at best I'll be involved peripherally with the actual ongoing accumulation of data, and development of new ideas. But there is an upside to the promotion, too. One I really hadn't thought about before now. The responsibilities are greater, but far more structured, in terms of work hours. I'll actually have more free time. I can take weekends off for a change. Most evenings will be my own. I could even have a real vacation."

She smiled. "Let me guess. Springtime, Midwest?"

He grinned. "If that's the only way to keep a hand in, yes. It's been a long time since I've storm chased without having to follow specific protocol. Who knows, I might stumble across something new. At best it will give me a chance to play with whatever toys the team has developed."

"And maybe offer a suggestion or two on improvements?"

"You know me pretty well," he said, grinning. "Would that bother you?"

It took her a second to follow. "You mean, if I were part of the team? Of course not. Why would it?" She wasn't sure where he was going with this and tried hard not to let her mind run too wild with hope. "I can't imagine your team would, either," she added cautiously. In case he was getting ready to explain that he wanted them to have the opportunity to work together at NSWC, and that was all he wanted. "It was your research and foresight that got them the funding they have now in the first place."

"You wouldn't feel awkward? Uncomfortable?"

"No," she said, dread beginning to creep in. He was going to let her down easily, be a nice guy about it, make sure she was okay with it. "I'm a professional. When I'm working, the job is the focus. And, to be honest," she added, speaking the truth despite the crushing disappointment beginning to fill her, "I'd enjoy the chance to work with you again. Even if it's only occasionally." *Even if it rips my heart into pieces every time I see you, knowing you didn't want me badly enough to fight to have both.*

Which was when she realized that she wasn't exactly fighting here, either. She was taking his smooth dismissal, literally lying down. But, her little voice argued, is it worth fighting when only one side wants it?

So why don't you come out and ask him? Maybe he did want it, but was doing what he thought was best for her. If she didn't put it out there, she'd never know. The truth might hurt, but the what-if would kill her. "Cooper…" she began, but he stopped her.

"Let me finish getting this out. Before I lose my nerve." He slid down a little then, so their faces were parallel, his gaze intent on hers.

She frowned. "If you think you need to walk away to protect me, protect my job for me, I don't need protecting, okay? But if you just don't want me—"

Before she knew what was happening, he'd rolled her onto her back amidst the pile of blankets. Looming over her, his expression as piercing as she'd ever seen it, he pushed his hands into her hair and framed her face so she couldn't look away from him. "I wasn't walking away. I was making sure you didn't want to. I do want you. Or at least the chance with you."

Her heart stopped, then went into overdrive. "What was all that about the job, about working together?"

"It might be awkward. The team is going to know we're having a personal relationship. I wanted to make sure you could deal with that."

"I'll do whatever I have to," she said, shaking as the reality of what he was asking her began to sink in. "I'll fight for the job, to get respect for my work." She swallowed hard, and stepped out on that emotional ledge next to him. "And I'll fight for you. If I'm going for it, I'm going for it all."

His grin was fierce, and his fingers tightened on her skin, but he didn't kiss her. "One of the reasons I was so afraid of leaving the lab, of taking on this new job, was because at the end of the day, I wasn't sure what was going to be waiting for me. I've been married to my work for a very long time, so the concept of having time to do whatever I wanted…well, in the past any answers I had to that were work related. Now, suddenly, I'm thinking that maybe having a life outside of work might not be such a bad thing."

Her heart wasn't going to settle into any kind of regular rhythm anytime soon. But that didn't matter. "No, not a bad thing at all," she said, then laughed out loud at the absolute joy filling her, leaving her giddy and light-headed with relief.

He blew out a long breath and laughed, too, sounding as relieved as she did. "Now why was that so damn hard for us?"

"I don't know. But it feels much, much better now."

She felt his body tighten on top of hers. "Does it now?" His eyes darkened and suddenly the light moment was over.

She wondered if it would always be like that between them. She couldn't wait to find out.

He leaned down for a long, drugging kiss. There was urgency still, but it was different now. Banked. The curiosity and need to explore were greater than ever, but they had time now. To indulge, to play, to see where things would lead.

"It's not going to be easy," she warned him between kisses.

"Nothing worth having is."

It made her heart swell, hearing him say that. And it was then she understood fully the importance of not holding back, and vowed she never would again. It was going to be difficult, forging this relationship while so many other changes were happening for them both. But this was the time they'd been given, and she didn't want it to pass her by.

Thank God, neither did he.

She wanted to let him just have his way with her, but there was one more thing she had to voice before they went any further. She pressed lightly against his chest, secretly pleased when he merely shifted his attentions from her mouth to the side of her neck. She liked the way he nuzzled her, the way he couldn't seem to keep his hands off of her. Yes, she could get used to that. "One thing," she said, gasping briefly when he bit her earlobe.

"Mmm-hmm," he murmured, intent on driving her insane by alternately nipping her lobe, then pulling it between his lips and soothing it with his tongue.

"If things don't work out," she whispered, "I want you to know I won't make things difficult. At work. I want us to stay together because we want to, not because we're worried about—"

He paused, but didn't lift his head. "What if we never make it out of this shelter?"

She shifted her head to one side until he lifted his and looked at her. "What is that supposed to mean?"

"It means that we both seem to have a penchant for letting the possible negative keep us from reaching out and grabbing the positive."

She thought about that for a second, then said, "Okay. You have a point. But—"

He silenced her with a kiss. It wasn't hard and fast like last time. No, this was quite different. From any kiss they'd shared. It was soft, tender. And when she relaxed and finally kissed him back, he didn't end it, but let it spin out. Leisurely kisses, needy kisses, but confident and certain, too. He was showing her he wanted this, wanted her, that he wanted to uncover her secrets, explore every part of her. Body and, she was certain, soul.

His eyes were dark, soft and filled with emotion she'd never before seen in him. "We can't know what might happen. But I do know that I'll forever regret not finding out. So if this is what I want, if you're what I want, then I really don't see any other option but to take the gamble and find out." He framed her face. "And you're what I want."

CHAPTER NINE

HE MOVED BETWEEN HER THIGHS and she shifted to accept him, accommodating him as naturally as if they'd come together like this for years. As he pushed deep inside of her, the sound that rose from his chest was a deep, guttural groan of pleasure, matched only by her own soft sighs of satisfaction. It was a homecoming he'd never forget.

Last time their coupling had been frenzied, wild. Primal. This time it was slow, purposeful, and yet every bit as visceral for the intimate new bond they were creating. Last time it had been an ending. This time it was a beginning. A foundation to build on.

She lifted her legs to hold him tighter, deeper. Her nails raked his back, then sank in as she clung to him while he drove her—and himself—higher, then higher still. He took her mouth, swallowed her cries as she reached her climax, fiercely happy he could bring her such pleasure. Then the feel of her body, so warm and pliant beneath his, wrapped so tightly around him, holding him so deeply as she quivered through her release, surprised him by immediately wringing a slow, shuddering climax from him, as well.

With his face buried in the crook of her neck, he rolled to his side and gathered her in his arms. "You know," he said eventually, his voice hoarse, rough with the emotions he'd yet to name, but which he no longer wished to deny, "at some point we're going to have to do this on a bed."

She lifted her head and regarded him with those big blue eyes, for once looking drowsy and sated. "I'm hoping we won't have to escape death every time, either."

"Oh, yeah," he teased. "That." He sighed and tucked her back against his side. "Do you think the team will get suspicious when I always request you as my navigator, then consistently opt for a different route than everyone else during a chase?"

"Might raise an eyebrow or two."

He nudged her chin up so she looked at him. "Will you care?"

Her smile, before she settled herself in his arms again, was perhaps a tad smug. "At the moment, the second cavalry could ride in and I wouldn't care."

He laughed. "We might wish they had if there's no ax down here to help us bust our way out."

Marty propped her chin on his chest. "They're probably worrying about us. We really need to get up and figure out what we're going to do."

Cooper smiled when she didn't make even the smallest effort to get up. "I know."

"Do you think the wedding is still going on as planned?"

Taking the initiative, he sat up and began gathering his clothes. "I hope so. If this was the worst of it, then it stayed to the west of town. But we can't be sure what the hell that storm cell spawned." He realized it was selfish, but part of him didn't want to think about Ryan and the wedding, or anything else for that matter. Once again he'd made love to Marty McKenna, and once again it had been a turning point in his life. Was it so wrong to want to revel in that moment, at least for a little while?

So maybe a tiny part of him still worried that when they were above ground and dealing with reality once more, Marty might come to her senses and decide not to risk her new career by trying to have a relationship with him at the same time.

Both of them made sounds of disgust as they pulled on their damp and dirty clothes. Cooper's thoughts were still on what would happen when they got back in his truck, and by the time he was all tucked and zipped, he realized Marty was dressed and rummaging around the tangled pile of farm tools cluttering the rear part of the storm shelter.

"Aha!" she cried, then turned, triumphant with an ax in one hand and a scythe in the other. "Not sure what we'll use this for," she said, lifting the curved blade, "but it looks like we could do some serious damage with it."

She stood there grinning, dressed in mud-caked, wrinkled, wet clothes, her hair so stiff and spiky she could give the Wicked Witch of the West a run for her money, but her eyes so luminous, even in the faint glow of the lantern, that he felt his heart stumble inside his chest a little bit. She was doing serious damage all right. To his heart.

Smiling, he stood and crossed the small space, took the tools from her hands and tossed them near the stairs behind him, then pulled her into his arms and soundly kissed her. Her surprise at the move lasted only seconds, and then she wrapped her arms around his waist and gave every bit as good as she got.

And that, right there, was what he loved about Marty McKenna.

"What was that for?" she asked, smiling and a little breathless when he finally lifted his head.

He rested his forehead on hers, feeling poleaxed, but not minding it all that much. "I don't want to screw this up," he told her baldly.

Her smile grew and her eyes were a little misty as she stroked the side of his face. "Me, either."

"Just don't hide from me, okay? And if I'm being obtuse, tell me. I get sucked into work and the world ceases to exist. I won't mean to hurt you, but I'm afraid—"

She kissed him quiet. And now it was his heart pounding a bit faster when she pulled away. "Wasn't it you who said moments ago that we worry too much about the negative?" She fisted her hands in his shirt and walked him backward until he came up hard against the shelves. She was grinning, looking cocky, and he thought maybe he'd met the one person who wouldn't let him hide, either. "I get caught up, too. So we'll just have to keep each other on our toes."

He laughed at her aggressive maneuvering. "Somehow I don't think that's going to be a problem for you."

"If you're really nice to me," she said, a wicked grin curving her lips, "I might let you come play in the lab with me after hours. I might even let you play with my equipment."

"Oh, really? This partnership is sounding better all the time."

She tugged his shirt, until their mouths almost met. "Worst case is we build a storm shelter of our own. And then we'll both have a place to hide," she murmured.

"Deal. Except I want more than a dirty cement floor and a pile of blankets."

Marty laughed, then stopped abruptly and cocked her head. "Do you hear that?"

Cooper leaned around her, straining to hear whatever it was she thought she'd heard. It took a second, and then he heard it himself. A buzzing sound that wasn't much more than a distant hum. But it was still distinctive enough that he knew what it was. "Chain saw?"

They both scrambled over to the stairs. Marty grabbed the ax, but Cooper climbed the stairs first. The doors were bowed in from the pressure of whatever lay on top of them. "I won't be able to get the bar out," he told her. "And I'm afraid if we start chopping, this whole thing is going to cave in on top of our—"

He broke off when the buzzing stopped and what sounded like shouts came from outside.

"We're in here," Marty started shouting.

Cooper yelled, too.

Then the buzzing started up again, only this time it sounded louder. Closer. There was no point in trying to yell over the sound, so they both moved back down the stairs and backed away in case the doors caved in.

"Sounds like someone out there found us," Cooper told her.

The buzzing grew louder, and louder still, until it echoed through the doors so loudly they both covered their ears.

After what seemed like an eternity—and still no light seeped in from above—the chain saw abruptly quit and someone yelled, "Cooper? Marty?"

They both moved to the foot of the stairs. "We're down here!" they both yelled, as loud as they could.

Cooper looked at Marty. "I swear that sounded like Ryan. What the hell is he doing here on his wedding day?"

"Back away from the doors," another voice shouted.

If Cooper wasn't mistaken, it sounded like another member of his old chase crew, Scotty Turner. Cooper and Marty moved to the other side of the room as the chain saw ripped back to life.

They could hear loud thumps and several muffled crashes. Then the chain saw died again and there were sounds of men shouting and lumber scraping, until finally something was lifted from one side of one door and a tiny sliver of light seeped through.

"Ryan?" Cooper shouted. "Is that you up there?"

"You two okay?" someone shouted back, he couldn't make out who this time. "Marty's there with you? Is she alright?"

"I'm fine!" Marty called out.

There was a pause as someone shouted something that was too muffled for them to make out, and then Ryan's voice came down to them again. "Well, if you two are all done playing Dorothy and the Wizard, how about we get you out of there?"

"That would be nice," Cooper called, grinning. "We're late for a wedding."

The only response was the buzzing starting up again.

Another half hour went by as more wood was cut up and moved off the shelter doors. The shouts of the workers overhead grew clearer and clearer, and more light began to filter through the slats of the doors, until finally, with an echoing groan, then a shuddering thud, the final section of wood was lifted off the door.

"Is it clear?" Cooper called, edging closer to the stairs. "I'll try and slide the beam out."

"Clear enough," came the reply.

Cooper climbed the stairs, but the beam wasn't moving easily. "Pull up on the door handles," he shouted through the doors. "It's still a bit warped from the weight and water."

The doors lifted up, making the hinges squeak and groan.

"Let me help," Marty said, climbing the stairs next to him. "I'll push and you pull. We only need to get one door free."

With a grinding squeal as the bar ground against the metal brackets holding it into place, they alternately dragged and shoved at it until it finally slid through the last bracket on the left-side door. Marty immediately shoved at it, and someone on the other side yanked it open.

Even though the sky was still overcast, it was so much brighter than the shelter, both Cooper and Marty swung their arms across their faces. Then they stumbled through the doors and onto the mounds of cut and busted-up lumber.

What they saw when their eyes adjusted, a round of cheers going up around them, was more than a little humbling. Clutching Marty's hand, both of them stood and stared at the destruction around them. The huge weathered barn had been reduced to nothing more than a heaping pile of busted wood planks. A whole row of towering pine trees behind the barn had also been ripped up. Some were tossed nearby, like they'd been nothing more than plastic pickup sticks. Who knew where the rest had landed? The roof was nowhere to be seen. Or maybe it was part of the pile of lumber that had once been the barn.

Marty moved in closer to Cooper's side as they turned full circle. Ryan and most of their former college chase crew had been standing on various chunks of barn and piles of cut-up planks, but now gathered to come up and shake hands and dole out hugs.

"What the hell are you doing here, man?" Cooper asked as Ryan moved in and gave him a one-armed hug and back slap. "How did you find us? And why the hell aren't you drinking champagne right about now?"

"What about the wedding?" Marty asked after accepting a hug from her old college pal. "How's Susan?"

"Susan is wishing she were here with us, trust me. Everyone was evacuated from the hotel to the town shelter not long after I talked Cooper into looking for you. No funnels in town, but the winds downed power lines and we've got some major flooding issues. The caterer finally showed up, just in time to join us in the shelter— so we're all being fed quite well, but the florist couldn't get in, and, most importantly, neither could the preacher. They were coming in from Smithville and both the bridges between there and Denton are out. So we're kind of stuck at the moment. Susan is keeping things calm at the shelter, with her family and the rest of our friends. But when neither of you checked in, I got worried. As soon as the worst had passed through, I rounded up the old gang and we headed out to see where you were."

"Convenient excuse," Marty teased, even as she beamed a smile of thanks for what they'd all risked to come find them.

Cooper and Marty held on to each other for balance as they climbed down off the worst of the pile. The other half dozen guys crowded around them, passing out hugs and handshakes. "I can't believe you all did this," Cooper said. "But I'm sure as hell glad you did. I'm not sure we'd have gotten out of there without you."

Ryan glanced down at their still-joined hands, then smiled knowingly at the two of them. "Yeah, I can tell you two were heartsick at the idea of being trapped together a minute longer."

Cooper glanced over and found Marty grinning even as she mock-punched Ryan in the gut. The flush on her cheeks brought color back, but now in the daylight he noticed the bruises darkening her skin. Without thinking he softly stroked his thumb next to one of them, making her look up at him.

Whistles and jeers erupted from the small ragtag crew. Cooper just smiled and figured he might as well make his intentions clear. He pulled Marty into his arms and kissed her.

Shouts of "get a room" and "it's about time" filled the humid, late afternoon air. Marty didn't seem to mind, and she snuggled up to Cooper when he put his arm around her shoulders and kept her close.

"How'd you find us?" he asked Ryan.

"We found your truck back there stuck between a few pine trees."

"What?" Cooper had forgotten about his truck. He turned back toward the road, but it was too far away to see anything from this point anyway.

"You're a lucky son of a bitch," Ryan told him. "Trees went down in front of and behind your truck. Somehow you got away with nothing more than a bent-up rear bumper. But being wedged in like that was probably what kept the thing from being sucked right up. It was right in the path." He looked to Marty. "Your car—"

"Went belly-up," she said, grimacing.

"It gave us all a heart attack when we saw that."

"I wasn't real blasé about it, either," she told him with a laugh.

"You sure you're okay?" Ryan asked.

Cooper felt her fingers tighten around his waist. "Never better."

"Even with the storm, we saw the tracks across the field. Scotty was the one who discovered the foundation of the farmhouse. Frank figured out there was a shelter. We were just glad Tommy and Brian had their trucks with all their gear."

"Thanks, guys," Cooper told them, reaching out to shake hands with each of them again.

Marty followed suit. "We all still make a pretty good team, if I do say so myself."

"You were trained by the best," Cooper said dryly, making everyone laugh.

"Speaking of that," Ryan said, pausing long enough to exchange looks with the rest of the team. "The first supercell went west of Denton, on through here, then pulled east of Cincinnati. But the system isn't done yet."

Cooper frowned. "What's up?"

"You know how huge this system is. Two more cells have formed north of here, heading south, southeast."

Marty frowned. "Denton might take a direct hit then."

"We're tracking it best we can, but with spotty power, it's been a bit risky."

"So what are you proposing?" Cooper asked, although he already had a feeling what was coming.

The rest of the team came to stand behind Ryan. "You, uh, you two up for some chasing?"

Cooper looked at Marty, and despite everything that had happened to them today, there was no denying the spark he saw in her eyes. "I'm guessing that's a yes?" he asked her.

"Might as well find out how well we still work together."

"Oh, we work together just fine," Cooper assured her, his eyes only on her.

More catcalls followed, until Ryan jokingly pulled them apart. "Hey, hey, if I don't get to have a wedding night, you two don't get to be all googly-eyed and mushy with each other, either. I'm tempted to break you guys up just so we make sure we focus on the storm."

"Where he goes, I go," Marty told Ryan, causing a few more whistles.

She ducked around Ryan and slid her hand into Cooper's, who gripped it perhaps a bit more tightly than necessary. It felt good, being part of a team. A team of two.

"So what are we waiting for?" she asked the group. "Let's go find us a twister."

They all crossed the field toward the group of trucks clustered on the side of the road. As they got closer, Cooper saw they'd cut the downed pine trees into sections and rolled the chunks out of the way so they could get through.

Ryan noticed the direction Cooper was looking and said, "Nothing stops us from getting down a road if we need to."

"I'll be sure to pack my own chain saw next time," Cooper assured him, and then he and Marty began walking down the road toward his truck. He leaned down and asked her, "You sure you're up for this?"

"I feel strangely energized," Marty told him, lips curving in a deep smile. Then she looked back over her shoulder and called out, "Hey, Ryan, what direction are we heading?"

"Heading back the way you came, then up 17. We can call in from the gas station in Pike and get an update, then plan from there."

"Okay, thanks!"

Cooper examined his truck, but it looked pretty much as Ryan had said. The back bumper would need replacing, but all in all, he'd been exceedingly lucky. He glanced inside the truck to find Marty was already in the passenger seat, strapped in, with his maps spread across her lap. Exceedingly lucky, indeed, he thought.

He climbed in and pulled on his seat belt. "All ready, navigator?"

"Yep. Turn around and head straight that way." She pointed behind them.

"I thought Ryan said we were heading north."

She just smiled at him.

Cooper caught on. His grin was slow and full of appreciation. "Isn't this sort of risky, heading off into the unknown without any maps or charts?"

She leaned across the seat, heedless of the maps she was crushing as she tugged him to her for a resounding kiss. "We seem to do pretty well in risky situations."

"You're right," he said, kissing her back as he revved up the truck. He spun gravel as he whipped the truck around, waved to Ryan and the crew, and took off in the direction Marty had given him. "I'm thinking I wouldn't have it any other way."

Dear Reader,

There's nothing more satisfying than a love story—unless it's a love story with a dash of adventure. Leah Taylor and Wyatt Stone both go to work one day thinking everything is status quo, but a terrifying storm and a blast from the past change everything. Soon they find themselves facing danger and their own hearts.

Perilous Waters was an exciting story for me to write. The research for my hero was especially interesting and I met quite a few new friends interviewing real-life heroes.

And look next month for Wyatt's brother's story in the Harlequin Temptation line. *Free Fall* is a March 2005 release!

Happy reading!

Jill Shalvis

PERILOUS WATERS
Jill Shalvis

CHAPTER ONE

LOOKING AT HER was like getting sucker punched. Wyatt Stone put a hand to his gut and watched with disbelief as the elegant blonde got into his Bell helicopter. Everyone around them stared as well, and he couldn't say he blamed them. At five foot ten, no one could miss her, but it was more than her height. She had the kind of face and willowy body a man remembered.

And Wyatt remembered perfectly well. Mostly he remembered the look of her excellent backside as she'd sashayed it right out of his life.

These days, no one got the best of him, but once upon a time, this woman sure as hell had. Leah Taylor had not only broken his heart, she'd ripped it out and run it through a shredder.

But that had been years ago and Wyatt was over it. He was here working, piloting the local TV station's reporter for her morning traffic report, as he did every morning. He'd heard that Sherry had transferred to desk duty, but not who was going to replace her.

Apparently, that would be Leah. She seemed startled, too, for a single beat. Then she recovered and smiled with warmth in her eyes.

He simply hardened his and faced forward again, glad to already have his helo running so he couldn't hear her greeting over the roar of the engine and whipping blades.

Maybe he was hallucinating and it wasn't really Leah. After all, he'd had a harrowing night last night. As a member of the Search and Rescue squad, he'd pulled two teenagers out of a raging river after they'd brilliantly decided to go swimming after a series of tornadoes had passed through. The rescue had been brutal, but he wasn't *that* tired. And unfortunately, neither was he hallucinating. Though it'd been ten years, there was no mistaking Leah.

She seated herself and slipped into a set of headphones. She spoke into the mike with that devastatingly soft, husky voice, the one that had always brought to mind hot, screaming sex. And just like that, all those years melted away and he was a stupid, horny eighteen-year-old all over again.

"Hello, Wyatt."

He actually twitched at the sound of his name on her lips. The chopper matched his heart's pounding beat, but he purposely calmed himself the way he did before heading into one of his treacherous search and rescues. Unfortunately this was no SAR, but just the routine flight he took five mornings a week. To support his helicopter habit, he rented himself out to southern Ohio radio and TV stations, flying their reporters on their various beats.

"Aren't you going to say hello back?" his biggest heartbreak asked, as if she really were thrilled to see him.

Odd, given how far and fast she'd once run from him. "What are you doing in my chopper?"

She blinked. "I'd have thought the small-town gossip would have preceded me. I'm back in Denton. I'm reporting for KROM, working on morning traffic and human-interest stories."

"Maybe you coming back to Ohio wasn't a big enough deal for the gossip train."

She cocked her head, studying him as if startled and confused by his unwelcoming reaction. "I just thought you'd have heard, is all."

He said nothing as the station's cameraman climbed aboard. Wyatt flew with Jimmy Austin often. Jimmy handed Wyatt a can of Red Bull, and in return Wyatt tossed him half of his convenience store breakfast burrito, a morning ritual.

Jimmy grinned broadly at Leah. "You're new, but I'm willing to share. No cooties, I promise." He offered her a bite, which she refused with the smile that had once decimated Wyatt, making him sweat beneath his breath as he took them in the air, probably more abruptly than he might have. Leah slapped her hand on the armrest and fought for balance as she hurriedly strapped herself in.

Wise move, sweetheart. His brief satisfaction was ruined by her self-deprecating grin to Jimmy.

"For your first day on the job, you're doing just fine," Jimmy told her, smiling back.

Suddenly Wyatt felt like snarling. Instead he concentrated on the sticks in his hands, on the pedals beneath his feet, all of which kept the helo stable.

"So you're a pilot," came her voice in his ear. "I think that's wonderful, Wyatt."

He glanced into his rearview mirror and met her fathomless sea-green eyes. "And you're a TV morning traffic reporter. I'd have thought checking for errant cows would be far too boring for you." It used to be he'd look into that turbulent gaze of hers while buried in her body to the hilt, feeling like he could happily drown in her.

Because the memories of that got to him good, he

pitched to the right—again too sharply, but sue him—and gave her an up-front and personal view of County Road 275E below. Yeah, maybe love had been enough for him once, but now he cruised through life on a different high, the rush of adrenaline and danger.

"I came back because I needed a different pace." She was looking at him instead of the road beneath them. *Damn it, Leah, stick to the job.*

"New York can burn out a person," Jimmy said helpfully, closing his mouth and shrugging when Wyatt glared at him.

"Yes, it can," Leah agreed softly.

Wyatt looked away, concentrating on anything else, the light wind, the bright sun, keeping his feet on the ball, holding them even. He didn't want to hear the world of sadness and regret in her voice, didn't want to hear or see her at all. She reminded him of a different time, of high school dances and late night make-out sessions, of stargazing on his tailgate and sharing ice cream and hopes and dreams. He stared hard at the world below, forcing himself to take in the green rolling hills, the broad-leaf forests, the farms, the recent flooding they'd suffered due to an extremely wet season.

"I'd hoped to run into you, Wyatt." Leah was gripping her clipboard to the front of her expensive, chic-looking suit that seemed far too…New York. "It's been a while."

"Yeah. Look, could you do your job? We're wasting fuel."

Hurt flashed in her eyes, which made him feel cruel. He told himself he didn't care.

Jimmy divided a confused look between them, as if trying to follow a tennis ball in a long volley. "So you guys know each other."

"No."

"Yes," Leah said, meeting Wyatt's gaze, then looking away from the mirror at what she saw in his. "But it was a long time ago," she added softly.

"Oh, I get it. You two used to…" Jimmy waggled his finger back and forth between them and lifted a suggestive, amused eyebrow. "Really? Right?"

Wyatt narrowed his eyes and Jimmy obediently shut his mouth.

Leah fiddled with her equipment for a moment, before gesturing to Jimmy that she was nearly ready for her live broadcast.

Apparently, she'd dismissed him, just as she had all those years ago.

Not this time. Oh, no. If there was any dismissing to do this time around, it would be *him* doing it. All he had to do was live through the next twenty minutes with the sight of her in his mirror, the scent of her teasing his nostrils, and the memories of far more floating in his head.

CHAPTER TWO

TWO DAYS LATER Leah was still reeling. Coming back to her hometown after so long away had been her own doing, for reasons she still couldn't think about without losing it, but she hadn't given a lot of thought to how it'd feel to actually be here.

Or how hard it'd be to face certain parts of her past.

Or one particular part anyway. Wyatt looked the same as he had ten years ago, and yet…not. He'd grown into that once-thin, lanky, too-tall eighteen-year-old body, adding bulk in the way of sleek, tough muscle. His eyes were still cobalt blue, but colder than they'd been, at least when he'd looked at her.

Don't go there. But it was hard not to. Once upon a time they'd shared everything. Homework, their love of movies, the back seat of his truck. As seniors in high school, they'd been lost in the moment.

Until a bigger moment had come along for her. A chance to get out of Denton and make something of herself.

She blew out a breath and walked the length of the house she'd rented, dodging all the boxes around her still waiting to be unpacked. It'd been a month since the nightmare. It'd taken three weeks to close things up in New York—quit her job, lease her apartment, say good-bye, something she'd never been good at. For lack of a better idea, she'd come here.

Her new job had the same title as her New York one, *reporter,* and yet the day-to-day implementation of it couldn't have been more different. In New York she'd tackled big critical issues, politics, war, economics. She'd traveled far and wide, and seen and done things she'd never forget.

She'd loved it, thrived on it.

And in the end, it'd nearly killed her.

Don't go there either, said her sensible inner voice, the one that had gotten her through some very rocky times. Leah prided herself on being tough and impenetrable on the outside, but she happened to have insides as soft as a marshmallow—attributes that had served her well on the job, not so well in relationships.

As proven by her absolute and utter lack of relationships at the moment.

In any case, she was ready for a new beginning, in a small town where crime was practically nonexistent and the big story of the day was the weather. Granted, it'd been a devastating spring for much of the Midwest, with a historical number of tornadoes. But the end of June had finally arrived, and soon the season would be over.

After slipping into her shoes, she left her place and got into her car to drive toward her day's assignment. She was going to meet Jimmy at Diamond Lake to interview a group of college students for tomorrow's show. The plan was that the budding photographers would take them out on their new roaming lab, a refurbished houseboat, to show off their techniques at sunset.

Driving down the two-lane highway toward the lake, she passed farm after farm. The wide open spring-drenched green hills weren't anything like the concrete city she'd gotten so used to in the past ten years, and yet she didn't feel homesick for New York at all.

In fact, as she drove the tension fell away from her in waves, and so did the tarnished, cynical cloud she'd worn like a cloak. By the time she could see the sparkling, deep blue water, she felt as if a huge weight had been lifted off her chest, one she hadn't realized she'd carried.

She was home now. *Home.*

She liked the sound of that. Hopefully here she could find herself again, relax, take a deep breath. Maybe even be happy again. She could grow some roots, re-connect with old friends, possibly settle down.

Easier said than done, of course. She was perfectly aware that people found her too direct, but that came from honing herself to a sharp point for her job. Few ever saw past it.

Once upon a time, Wyatt had. They'd been best friends, and more. At least as *more* as she'd been able to offer him, but even then she'd still been reeling from her parents' devastating divorce. It had irrevocably changed her, made her more reserved and careful with her heart.

As Wyatt had learned all too well.

The lake was clear, choppy from the winds, and so many miles across she couldn't see the far shore. Jimmy was on the dock, along with six students, all waiting for her with a palpable excitement. Their professor had got-ten sick, so his TA was there instead, a grad student named Stu who'd been trained in driving and handling the houseboat.

The houseboat itself was two levels, with open deck-ing around each. It was more than fifty feet long by the looks of it, and just scruffy enough that she'd guess it'd been in service for a good long time before being donated to the school by a retired, wealthy alumnus. Both the upper and lower decks had once upon a time been painted white with red trim but that had faded to a gray-and-rust color. The fly deck was wide and spacious, though, and the sun awning protecting it looked new.

In any case, it was the interior that meant anything to the students, which had been set up as a roaming photographer's wet dream, complete with darkroom, full galley and bunk room for overnight excursions.

It took them a few moments to get the cranky old engine started, but they finally got it moving and set off a good hour and a half before dusk so they could catch the sunset. They all stood on the upper deck just behind the flying bridge, in front of the boat's controls, the winds whipping at their hair and clothes. Leah had checked the weather channel and gotten a good report, but now she had to hold her skirt down in the gusts. Probably pants would have been better, but her new boss was old-fashioned enough to request his women reporters wear skirts. She wasn't in New York any longer, that was certain.

It would take them an entire hour to get out to the middle of the lake, and Leah was thinking they probably could swim there faster but the water was beautiful and the students so excited she didn't mind. While the boat crawled along to their destination, she talked to the students, getting an angle for her story on their photo studies and how it would appeal to her viewers.

"Tell me why you love photography," she asked Stu at one point, having to talk loudly over the unexpected wind.

Stu smiled as he staggered about like a thin, lanky sailor without sea legs. "I love the expression of it. Showing people how I see things."

She asked Debbie, a sophomore, the same thing.

Debbie grinned as happily as Stu had. "I love photography because the teacher gives us freedom to do what pleases us." She leaned in, her hair whipping them in the face. "And because the guys are hot."

Leah asked Ronnie why he loved photography. The senior laughed as easily as the others had. "Because I can take pictures of whatever I want. Look at us, out of school and on the lake. What other class could be this cool?"

Expression. Freedom. Hot guys. She showed her notes to Jimmy, who sighed. "Ah, to be young and free and stupid again," he said.

Young and free… Most adults, locked into their daily routine, fondly remembered their youth. These guys were living it. Maybe she had her angle. She scribbled notes for the rest of the hour it took to get out to the middle of the lake.

And then suddenly the clear skies weren't so clear. Clouds were rolling in from the northwest at an alarming speed. The students set up their equipment anyway, but ten minutes later the rain had begun, a slashing downpour that seemed to come from nowhere. Thunder cracked, lightning lit up the sky with a shocking violence, and though she'd grown up with this weather, Leah started to get nervous.

Twenty minutes later, the storm had stirred the lake into frenzied whitecaps. In the north, the sky had darkened considerably. Thunderous gray clouds churned, making their way southeast. Leah's nerves went straight to her throat. It'd been ten long years since she'd dealt with a twister, and she didn't want to be out in the middle of the lake for her first one since then. "This isn't good."

"Are you kidding?" This from Trent, one of the seniors, who began clicking away at the sight of the sun, still blazing yellow and red and orange in the far west, being chased and beaten back by the storm overhead. "This is amazing."

Leah pushed her now-wet hair out of her face and turned to Jimmy. With the lake so choppy, the boat had been rocking and swaying, and the poor guy looked green. "I don't like it," he said. "My stomach doesn't like it, either. Make it quick."

Leah lifted her microphone to begin her report, but a flash of lightning kicked her heart into high gear. The accompanying booming crack of thunder nearly startled her right out of her skin. Waaaay too close. "No. We've got to go back."

Though the students looked disappointed, Stu agreed with her, but even as they stood there, Mother Nature let loose. More thunder and lightning strikes, so close the hair rose on Leah's skin. The rain came in sheets now, drenching everything. Looking shaken at the speed with which the storm had gone from bad to worse, Stu leaped into action, jumping back into the flying bridge to start the houseboat.

The engine wouldn't turn over. "Uh-oh."

"No." Leah squinted through the rain and shook her head. "No 'uh-oh.'"

Stu tried again, but the engine didn't catch. Jimmy moved next to him to give it a go, to no avail. "Where's the engine compartment?"

Stu bit his lip. "I don't know."

A general panic began among the students. "It's all right," Leah shouted over the wind, needing both hands now to keep her skirt down while the hard-hitting rain beat them up. "We're going to be all right. Get below deck."

"And get life vests on, all of you!" Jimmy demanded, gripping the rail to hold steady.

Leah staggered over to him. "Radio this in. Get another boat out here now. We need to get these students off the water."

Jimmy got on his radio, but a moment later turned to Leah with an expression that had her stomach clenching.

"What?"

"I've got bad news, and badder news," he said. "Which do you want first?"

"Jimmy." She gripped the railing to keep from falling over when the boat pitched. "Now's not a good time to mess around."

"I'm not messing around, trust me."

She looked into his green face and her skin prickled with fear. "How soon until someone gets here?"

Jimmy held on, too, as the boat bumped in the waves as if they were on the ocean. "That's the problem."

The students were all huddled together like a litter of kittens as they moved carefully below deck. Leah kept one eye on them, worried about someone getting tossed overboard. "Tell me."

"There are no boats that can come out for us."

"What?"

"The two coast guard boats are employed in rescues, one twenty miles from here, the other twenty-five miles."

Oh, God. They were at least five miles from shore, unable to go anywhere, and no rescue in sight. She swallowed hard. "And the other bad news?"

Sirens went off from shore, carrying across the water with ease, signaling a twister warning.

Jimmy smiled grimly. "They've just issued tornado and waterspout alerts."

CHAPTER THREE

WITH THE DRIVING, punishing, icy rain beating down on her, Leah pulled out her cell phone and called the TV station. She could barely hear them over the roar of the winds and the clatter of the rain on the deck and canvas overhang, but they told her to hang tight, they were already doing what they could to get a rescue effort going. Unfortunately the entire county was being devastated by the drenching rains, on already oversaturated ground. Flooding was imminent.

Jimmy stood at the railing, divesting himself of anything he'd ever eaten, but it wasn't motion sickness churning Leah's stomach, just good old-fashioned terror. Quickly as she could, she got Jimmy below deck with everyone else. There they sat, only five of them in life vests because that's all they'd been able to find. They were on the galley floor, their backs to the cabinets, figuring it was the safest place for now. But as the rain bombarded the boat around them, shuddering the roof and windows, there seemed to be no true safe place.

Outside, the sky had darkened ominously, which somehow magnified the fear. Yet there was little to do but remain as cool and calm as possible and hope that any tornadic activity would bypass them…instead of ripping them open plank by plank.

Then suddenly Leah heard the unmistakable *thump thump* of a helicopter over the driving rain. After staggering to her feet, she climbed the stairs and opened the hatch door leading to the open upper deck.

Sure enough it was a helicopter, hovering as steadily as it could above them. Shading her eyes from the drenching rain, she squinted upward and saw it was black with a bright yellow stripe…the same helicopter from the other day.

Wyatt?

She staggered out onto the upper deck, followed by an equally startled Jimmy, only to be shoved back against the bulkhead by the wind.

"What is he doing?" she gasped.

"He's on the SAR squad. Search and Rescue," Jimmy

yelled. "I didn't think he'd fly in a storm like this, but then again, Wyatt's pretty crazy."

Behind them, one of the students poked her head out from the lower deck. It was Sally, a freshman, and her wide gaze shot straight to Leah's. "I can't stay down there!" she cried. "It's too closed in, too tight!" She began crawling toward them.

She was tiny, and no match for the weather. Halfway to Leah, she lost her hold and went flying toward the fiberglass rail.

"No!" Jimmy dove after her. Unable to stay upright on the slick deck, they fell, sliding across the planked wood, slamming into a steel railing post.

"Oh, my God." Sally was sprawled over top of Jimmy, who hadn't moved. Her face was so pale her freckles stood out in bold relief. "He hit his head!"

Leah crawled toward them and gripped the front of his T-shirt. "Jimmy!"

"Did I kill him?"

"No, he's breathing."

Above them, the helicopter lowered, hovering. A man exited the craft and began to rappel down toward them.

Leah shrugged out of her drenched blazer and shoved it beneath Jimmy's head, which was bleeding freely out of a gash at his temple. She glanced up at their helmeted rescuer and gasped. Wyatt wasn't flying the helicopter, he was rappelling, landing easily on the balls of his feet only a few yards away from her.

For a single heartbeat, their gazes met, and for Leah, time stopped. How many times all those years ago had she looked into his eyes and just known everything would be okay? When she'd lost her student council election. When she'd been in a fender bender with a mailbox in her dad's car. When a bully had cornered her at the park. With one touch, one look, Wyatt had always imparted a sense of composure, a reassurance that everything would turn out fine, no matter how crazy it all seemed.

And with just a look, he did it now, as well.

He unhooked himself and jerked once on the rope, giving a thumbs-up sign to the man peering down at them from the helo above. Then he swiveled back toward her, dropping to his knees beside Jimmy. Though water drenched behind the lenses of his goggles, his eyes glittered with adrenaline and authority. "How many of you are here?"

"I can't remember." Sally burst into tears.

Wyatt looked at Leah.

"Eight," she said quickly. "No one else is injured."

Jimmy groaned, and Wyatt put his hand on his shoulder. "Gotcha buddy. Just relax now."

"I would but my head is going to fall off."

"Nah, you're hardly nicked." He met Leah's worried gaze. "He goes on the first run, with two others. If we hurry, we can make the additional runs needed to get all of you before we're forced to wait out the winds."

His voice was tense and urgent, and yet somehow calm, and even though she was a woman who prided herself on being independent and levelheaded in an emergency, she had the ridiculous yearning to put her head down on his chest and let her fear rule, knowing he would take care of her.

To keep herself from doing anything stupid, she leaned down and hugged Jimmy, then backed up to let Wyatt work his magic. The next few moments were tense, the air filled with fear along with the shuddering thunder and lightning, and the ever-present driving rain.

Some sort of winch pulled Wyatt and Jimmy into the helo. Wyatt rappelled down again, taking Sally next, while the others remained huddled in the galley below on Wyatt's orders. With the wind as heavy as it was, and the pilot fighting just to stay in place above them, he didn't want to deal with anyone being blown overboard.

There wasn't time to talk, not with the storm growing more violent by the second, and their very lives at stake. Wyatt handled everything with the same natural confidence he always had. Leah found herself staring at him, shaken by how familiar, yet utterly unfamiliar he was at the same time, as well as how, when he had reason to look at her, he did so with a challenging gaze void of any of the fondness she felt swamping her.

Since she'd been the one to end their relationship, and had done so badly, she had no one to blame but herself. But damn it, they'd been teenagers, just kids really. No one in their right mind would have expected them to make it. They hadn't been old enough, hadn't known themselves yet, hadn't the experience to make it work—

Excuses. He'd loved her and she'd known it. And though she'd felt more deeply for him than she'd felt for anyone before, her past was such that she hadn't trusted it. Or, when it came right down to it, him.

Once again, he landed on the deck.

"Come on," he said, wiggling his fingers for her to move closer. "We can take one more."

She twisted around and yelled down the stairs for another student. Debbie showed her terrified face, and Leah grabbed her, thrusting her at Wyatt, who was staring at her, clearly surprised she hadn't elected to go herself.

She understood what it meant for her when she put Debbie ahead of her. She was risking that he might not be able to come back until the storm was over, and just about anything could happen out here while they waited. A twister that could break up the ship, or even sink them.

But she couldn't go ahead of the students still below, she just couldn't. "Just go!"

"Get below with the others!" He hooked Debbie up to the harness. Winds whipping at them, they began to rise, and the momentum turned Wyatt away from Leah. But he craned his neck, finding her gaze again, and for one split second, his icy calm cracked, revealing a tortured regret, even fear, at having to leave her and the others in the choppy dangerous waters.

She stared up at him, lifting a hand, not wanting him to worry, and yet oddly touched that he did. She didn't fool herself though, this was a job for him. He'd be stressed about leaving anyone in this. Still, something loosened deep within her, and warmed.

"Below!" he shouted down at her, through the slashing rain.

She nodded, and shoving her wet hair out of her face, did as he commanded. The way was slippery, dangerous, but she crawled to the hatch and then inside. Sitting on the top step, she gripped the railing. There, she dropped her head to her knees and took a couple of careful gulps of breath. "It's going to be okay," she whispered to herself in an old mantra. "It's going to be okay." She'd gotten good at believing this, starting years ago when her mother had left her and her dad.

Back then, Leah had thought she'd never be okay again, but she'd gotten through it. Her dad had done his damnedest to help her. His own life had been hell, but he'd never let her suffer for it.

She'd survived. And given what she'd gone through to get to this point, she could survive anything. She had a drive, a hunger within her. Once it'd been borne of a burning desire to prove herself. She'd been bound and determined to go off to college, then rake in her fame and fortune. Nothing would hold her back, not her love for her hometown, or her friends, or even Wyatt.

Wyatt himself had had different dreams. His childhood had been spent riding shotgun in his father's big rig. They'd landed in Denton when his dad had fallen asleep at the wheel one night, hitting a telephone pole. Shaken, he'd turned in the wrecked truck for a job wrenching at Bob's Motors. Wyatt had gotten the most out of that deal, thriving on having a real home for the first time in his life, thriving on creating lasting relationships...like the one he'd forged with Leah.

But then Leah's dream had come true. She'd been accepted at New York University, full scholarship. In a testament to how much she'd let herself care for Wyatt, she'd actually hesitated, knowing Wyatt was going to a junior college here. But in the end, there'd been no choice. She had her father to repay for all he'd given her, and her future to grab. She'd broken up with Wyatt and left.

It hadn't been easy. Wyatt had been quietly furious, and hurt that she'd refused to see their relationship through to the end. But she'd been young and so damn

sure that being on her own in New York was what she
needed to do.

At first, the loneliness and fear had nearly done her
in, but out of sheer grit and determination, she'd done
what she'd set out to do. She'd made it in her fast-paced
world of war and politics. She'd been able to support her
father all the way up until his death a few years back.
When she'd sold the house she'd bought for him, she'd
put the final vestige of her past behind her.

Then the unthinkable tragedy had come along, shat-
tering her dreams along with her confidence and drive
to do her job.

Just the thought made her heart race and her palms
go damp. She could still taste the panic, smell the death
and destruction, and remember what it felt like to stand
in the middle of the horror and be the only one alive.
She hadn't been able to reconcile that, to the point that
nothing in her life had made sense.

Lost and unhappy, she'd come back to her starting
point, back to Denton, thinking she needed to find a way
to begin again. Somehow.

Up until now, it'd been working.

She'd known she'd run into Wyatt eventually, but
she hadn't expected it to be so soon, or in a capacity that
could involve working with him. He still had the abil-
ity to steal her breath. He was different yet so much the
same. There were tiny lines of life experience imprinted

around those knowing eyes now, eyes that still reflected only what he wanted them to, and laugh lines bracketing his wide, firm mouth.

Not that he'd flashed her a smile.

What had he been doing with himself all these years? Was he married, maybe with kids? As she sat huddled on the stairs, wet and cold and scared spitless, thinking too much, she knew she had no right to care one way or another. And in any case, it was all water under the bridge. Wyatt, and what they'd once meant to each other, didn't have a place here.

The boat pitched and swayed, and she gulped hard, hoping to hell that *she* had a place here, and that it wasn't the last place she'd ever see.

CHAPTER FOUR

"Nearly there."

Wyatt nodded at his partner and best friend Logan as he flew them back over the lake. Dominic, their flight mechanic and winch operator, rode along. They were racing against time and high winds to get to the houseboat where they'd left five stranded victims.

That one of them was Leah shouldn't matter. *Didn't* matter. When he'd found out her station had called for help for her and Jimmy, he'd had time to brace himself. But still, he'd felt a hard kick to his gut when he'd seen her, drenched and battered and terrified. "Punch it," he said to Logan.

"I am." Logan flew with a calm skill that matched Wyatt's. They'd purchased this helo together, and had done incredibly well business-wise. Flying for TV and radio stations had been a stroke of genius, and good for their bank account, allowing them to work volunteer for SAR. They'd done this for five years now, earning quite the reputation for daring escapades, but even they rarely flew under as harsh conditions as they were now.

"There." Dominic pointed to the houseboat being tossed around on the water.

Squinting against the lashing rain, Wyatt wondered at the boat's chances of surviving if a waterspout formed or a tornado from shore found its way onto the lake. Probably zilch. He didn't care, as long as they got everyone off of it.

Then Dominic shook his head and tapped his headphone. "Tower says weather's going downhill."

"This is the last run, then," Logan said. "How many are down there?"

"Five," Wyatt said. His gaze met Logan's and held. Eight of them in total, far over the limit for the helo, and in these winds they didn't dare go overweight. "Where the hell are those rescue boats?"

Logan checked status on his radio. "One's still on a rescue twenty miles away, the other's beached with weather-related mechanical failure."

"Up to us then."

Logan nodded grimly. He'd been with Wyatt through too many disasters and treacherous rescues to count, pulling people out of raging rivers or from their own homes when the floods had come; whatever it took, wherever they were needed. Over the years they'd saved people who shouldn't have been savable. And in some cases, they'd just managed to save their own hides, like when they'd been in a small plane crash together several years ago during a training session, and had been surprised to discover they would live to tell the tale.

They'd do whatever it took, they always did. With Dominic running the winch, Wyatt rappelled out of the chopper and landed on the houseboat, which was in much worse condition than it had been eighteen minutes ago. Half the canvas shading had torn free, the rest threatening to go at any minute. The upper railing had pulled loose on the port side. It was only a matter of time before it went, as well.

Leah popped her head out of the hatch and Wyatt took his first deep breath since he'd left her. "Let's go," he yelled through the winds and the chopper noise.

"The students first!"

It was the second time she'd put them ahead of her. Admiration, reluctant or not, was not what he wanted to be feeling for her. "Get them!"

Ignoring the brutal elements, she helped him with Stu, who'd apparently fallen below deck and had possibly broken his ankle. Two more students went after him, while Leah stood helping through the drumming rain. Finally there was one student left, and Leah.

"Stop. That's it," Dominic said in Wyatt's earpiece. "We're maxed, and Logan can't hold her steady."

Wyatt looked at the remaining student and the woman he'd once loved beyond all else. "No. We're taking more," he said into his mike, wanting to reach for Leah. He knew she'd shove the student at him even before she did, and for the first time ever on a rescue, he hesitated. "Leah—"

"Do it."

He couldn't even hear her words over the roar of the wind and the whipping helo blades but he read her lips. He got the last student on the line, signaled Dominic, and they began to rise. The terrified student clung to him, but still he craned his neck and watched Leah from her precarious perch on the damned houseboat as she got smaller and smaller—

The lift seemed to take forever. In his ear he could hear Logan's low oath as he struggled to keep the helo in check, fighting for all of their lives.

When the trembling student was in the helo, Wyatt stood in the opened door. "One more."

Despite the freezing wind and rain all around them, Logan was sweating as he worked the controls, jaw tight, teeth gritted. "No."

Dominic, looking bleak, shook his head.

Logan was the best there was. If he said no to saving a life, then they were hanging on by a thread. He met Logan's determined gaze in the mirror. "I'm going back to stay with her."

Logan didn't waste time telling him he'd just given himself a possible death sentence. They both knew it. But Wyatt couldn't leave Leah down there alone, they all knew it, and would have done the same.

"I'll be back as fast as I can," Logan vowed tightly.

Looking grim, Dominic operated the winch, and with a terse nod to them both, Wyatt rappelled back down to the houseboat.

To Leah.

CHAPTER FIVE

PELTED BY THE WEATHER and rotor wash, Wyatt eyed the houseboat below him as he rappelled the last twenty feet. Darkness had nearly fallen now and Dominic directed a spotlight down for him.

He dropped to the empty deck, staggered for balance and then unhooked the rope. Legs spread wide, he squinted into the bright beam of light and gave Dominic the thumbs-up sign. He watched the helo struggle in the face of the heavy winds. For a moment it seemed it wouldn't react to the demands Logan was making of it, sort of shuddering in indecision, and Wyatt shielded his eyes, crouching low to avoid being blown away while he held his breath and prayed.

They'd cut it too close. Theoretically they shouldn't have come back for the second run. It had been crazy dangerous to do so. But though Wyatt had no doubt Leah Taylor knew how to take care of herself after watching her on the news over the past ten years from various hot spots around the world, he didn't know that of the students. These were extreme circumstances to say the least, and even the best of the best could perish out here.

The hatch door to the deck opened, highlighted in the helo's spotlight. The wind caught the door, slamming it to the bulkhead just as Leah's head appeared. Wet hair wild, eyes wide, she sought him out, visibly slouching in relief when she saw him.

"Get down," he shouted, doubting his words could reach her, so he added an arm gesture.

Above them, the helo continued to falter and Wyatt swore, but then Logan somehow managed to execute a one-hundred-and-eighty-degree turn, and headed toward safety.

Lightning lit his way now, piercing the utter darkness. Wyatt reached for the flashlight at his hip. Only one victim left to worry about, a stubborn woman who hadn't stayed below as he'd asked. She never had been good at following directions.

But she'd been good at making him feel amazing.

He ignored the thought and backed to the bulkhead, running his small beam of light over the shelter they were stuck with for the duration. It was hard to see much with the wind blowing the rain in sheets across the deck and the lightning blinding him, but he took quick stock.

The weather had gone downhill in just the past two minutes, and as he thought it, the rain turned to marble-size hail that, slung around by forty-knot winds, slammed into him and the boat like BB shots. Bad as that was, he knew it could get even worse yet. The boat was hurting. The canvas sun guard was nearly entirely gone, and every time he blinked and focused again, something new had ripped away. Ducking to avoid an airborne piece of wood, he lurched toward the door to go below deck.

"Wyatt, look out!"

It was the look of sheer terror on Leah's face more than her words that actually conveyed her warning, and since instincts had saved his life so many times, he never hesitated to act on them. He flattened himself to the deck, just as a jagged piece of wood the size of a two-by-four flew past him, nicking his helmet by his ear…instead of decapitating him.

Leah flew out of her safehold and crawled toward him. She'd given Jimmy her blazer as a pillow, which left her in a white blouse that was so drenched she might have been wearing nothing but the white lace bra she had on beneath. She'd hiked up her skirt to her thighs to crawl toward him, revealing long, long legs that he'd once known every inch of intimately.

"Oh, my God," she cried. "Are you all right?" She cradled his head in her lap as she hunched over him, taking the punishment of the hail on her back to protect him. "Wyatt—"

"No, don't." He pushed upright and reached for her, tucking her against him to protect her the best he could. Another chunk of fiberglass freed itself from the top deck, barely missing them. Palming her bare head, he pressed her even closer to him. She wasn't wearing a helmet, or any protection, and his heart leaped to his throat. "Stay close!"

She fisted her hands in his jacket and held on, wincing through the pain of the pounding hail. "I didn't think you'd get back—"

"I wasn't going to leave you here."

She lifted her head. Her blond hair was plastered to her, long strands of it whipping her wet face, which was filled with fright and adrenaline-fueled intensity, and something else as she stared at him. Surprise.

She hadn't expected him to come back for her. She'd really believed he could leave her here to make it—or not—on her own.

Once upon a time, they'd communicated without a single word, and he'd loved that. But she'd walked away from that, and he'd gotten over her.

A very long time ago.

A large wave rocked the boat, accompanied by a wall of water that hit them with its icy blast. He whipped Leah around and gave her a not-so-gentle shove toward the hatch.

"Hurry!" he yelled. "Stay low and close to the bulkhead!"

"The what?"

"The wall, Leah! Stay close to it!"

On her hands and knees she began to crawl to the door.

He stayed directly behind her, his nose so close to her finely shaped ass he could have bitten her. Ten years ago he might have.

He was still thinking about that when, halfway there, another wave washed on deck, hitting them hard, knocking them both against the bulkhead. He reached out to anchor her to him and got hold of her ankle. Blindly now, as he couldn't see past the water rolling over them, he followed the line of her leg with his hand, over her thigh, her rear, until he got a grip on her hip and hauled her back against him.

When the wave retreated, he shook his head and spit out a mouthful of water.

Beside him, Leah gasped for breath. "Oh, my God, it's going to knock us over!"

"Below," he yelled, and when she didn't move, he pushed her to the hatch, following her below deck.

CHAPTER SIX

LEAH HIT THE STAIRS, slipped on the first one and fell. She landed on the floor in the dark and lay there for a moment, taking stock.

Wyatt flicked on a flashlight, tossed off his helmet and crouched beside her. "You okay?"

"Define okay."

He set the flashlight down, still on. It rolled around them, casting an eerie flickering light while he put his hands on her legs, then her ribs, checking for injuries until she covered his hands with hers. "I'm not hurt."

His sharp, blue eyes searched hers, and then he let out a relieved breath. With an exhausted groan, he flopped onto his back next to her. "Damn," he muttered, reaching out for her hand, which for some reason brought a lump to her throat. "That was the longest hour of my life."

"Was it only an hour?" She'd lost all perception of time.

"Since we first got the call and I found out you were stranded out here, yeah. An hour."

Startled, her gaze shot to his. "You knew it was me?"

Letting go of her hand, he raised his arm and covered his eyes. "I knew. I was slated for a different rescue but I heard you guys were stranded and traded. You shaved some good time off the end of my life on this one." He lowered his arm and pegged her with a long, unreadable stare that stabbed through the dark. "You owe me."

He'd known it was her and he'd still come. An entirely inappropriate little kernel of hope seeded deep inside her. "Thank you," she whispered.

"Don't. You're not safe yet."

But he'd keep her safe, or die trying, she knew that much. From all the times he'd been there for her, she knew he was that kind of man, and for a moment a yearning came over her, so strong she'd have staggered with it if she'd been standing.

It'd been ten years. In that time, she'd had relationships with other men, big city men, politicians, soldiers, world travelers…and yet she wouldn't have characterized any of them as a love connection. Not once in all those years had she ever felt…cared for. Cherished. Truly safe. At least not the way Wyatt had always made her feel. She'd never realized exactly what was missing; it hadn't hit her until this moment.

She'd missed him.

She lay there next to him absorbing that thought while wind whistled through the cracks around them. Thunder boomed. Hail beat down. The sound of parts breaking free and hitting the walls was disconcerting to say the least, and each crack made her jump. It had grown fully dark, the only relief in the utter blackness being the meager flashlight and the nearly continuous strobe of lightning.

"I need a better day job," Wyatt said.

That startled a laugh out of her and she pushed her weary body to a sit. The boat shifted, rocked, and she would have slid away on the wet, slick floor if he hadn't reached out and snatched her hand. After tugging her back, he wrapped a long arm around her waist, anchoring her to him. "Stay."

"I'm trying." The full body contact sent a confusing mix of emotions hurling through her. The boat rocked again, and Wyatt tightened his grip on her as he grabbed his flashlight. His expression was cool as he looked at her, though his gaze was anything but.

It made her breath catch all the more, because distant as he clearly wanted to be, he didn't seem quite able to pull it off.

"I'm going to check the engine," he said. "See if I can't get it running."

"What can I do?"

"Stay here. Don't do anything stupid."

"I do realize the direness of our situation."

"Do you?" His arm tightened around her. "Then why aren't you in a life vest?"

"There weren't enough."

"Then at the very least you should be in a safer place instead of here, unanchored, where you can fly around and get hurt."

It wasn't easy to think plastered against him as she was, but she managed a nod. "I'll do that now." As she came up to her knees, he did the same, still holding on to her.

Unbidden, an odd little shiver of thrill raced through her, and feeling it, he made a rough sound, running his hand up and down her spine. "Cold?"

Her extremities were numb, but oddly enough, her body felt vibrantly alive beneath his touch. "Yes."

He ran his gaze over her, reminding her that her blouse had gone sheer and that her skirt had shrink-wrapped itself to her lower body.

"We need to get you dry," he said a bit hoarsely, and shrugged out of his jacket, wrapping it around her.

Though wet on the outside, it was warm and toasty on the inside.

She clung to it with shaking fingers, realizing she was colder than she'd thought. "What about you?"

In a long sleeved T-shirt, he shrugged. "I'm used to conditions like these."

"I can handle it, too."

"Right. You can handle anything, all by yourself. I remember that much."

He wasn't talking about today, of course, but their past, which might as well have been the third person in the room. "Wyatt—"

"Not now," he said, dismissing that third person. She struggled with that, and the fact that in all likelihood, she was the only one of them with regrets.

"What's down here?" he asked.

"Um…" Hard to switch gears. "A bunk room, a stateroom that's now a classroom, a galley, a darkroom and two bathrooms."

"Bunk room, then. It's the safest place." He broke off at the sound of radio static and pulled a small handheld unit off his belt. "Go ahead," he said into the mouthpiece.

"What's your status?" came a male voice.

"We're hanging in. Weather?"

"Bad." The voice broke up a bit and the static got louder. "Tornadoes all over the place, slinging debris and causing major destruction. We're swamped with calls but forced to stay grounded until the winds die down."

"The rescue boats?"

"One flipped, no injuries. The other is also officially grounded until this passes."

Wyatt dropped his hand to his side and looked grim. His gaze ran over Leah, but his eyes gave away nothing of what he was feeling.

"I'll be back for you as soon as I can," the radio said.

Wyatt brought it back up to his mouth. "We'll be okay."

Because there wasn't much choice. Leah knew that much.

"You can make it until morning?" the voice asked.

Leah sucked in a breath. Morning seemed a long, long way off.

"That's affirmative," Wyatt said. "Assuming the boat holds. We've got a shot at it anyway."

"Call me," said the radio.

Wyatt pocketed the radio. "My partner," he said to Leah. "Logan White."

"We're going to stay until morning?" she asked in a very small voice that she couldn't help.

"Looks like it."

The winds howled. The lightning hadn't let up, nor had the accompanying thunder. If the tornado-warning sirens were still going off, she couldn't hear them over the unbelievable noise of the storm.

"Get to the bunk room." Wyatt handed her the flashlight. "I'll meet you there." He turned on his heels and once again moved toward the hatch door, hardly even staggering for balance as he went, his T-shirt and jeans stuck to him like a second skin, delineating every line and every muscle, of which he had many.

She knew she didn't have his catlike balance, so she stayed on her knees and did as he'd ordered, crawling through the rocking houseboat toward the bunk room, wondering how they could possibly survive until morning.

Wondering, too, what they'd do to spend the long hours until then. She'd known her body was at huge risk. She just hadn't realized her heart would be, as well.

CHAPTER SEVEN

THE HOUSEBOAT PITCHED and swayed as Leah crawled toward the bunk room. Twice she was knocked off balance, but the corridor was narrow enough that she didn't fly far.

With Wyatt's flashlight, she got herself to the door and then just inside, where she huddled in a corner. She hadn't realized how badly she was shaking until she tried to scoop a strand of hair from her eyes and couldn't get her fingers to work. Two stacks of three bunks lined two walls, bolted in place. There was a window running along the third wall, long and high, revealing nothing but inky blackness and staccato bursts of lightning. Each flash backlit the huge chunks of hail flung from the heavens above.

She eyed the blankets on all six beds, but even with Wyatt's jacket she shook so much now that her teeth felt like they were going to rattle right out of her head. Delayed reaction, she knew, but that didn't help her get warm. She was just considering crawling over to the blankets when a light appeared in the doorway. Wyatt stood there holding two life vests, a pack and a lit lantern.

"Found these." He tossed the vests down along with the small pack and surveyed the room in one sweep. "A hell of a storm, and it's not nearly spent yet."

"If you're trying to cheer me up…"

Striding to one stack of bunk beds, he hooked the lantern on one of the steel posts. He reached up to the top bunk and ripped the army surplus blanket free. Then he turned to Leah. "Lose the clothes."

"W-what?"

"You're turning blue, you're dripping water in our dry room and you're going to get hypothermia if you don't hurry."

"I'll just wrap the blanket around—"

"I'm not wasting a perfectly good blanket on a drenched vic."

"Vic?"

"Victim."

"I'm not...a v-victim." Her chattering teeth were helping to prove his point so she shut her mouth. Chin high, she went to kick off her pumps but realized she only wore one.

"It's long gone," he told her grimly. "Lose the rest, Leah."

She stood up. She needed height for this. "I don't see you stripping."

With a sigh, he tossed aside the blanket and strode back toward her, which took all of two steps.

"Don't." She had no idea what she was saying *don't* to, but she had a feeling it had to do with him removing her clothes for her. There'd been a time when she'd begged him to do such a thing, but that had been years and years ago, when he'd looked at her in a way that had never failed to take her breath. Now all she saw was anger and frustration. "Don't," she said again, in a plea this time.

He sighed and a real regret filled his gaze. "This isn't a game, Leah. This isn't fun."

"Do you s-see me l-laughing?" Damn it, she could hardly get the words out, and to make matters worse, the violent rocking of the boat was making it difficult to remain upright, forcing her to clutch his arms for balance.

He held her steady. "I don't see anything but you, in danger," he said more sympathetically. "You need to be dry and warm. Fast." Without a word he stripped his jacket from her. Then he tackled the buttons on her blouse, the backs of his hands brushing her breasts and belly as he went, causing more shivers. He made a rough sound that might have been sympathy, or just more frustration, but then he peeled the material away from her wet skin and looked at her lace bra.

Jaw like granite, eyes completely unfathomable, his hands went to her shoulders, turning her around to unzip her skirt. When it fell to the floor, exposing her purple satin bikini panties, he wrapped her in the blanket and said in her ear, "This is survival. Just survival."

Then he pushed her toward one of the lower bunks. He pulled back the blanket there and found bare mattress. "It'll do," he said and waited.

She supposed he meant for her to crawl in. With her knees threatening to buckle on her, she did, rolling into a ball facing away from him. The blanket came down over her and then she felt the weight of still another.

It didn't seem to help. Lying there in the dimly lit room, the shivers continued to wrack her frame, so much so that she no longer felt the wild rocking of the boat, she felt nothing but the painful beat of her freezing heart and the blood in her ears pounding with each beat. Her extremities were blissfully numb but the core of her was not, and she actually felt like she might burst into tears at the pain of the iciness filling her.

Then, over the roaring in her ears came a shockingly

quiet rasp of a zipper. A few thuds and one thump later, and the blankets lifted from her and Wyatt slid into the bed behind her. Wrapped like a sausage in that first blanket, she didn't care, but that thought backed up in her throat when he tugged on her blanket, slowly unraveling her, flipping her over to face him in the process.

One look at him in the lantern's glow and she slammed her eyes shut. "You're naked."

"Not quite. Besides, you've seen it all before."

Yes, but that had been a long time ago. A *lifetime* ago.

His arms slid around her, and as he hauled her up against him, three things hit her at once. One, he was right. He wasn't completely naked, he had on underwear. Two, he was every bit as damp and icy cold as she.

And three…the proximity of their bodies vividly slammed home memories of all the times they'd spent in each other's arms, less dressed than this.

"This is a mistake," she whispered, staring into his eyes, which glittered with something that was most definitely not a happy stroll down memory lane.

"The whole damn week is one big mistake." Against her he shivered, just as violently as she, and she realized she wasn't the only one in danger here. Softening at that, she relaxed against him, hoping that somehow their two cold-as-fish bodies could warm each other. But he let out a rough sound, as if in pain, and she quickly pulled back. "Are you hurt?"

"No."

"Are you sure?" Fear in her throat, she pushed back the blanket and looked him over in the meager lantern's light, an action that proved to be another mistake. As she took in his broad, sinewy chest, a belly ridged with strength, his blue knit boxers clinging to every inch of him, her heart just about died at the sight. Not her body though. No, her body remembered. *Yearned.* "I don't see an injury."

"Leah—just get warm."

The chill went so deep, she didn't know how she could ever get warm again, but she closed her eyes, pressed her face into his throat and tried to shut her mind off and heat up.

A tiny little flicker of warmth licked at her insides. She squirmed a little closer, desperately seeking another little flicker. But this time all she got was a low, thick moan—not hers.

"Stop moving," he grated out.

She moved again. "I can't. It's starting to work—"

His hands spread wide on her back, locking her in place. "Leah—"

"Don't you feel it?"

One of his hands skimmed down and palmed her bottom. "Yeah, I feel it. Every time you squirm, you glide more of your flesh over mine. Just like old times." His other hand joined the first, and squeezed. With a rough groan he let go, sagged back and closed his eyes. "This has got to stop." He threw an arm over his eyes. "I know you're back in town for a while, but—"

"For good," she admitted into his bleak face, wishing he hadn't stopped touching her, even though she couldn't come up with a reason she should be wanting his hands back on her, other than nothing had felt so right in so long. "I didn't realize that until now," she marveled softly. "But I'm back for good."

"Why?"

Because she'd seen and done it all, and it'd left her cynical, tired and carrying a sense of hopelessness that dogged her every step. Because she'd watched a van full of comrades die right in front of her for no reason other than to satisfy some need for revenge she'd never understood. Now she was losing herself, or had been until she'd come back to Denton and taken a big gulp of air and understood life didn't have to be lived at one thousand miles per hour. "It's complicated," she finally said, and unbelievably he laughed.

"Hell, babe. It always was."

CHAPTER EIGHT

SHE WAS BACK. To stay.

It shouldn't have mattered to Wyatt, he'd have sworn it never would, but here in the moment, holding her trembling body to his like the past ten years had never happened, like they were still in love, like she hadn't crushed his heart and shattered his idealistic view of romance, shook him. Shook him deeply.

He'd long ago stopped thinking about her, missing her, but now time seemed to evaporate, and he stared down at her in the lantern's glow. "I don't think I'm going to like you being back."

"I know." Her lashes swept along her high cheekbones as she shut her eyes, hiding from him. Her naked lips, always full and kissable, parted slightly, and he forced his gaze off them.

If she'd started out the day fully made-up for the camera, and he suspected she had, every ounce of it had long been washed away. His gut clenched at that, and what could have happened to her on deck.

Then she opened her eyes and met his. "Coming back here, to Denton, I didn't think about how it would affect me. Or you. Didn't think about it because there wasn't time…" A spasm of pain crossed her features. "I really needed to be here," she whispered. "Badly. So badly that even if I'd known I'd hurt you, I'd still have come."

"There's a lot you're not saying, Leah."

"I know."

He'd told himself a hundred times today he didn't care, and yet he stroked her drying hair off her face and asked, "Are you okay?"

"Still cold."

"I meant…New York. Were you hurt?"

Again she closed her eyes.

Shutting him out, damn it. He was such an idiot, doing this. He'd sworn he wouldn't and yet holding her, feeling the shivers that still occasionally wracked her, he knew he was screwed. He could talk to himself until he was blue. It didn't matter. Everything he'd once felt for her was shoving its way to the surface regardless. Shaken to the core, he jerked away from her as far as he could in the small cot and still share body heat, which wasn't that far. He was done—he'd given her all he had—and now he was spent.

She let out a soft sound of distress and he hardened himself against it. Outside, the storm continued to batter the boat. Inside, everything churned just as violently.

For something to do, he reached down to the floor and grabbed the emergency pack he'd rescued from the galley. Because he wasn't completely heartless, he unwrapped a power bar and handed it to her. She sank her teeth into it, stroking her tongue over her lower lip to catch a crumb, and damn if something deep inside him didn't get all hot and trembly.

He had to shake his head. Never again, he reminded himself. Her tongue was never again going to be anywhere near his. He needed to remember that.

But then she took another bite, hummed out a little "mmm," and Wyatt heard a rushing in his ears.

She offered him a bite. Leaning in, he opened his mouth, eyeing her as he did, wondering if he was doing anything to her, anything even close to what she was doing to him.

"Do you think the lantern will last?" she asked.

Probably not. He lifted a shoulder, not wanting to lie to her.

She looked at him for a long moment. "What are the chances of us dying out here?"

"We're not going to die."

"No." She pressed just a little closer. A strand of her hair caught on the stubble of his chin. Her eyes never left his, and though fear still lurked, she was calm. "Not on your watch."

"Damn right."

She let out a warm little breath that blew over his lips and made him shudder with more memories—lying with her just like this, his hands all over her, bodies entwined.

"You always were a take-charge kind of guy," she murmured. "Remember our senior prom? There was a storm then, too, and the lights went off. You rigged the generator and saved the night."

And after the dance, they'd sneaked out to the lake and made love beneath the stars.

"Wyatt…"

God, the way she said his name. Around them the crazy wind whipped, huge hail pelted the windows, while adrenaline raced through him. Her gaze dropped to his mouth, and he knew. She was remembering, too. She was going to kiss him and he wouldn't resist. In fact, when she touched her lips to the very corner of his and nibbled softly, he let out a rough groan of sorrow, of frustration, of need, and clamped her head in his hands, properly lined them up, opening his mouth over hers.

A take-charge kind of guy she'd called him. He sure as hell wasn't feeling in charge of himself as he dove right in. With a low throaty moan, she was right there with him, her tongue sliding along his, making him quiver like a damn teenager. She tasted like forgotten dreams and missed chances, and though he could hardly stand it, he couldn't pull away. And he didn't, not until they needed to come up for air, and then they stared at each other in mutual shock.

Breathing unsteadily, she let out a sigh filled with pleasure, and reached for him again, eyes already closed, lips wet and parted....

And though his body protested greatly, he managed to hold back.

Slowly she opened her eyes, the shiny green orbs filled with a question.

One he had no answer for.

He had to be crazy not to give in and warm up in the good old-fashioned way, but his brain had finally kicked into gear. "Bad idea."

"But—"

He settled a finger on her lips. "No buts." A mistake, touching her in any fashion, but he had to make her understand. "You're hard on my mental health, Leah."

She frowned and ran her hand up his chest.

Even that little movement was sexy enough to make

him want to cave. He couldn't. He wouldn't. "Look, we're over. Ten years over."

"Things change."

He shook his head, letting out another ragged groan when she pressed her heat-seeking body tighter to his. "Leah." God. He dropped his forehead to hers, fisting his hands to keep them off her. "If you cared for me at all—"

"I did, you know I did—"

"Then stop. *Please,*" he added very quietly and closed his eyes, hoping to God she was listening, because his body, hard and aching and plastered to hers, sure wasn't.

CHAPTER NINE

"I JUST THINK WE SHOULD TALK about it," Leah said softly. "About our past." The boat tilted roughly and she clung to him. "I *need* to talk about it," she added desperately.

Again they rocked, so that they nearly fell out of the cot, but he held them in. Leah let out a worried whimper, and with a sigh, he tightened his grip on her. "Shh, it's okay." He stroked a hand down her slim spine, and again the inner kick came from just touching her. He could only imagine if he tried touching her anywhere else. It was bad enough that, pressed against him, he could feel her breasts, her belly, her thighs….

No. Bad. Stick to the situation: tornado conditions,

trapped on a houseboat with the last woman on earth he would choose to be stuck with and no rescue happening tonight.

At least she wasn't shivering as violently anymore, and neither was he. Hell, he was beginning to feel like he was in a sauna.

"Wyatt? Do you remember our first date?"

Hell, yes. She'd been the hottest thing in his English Lit class, and just a little snooty, which for some sick reason had turned him on. It hadn't been until later he'd realized she wasn't stuck up at all, but shy.

They'd gone to dinner, and had been in the middle of dessert when a tornado warning had come through, and for two hours they'd huddled with twenty others in the diner's cellar. It'd been cold and dark and she'd cuddled up to him, shaking and scared.

He'd been in heaven.

"We were stuck in that horrible, damp cellar for so long, no electricity. You started talking to me to keep me sane."

"I remember." Damn it.

"You told me how your father was recovering from his terrible trucking accident, how you'd walked away without a scratch. You felt bad," she whispered.

"I said I remember."

"I told you my mother had left my father and me, and you said your mother had died when you were a baby. I felt like we were kindred spirits, Wyatt."

"Leah." Her hair was poking him in the eyes and he stroked the silky strand away. "We don't need to relive it. We had something good but then something else, something better came along for you and you were gone."

"There was nothing better than you." She let out a breath. "I'm sorry if I ever let you think otherwise."

"Then why did you walk away so completely that we haven't even run into each other, not once in all this time?"

She dropped her gaze, staring at his throat. "Because I told myself that my past didn't matter. That I was making something of my here and now, and that was all I needed."

"So what changed?"

Dark, haunting emotions flickered across her face and she swallowed hard. "A lot."

He wasn't going to go down this road. Wasn't going to let whatever had gotten to her affect him now. "Maybe. But as you once decided, what we had no longer matters."

"But I was wrong. It *does* matter, especially if you're still angry."

Well she had him there. "Leah. I don't want to do this. I can't do this."

The admission made him want to cut out his tongue but she put her hand on his chest, looked right into his eyes and said, "I knew the day I left that I'd hurt you. I'd hurt myself. I don't expect you to believe me, but I went on hurting for a long time. As for the job, I loved it, and because I did, it soothed the ache that I got when I thought of Denton, my father, you. My job as a reporter, traveling to every corner of the earth, was everything to me." Her lips twisted wryly. "For a long time, anyway." Her eyes clouded now. "It satisfied my curiosity, my hunger, my drive. Everything."

"Good for you."

"Until the end."

He didn't want to see the fear and hurt in her eyes. He wanted to hold on to his righteous anger.

"I'd gone to Somalia for a story on orphans," she said very quietly, "and fell in love there."

He tried, unsuccessfully, not to feel the gut ache at that.

"Eli was three years old."

Wyatt blinked, hating himself for the relief that she'd meant a child. Until her next words.

"He died of AIDS in my arms."

The pain made her voice soft yet serrated, and he had to lean close to hear her as she continued.

"I'd seen death before, of course. Too much of it. This was far more personal than all that. It put a chink in my armor, but I didn't have time to think too much because I had to go directly to Tel Aviv, to some international press event. I was preparing to load a bus filled with members of the press, my colleagues and friends."

He had a very bad feeling about this and opened his

mouth to say something, though he had no idea what he could possibly put out there to ease the pain in her voice.

"I'd been held back by a cell call that had irritated me," she continued before he could speak. "A New York friend wanting to say happy birthday, and to hear her I'd stepped back into the hotel." She let out a harsh laugh. "I'd practically forgotten it was my birthday, and I wanted to blow her off because the bus driver was waving at me to hurry. I could see the bus was filled to the limit, and I was worried about where I'd sit. As I disconnected, the bus exploded from a planted bomb. Parts blew into the hotel, shattered windows. I was cut up, but the brick wall of the building protected me." She closed her eyes. "Everybody died." Her breathing was the only sound in the room. "Except for me, of course. I didn't die. I only wanted to."

"God, Leah." His arms tightened around her. He remembered reading about the tragedy, seeing it on TV, but they'd never released the name of the one reporter who'd lived, and he'd had no idea. If he'd thought he hadn't known what to say to her before, now he felt flummoxed. "I want to say I'm sorry but—"

"But the word is woefully inadequate, I know." She shook her head. "The thing is, I didn't have more than a few scratches on me, and I couldn't get that to make sense. It screwed me up. I couldn't eat, couldn't sleep. Couldn't work."

"So you left New York."

"And so I left New York."

He found it interesting that she'd come here, a place she'd once run from as fast as she could. He might have even said so but a gust of wind hit the boat hard, whistling through the windows with so much velocity, he was surprised they didn't shatter. Instinctively he tucked Leah closer to him, palming her head in his hand, covering her with his body.

When the wind lessened slightly, he took a breath and let go of her.

Leah's smile was a bit tremulous. "Even now, you protect me."

"It's my job."

"It's more."

His heart squeezed because he didn't want it to be true. He didn't want to think about what had happened to her, or dwell on what could have happened, but he was. The thought of how close she'd come to death scared him in a way he hadn't known he could be. But that didn't mean there could be something between them again. "Maybe some things never truly die in your heart," he conceded. "But my brain knows better. I moved on. Completely. I'm sorry for what you went through. I'm so damned sorry, but—"

"But you moved on. Yeah, I hear you." Eyes dark and

unreadable, her thigh nudged against the unmistakable bulge behind his clinging knit boxers.

"I did move on," he repeated harshly, the part of him in question twitching. "Look, we're stuck in an unusual circumstance that I wish to hell we weren't, but there's nothing I can do about it. We're fighting hypothermia, we're exhausted, and frankly, we're having normal bodily reactions to the situation."

"We?"

His eyes narrowed. "Yeah, *we*. I'm hard as a steel beam, and so are your nipples, sweetheart."

"I'm cold," she reminded him.

"So that kiss did nothing for you?"

"It was just a short little one…."

Short and little, huh? He skimmed his fingers along her back, to her ass, squeezing before he could stop himself. Then he slid his fingers down a little, until they met in the middle over purple satin. Purple *wet* satin that had nothing to do with the violent spring storm still raging outside.

She didn't kick him, as he half anticipated. She didn't rail at him, or pull his hair, or do anything else he deserved.

Instead she planted her palms on his chest, arched into him and let out the sexiest little sigh he'd ever heard. It used to be when he kissed and touched her she'd make that sound and he'd have to physically pull back and recite the alphabet in order not to lose it in his pants. But that had been when he was nothing more than a horny teenager—which didn't explain his current situation.

Sleep. Though *he* couldn't sleep in this situation, she could, and should. He opened his mouth to tell her so and instead said, "Purple satin and white lace. Lethal combination."

In answer, she opened her legs, giving him better access, making him realize how intimately he was still touching her, that his fingers were even now slowly stroking up and down, outlining her every dip and curve, spreading the hot wetness—

He jerked back as if he'd been licked by fire.

Her chest rose and fell too quickly, her eyes clouded with desire. She wet her lips as if parched, maybe for him. His body reacted to that, and when she made a little sound of appreciation in her throat, he knew she'd noticed. "Maybe when we wake up it will all be just a bad dream," he said, sounding a little desperate to his own ears.

"Do you really believe that?"

"Yes," he lied and closed his eyes.

"Wyatt."

He didn't answer.

"Wyatt."

He was feigning sleep, Leah knew it. Or maybe he could really sleep through this—she had no idea. She waited for her sensible inner voice to tell her what to do, but it had deserted her.

Outside the storm still raged on and on, while inside this small bunk room, buffered only by wool blankets and their own private thoughts, a storm of entirely another kind raged. Wyatt was breathing deeply, his hard chest against her hand, his hot mouth closed now, but when she thought about how it felt on hers, she got warm all over again. "Wyatt, do you really believe we'll be able to forget tonight?"

Nothing.

His lashes were inky black smudges on his tanned skin, and even though she knew he couldn't possibly be asleep, she didn't say another word.

She couldn't, because just being this close to him took her breath. He hadn't shaved this morning, and probably not yesterday either, but the light, rough growth didn't detract from the strong jaw. She noted fondly his slightly crooked nose, which he'd broken playing all-state point guard in his senior year. Fine laughter lines bracketed the mouth she'd just kissed as if she needed him more than air.

And she had needed him. She'd had no idea how much or how thoroughly she'd closed herself off, but lying here like this, so close to the only man she'd ever come close to letting in her heart, was both unexpectedly painful and joyous at the same time. It was as if everything within her had opened at the sight of him, and she couldn't stop the floodgates of emotion. Not even his abruptness or frustration could change that. And when he'd tried to scare her off by touching her, he'd only accomplished the opposite, because now they both remembered exactly how explosive their physical relationship had been.

Could still be. That deep, soulful kiss they'd just shared hadn't been any simple release of adrenaline, or even a way to escape from fear. Yes, she was frightened, and yes, she felt safe in his arms, trusting even, that he would do everything in his power to get them through this, but the kiss had been about much, much more than that.

The boat continued to rock and shift, and when another gust hit them hard, the boat protested the abuse with a loud groan, making her gasp.

Wyatt tightened his arms on her. "I'm right here," he murmured.

Not "it's all right," she noticed, because he wouldn't lie to her. They weren't all right. But he was here for her.

He opened his eyes. They were as hot and deep as always, and she nearly fell into them as he stroked a strand of hair from her cheek. He looked halfway tortured to be holding her like he was. Halfway tortured and halfway accepting, with a dash of arousal to go with it.

A devastatingly sexy combination. "I'm sorry," she

whispered and cupped his face, running her thumbs over the rough stubble on his jaw. "I'm so sorry."

"Being here isn't your fault."

"But our past was." She held his face when he would have turned away. "Wyatt…I don't want anything bad between us anymore."

"It isn't. It's over."

"Yes, but—"

"It's been over since the day you left," he said quietly. "So don't apologize now."

"I'm not apologizing for leaving town as I did, that would be a lie. We both know I wanted to go—I had to go. What I'm sorry about, really sorry about, is that I hurt you."

"I guess I just never understood why it had to be over. It seemed like a careless destruction of something that was…" He closed his eyes. "You know what? Forget it."

"No, I can't. I won't." She waited until he opened his eyes again, which now so carefully shielded his thoughts from her that it broke her heart. "Oh, Wyatt. I ran out of Denton like a bat out of hell. You have to understand—for so long, it was all I ever dreamed of."

"I know."

"New York was…"

"Leah, I *know.* You always said you were going. I got that, I got why. You needed to make something of yourself, see the world. Believe me, I never intended to hold you back."

"I never told you all of it." It'd been wrong not to, but back then she hadn't had the words. "You know that my mother left when I was ten."

He made a sound of regret. "I didn't know how young you were."

"Fourth grade. She took me to school that morning, as usual. But instead of going to work, she let the movers into our house. She took everything: her clothes, the art on the walls, the furniture, everything. Except the photos." She stared at his jaw. "She didn't want those."

He stroked a hand down her back and the gesture warmed her in a way nothing else could have.

"You've never heard from her?"

"Not once in all these years." She shrugged. "It doesn't matter."

"Of course it does. She took something from you."

"No, she took something from my dad. She left him a broken man."

"It was wrong what she did, Leah. To both of you. You didn't deserve that, and neither did your dad. He was a good guy."

"She left him with nothing." Her voice hardened at that, her eyes burned at the memory. "And because of me, he had to quit his sales position."

"He didn't want to travel so much and be away from you."

"He had to work at the hardware store in town."

"There's no shame in that, Leah."

"Of course there's not. But damn it, he deserved more. He gave me everything, Wyatt. He was at every softball game, every silly little ballet concert, wherever I needed him. All my life I knew what he sacrificed for me, and I wanted to live up to that."

"You did. You were an amazing student. You got straight As with honors."

"So that I could get into the right college, to get the right job, to earn money so that I could give him something back."

"Is that what you thought you had to do?"

"It's what I wanted to do."

"I'd bet every last penny I have that he didn't want to be paid back."

"I know that now." She looked deep into his eyes, saw compassion, and felt her throat close up. "But back then, in the moment, I thought I had to sacrifice everything to do the right thing."

"I think it was more than that though."

His gaze was steady on hers, and because of it, she could admit the truth. "Okay, yes, it was more than that. I didn't believe in love. And because I didn't, I truly thought I could walk away from you. I didn't expect it to cost me, though it did."

"You don't expect sympathy for that." It was an observation.

"No." She shook her head. "I just really wish I hadn't left the way I did." She looked deep into his eyes. "I wish I'd kept seeing you…because I was wrong. Cutting us off like that was wrong."

He closed his eyes. "Get some rest, Leah."

"Wyatt—"

Reaching out, he softly glided his hand down over her eyes until she closed them. "Rest."

"You said not to sleep."

"That was then." He shifted slightly, trying to get comfortable, and she realized he was still aroused. "Hypothermia is no longer a problem," he muttered, then went still. His breathing evened out.

She didn't buy that he'd fallen asleep. She knew he wouldn't allow himself to relax in their situation. But she lay there for a long, long time, listening to the wind and hail beat at the walls and windows. Hypothermia might not be a problem, but dying still was. She had no idea how long she managed to stay still before she couldn't stand it any longer. "Wyatt?"

He didn't move but he'd stopped breathing. She could feel the tension in his body. His muscles were so rigid that when she ran her fingers up his sleek back, it was like stroking steel. "You're not asleep."

"No." He opened his eyes. "I can feel you staring at me, poking at me with your thoughts."

"Because I can't sleep."

"Why did you come back here, Leah?"

"I told you."

"No, you told me why you left New York. Not why you came here."

She looked away, just a little ashamed to admit she'd had nowhere else to go. No family, no real friends and no one to keep her warm at night.

Wyatt put a finger beneath her chin and brought her back, waiting. "I used to catch you on satellite sometimes."

"You did?"

He nodded. "And I'd marvel at all you saw and did. I also know you took care of your dad before he died. Whenever I'd go into the hardware store, he'd show me pictures from the vacations you sent him on. The house you bought him was beautiful." He smiled a bit grimly. "I wouldn't have said so then, but I was proud of your success."

Looking into his eyes, seeing the compassion, the affection, she found some of the courage to say it out loud. "I came here because running home seemed like my only option."

"A pretty common feeling, I'm sure, given what you went through."

"I didn't feel common, I felt alone. Desperately, frightfully alone. I needed a connection, something personal, something…real. Denton was the last real thing I remembered."

He stared at her for a long moment. "I can't tell you how many times I've been on a rescue," he finally said, his voice low and burning with compassion, "hanging off a rope into an endless chasm while being beat up by the elements, or swimming through raging waters after some kid stupid enough to go for a dip the day after a twister, certain I was going to die, and in that moment, wanted nothing more than to be home."

He was telling her it was okay, that he understood, and her throat closed. "But you never quit." She closed her eyes. "Hard to be proud of that."

"Anyone standing in your shoes would have felt the way you did."

"But would they have left their job? And moved home? Or would they have stood strong and plowed on?"

"Everyone's different, Leah, but there's no dishonor in the route you chose."

She sighed. "I don't even think I realized how much I needed to come until I drove through the hills. Until I breathed the fresh air. And then…"

When she didn't answer, he looked into her eyes.

"And then I saw you. And I knew for the first time in years it was time to think about me, about what I really wanted out of my life." She stroked a finger over his shoulder. Not a sexual touch, she just needed the connection, and touching him had such a grounding effect. "I'm sorry I hurt you. I know it's too little too late, but God, I'm so sorry."

He leaned in close and amazingly enough, kissed her softly on the lips. "It's okay."

She cupped his face and looked into it, needing to see his expression, needing to see he still felt something for her. "Do you ever think about it now? About how good it was?"

"I loved you, Leah. No doubt. I believed it was the forever kind of love." The slow shake of his head made her stomach clench. "And then you broke my heart." He smiled into her unsmiling face. "Don't look so stricken. It's been broken a few times since, and it's far tougher now."

CHAPTER TEN

WYATT WATCHED LEAH ABSORB what he'd just said, her skin pale and creamy in the low light of the lantern. At least she was no longer blue and shaking, and sharing the blankets as they were, he could attest to the fact she'd warmed up nicely.

"You've had your heart broken since me…a lot?" she asked, trying very hard to be casual, he could tell.

"Some people get their heart involved in everything," he said, reminding her that she had held back. He knew his barb hit home when she closed her eyes for a long beat, but instead of feeling victorious, he felt like a jerk.

"I wish I'd understood then," she said, "how much I was leaving behind."

"What do you mean?" He pulled back a little to see her face better. "You didn't believe I loved you?"

"I didn't really understand—why you loved me, or how you could."

He stared at her, totally blindsided by this. "Leah, I loved you more than life itself."

The misery in her eyes…damn it. He didn't want to know she'd hurt, too. That she regretted how she'd ended it. He didn't want to know she'd thought herself unlovable. He didn't want to know any of it.

"So what now?" she asked in a bare whisper of breath, wincing at a particularly loud crack of thunder.

He dipped his head so that they were nearly kissing, the very organ she'd broken pounding hard and heavy within his chest. "You could take another shot at me."

"What?" Her eyes were dark in the lantern's glow, her arms around his neck as the boat rocked around them.

"This time I'll make sure to enjoy the run while it lasts," he promised. "Every minute of it."

She stared at him like he was so familiar and yet an utter stranger at the same time. "Are you suggesting that we resume our relationship?"

"Our bedroom relationship," he clarified, "seeing as we're in a bed."

"So this would be a…sexual thing?"

His smile was grim as another boom of thunder echoed, reverberating in the small room. "It would certainly take our mind off our troubles." He traced her white lace bra strap down her shoulder, running his finger over the top edge of the cup, over the quivering full curve of her breast. "After all, we're here, keeping each other warm in the dead of the night, with no one else around for miles and miles, in the face of an incredible storm—that pretty much matches what's going on inside of us."

"How…" She stopped, licked her dry lips. "How do you know there's a storm inside of me?"

His finger slid up over her collarbone and settled right over the pulse beating faster than a hummingbird's wings at the base of her throat. *Gotcha,* he thought, and kissed the spot. "Your pulse is flying high."

"Maybe I'm just scared." She arched just a little, giving him better access and making her a liar at the same time.

"Don't be. We've done everything we can to stay safe."

"Maybe it's not the storm scaring me."

"Don't be afraid of anything." And then, though it was wrong, it was crazy, he took her mouth with his.

She let out a rough moan and fisted her hands in his hair. He hauled her against him, his hands sweeping up and down her spine before drifting lower, cupping the rounded flesh there in his palms, pressing her against his arousal.

When she felt how hard he was, she let out another low moan, one that went straight through him. The kiss went carnal at that, deep, hot and wet, and for long moments the only noise was the vicious winds, the creaking of the abused houseboat and the sounds of their passion.

Until a sudden thundering crash above them had them jerking apart. "What was that?" she gasped, holding on to him so tightly he couldn't draw a breath.

"More of the exterior decking, I think." The long sustained winds were taking their toll. He pulled out of Leah's arms and slipped out of the bed.

With alarm, she sat up, the blankets slipping down to reveal her shoulders, her long semidried hair streaming over them. "Where are you going?"

"Just to make sure we're holding up."

Terror leaped into her eyes. "Wyatt—"

"It's going to be okay." He pulled on his wet jeans and winced. "I'll be right back."

"Be careful."

"I always am." He jammed his feet into his wet boots, staggered with the rocking boat to the corner where he picked up the two life vests he'd found earlier. He tossed her one and slipped into the other, buckling it across his chest and abdomen. "Put that on."

"Oh, my God." With shaking hands she reached for it.

He moved to the door, then caught sight of her struggling to get into the vest. Moving back to the cot, he kneeled beside it and reached for the buckles. "Nice outfit, reporter Leah Taylor."

She let out a shaky laugh as he pulled the nylon straps across her lace-covered breasts. His knuckles brushed her soft, creamy skin while he buckled her in. Then she covered his hands with hers. "Be careful," she said again.

"Because you want that chance at breaking my heart again?"

She searched his gaze. "What if I said I wouldn't break it, not this time?"

His heart pitched in unison with the boat. "I'd say I don't want any promises." He went to rise but she snagged his wrist.

"Wyatt—"

"Shh." Leaning in, he gave her a quick, hard kiss. For a moment she clung.

"Stay safe," she whispered, then let him go.

ALONE, LEAH TRIED TO LIE BACK and close her eyes. She even managed to snuggle down into the body heat that he'd left behind. For a few moments, her thoughts rattled around in her head like the boat on the water, just as rough and unguided.

She'd kissed him.

He'd kissed her back and had looked at her with all

the heat and passion he used to. And she knew without a doubt, despite all the time that had passed and the men she'd seen since, nothing had ever equaled what she and Wyatt had shared.

Which meant she'd never gotten him out of her heart.

But he'd gotten her out of his.

Another resounding, shuddering crash had her sitting straight up in bed. "Wyatt?"

No one but the storm answered. Oh, God. What if he'd fallen? Or if a loose part had hit him? What if he lay unconscious and vulnerable? He could fall over-board and she'd never know. She quickly tossed aside the covers and immediately felt chilled again. She tried to slip her wet skirt up her thighs, but between not being able to bend very far because of the life vest and the fact that the material stuck to her like stub-born glue, she had little luck. Plus the boat kept tip-ping her over. When she'd fallen back to the bunk for the third time, she gave up, and wearing only her bra, panties and life vest, wrapped herself in one of the blankets.

She stumbled to the door. It took her a moment to wrestle it open with her shaking hands while keeping the blanket wrapped around herself but she managed.

The hallway was pitch-black, the walls around her seeming to be alive with the pounding hail around her. From outside the windows came the steady flash of lightning. She could hear the thunder, coming so regularly it was nearly impossible to tell when one boom ended and the next began. "Wyatt?"

Still nothing. Standing there holding on to the doorjamb, she hesitated.

He'd told her to stay.

But what if he needed her?

And then came another bone-shuddering thud, accompanied by a wave of movement, ripping her from her hold on the jamb, throwing her down the hallway. She hit the stairs to the upper deck and sat there for a moment stunned. It was as if the boat had just slammed on its brakes in the midst of a high-speed chase.

Suddenly the door above her bashed open. It got caught in the wind and tore from its hinges, leaving her staring up at the dark, burning night sky.

Then something came hurtling through the open doorway.

All she managed was a scream.

CHAPTER ELEVEN

"WHAT THE HELL— Leah?"

Before she could so much as draw a breath, Wyatt rushed down the stairs, pulled her up to him and brushed the hair out of her face. "Are you all right?" Wyatt demanded, yelling over the wind blowing in the open hatch.

"I heard a crash—"

"The rest of the canvas shading. The shaking of the boat was because we were drifting. No one had put the anchor down, but I got it. Come on." With an arm around her, he helped them both along the hallway.

Water sloshed under their feet now where it hadn't before. Back in the bunk room, he shut the door and leaned against it for a moment, then grabbed two blankets from the beds, which he rolled up. He shoved the two long, thick rolls against the bottom of the door. "To block the water coming in," he said and looked around as if looking for something else he could do.

"You mean…we're sinking?" This came out in a small voice, and though she hadn't intended to sound scared, she couldn't hold it back.

"No. But you saw the hatch door broke off in the wind just now, right? There's nothing to stop water from coming down the stairs now. Maybe this will help keep it out of here."

For now. He didn't say it, but he didn't have to. She saw the look on his face and decided not to ask any more questions that she wasn't going to like the answers to.

Satisfied the blankets were going to do the best they could, Wyatt put his hands on his hips and looked at her. In the dark night with only the glow of the lantern, he looked hollow. Weary. "If you'd come up above deck, you might have blown overboard. I'd never have found you."

"I wasn't going to do anything stupid."

"Other than leave this room, that is."

"I heard a crash. I was worried you were in trouble."

"So you were rushing to my rescue?"

"Yes."

He plowed his fingers through his hair, which stood straight up in response, reminding her he'd gotten wet and chilled for the second time tonight. Once again his clothes were plastered to him, and though he wore a life vest, too, she could have sworn she saw him shiver.

Not that he'd admit to being cold, not this stubborn, beautiful man. "Let's get you warm," she said, not surprised when he shook his head.

"I'm fine."

Yes, he was. Extremely fine. But his long, tough body was taut with cold and adrenaline. He always was the strong one, the rescuer. Well, now it was her turn. "Come lie down, Wyatt."

"I need to—"

He broke off when she let her blanket fall. He'd already seen it all of course, her entire package, but he went very still, apparently riveted by the sight of her in purple satin panties and the life vest. She sat down on the bunk and patted the spot next to her.

He shivered and tightened his jaw. "Cheap trick." But he came close, tearing off his clothes again, sliding under the covers next to her.

The life vests kept them apart, and she lifted her hands to remove hers but he covered her fingers with his. "It's got to stay on." He wrapped his frozen legs around hers.

"You think we're going to need them?"

He didn't answer for a moment, but reached up to stroke another stray strand of hair off her cheek. His gaze strayed to the door, to the water slowing seeping in past the rolled up blankets. "We might," he said after a long moment. "Does that scare you?"

"A little," she admitted. "I'm not a very strong swimmer."

"I'm not going to let anything happen to you."

A promise. He didn't trust her enough to accept her promise, and yet he'd made one to her.

"Leah." He turned her face up to his. "I won't."

"I know."

He stroked his thumbs along her jaw. "Then what?"

She stared into his incredible eyes and felt her throat tighten. God, she'd once been such a fool to toss him away. If she ever got another chance…

"Nothing," she whispered and pressed as close as she could get, sharing and receiving precious body heat.

"LEAH."

She was out, deeply asleep, and didn't answer. Back in his damp clothes and standing beside the bunk, Wyatt put a hand on her shoulder and gently shook her. "Leah, wake up. It's over."

She opened her lids and blinked up at him with those sea-green eyes that always made him feel like diving right in. There *was* swimming in his immediate future, but unfortunately not in her gaze.

"Wyatt?" She sat straight up in the bunk, hit her head

on the upper bunk, wincing as she slouched down. The blanket fell to her lap revealing the unintentionally hot outfit of purple panties and the life vest.

"It's over," he said again.

Her eyes widened. Her palms went to the mattress on either side of her hips. He saw the exact moment she registered the boat no longer moved. "The wind," she said, dumbfounded. "It's…gone."

"And the sun is out." He tossed her a granola bar. "It's stale, or at least mine was, but it's all the food we've got before I go."

She blinked again, slow as an owl. She'd never been a morning person, he remembered. If they'd only been in his bed at home right now, with her looking so tousled, hair in every which direction, that sleepy, sexy look in her eyes, mouth at half pout, wearing as little as she was, he could honestly say neither of them would be going anywhere.

But she wasn't in his bed, she wouldn't ever be in his bed again, and he needed to remember that, damn it.

"Before you go?" she repeated. "Are they here to rescue us?"

"Babe, I am your rescue. I've talked to Logan, and the town's a mess. The storm took out electricity to at least three thousand homes, and there's flooding across the entire northern side. Telephone equipment is down everywhere, and all SAR personnel have been called in to help. It's going to take days."

"Days?" His unhappy little camper didn't looked thrilled at this. "But what about us?"

"I told Logan we weren't injured and that I'd get you home safely. He's rescuing flood victims as we speak."

"But…"

"I'm going to swim to the east shore. There's a lot of homes there. I'll get a boat and come back for you."

"You can't swim that far. It's what, like two miles?"

More like five. "I can swim that far." He walked to the bunk and crouched beside her. He looked into her eyes and saw her fear. For him. That did something odd to him when he didn't want it to. "I'll be back for you," he promised. "Believe in me."

Her eyes never left his, though they went suspiciously shiny. "It wasn't ever you I had a hard time believing in," she whispered, "but myself."

He stood up, wanting desperately to remain unmoved and failing miserably. "I'll be back," he said again and walked out.

SWIMMING THE FIVE MILES wasn't a problem, though exhausting after the past twenty-four hours. It took him nearly two hours to do it, during which time he worried about Leah and how she was faring, and about everyone else the storm had affected, as well. When he finally got to shore, he went straight to a house he knew well, a neighbor of his. After making sure everyone there was safe, he borrowed their boat to go back and get Leah.

But by the time he got to her, his radio had been going off nonstop. He had to get to work and join the rescue efforts. It was his job.

His neighbor offered to drive Leah home from shore, and Wyatt knew it was the right thing to do. He needed to get her off his mind so he could concentrate.

Which turned out to be the hard part.

For the next twenty-four straight hours, he and all the other emergency workers in the county worked tirelessly, performing first aid, relocating stranded victims, performing daring rescues for people stuck on their roofs, in trees, clinging to rocks in the raging rivers…whatever it took.

All while Wyatt's mind was occupied by something else.

Someone else.

Leah.

It was foolish. What they'd shared, the magic they'd had, had been too long ago, and yet a part of him had wanted to believe he could do what he'd told her he would. *Take your best shot. This time I'll enjoy the run while it lasts, I promise. Every minute of it.*

But he'd lied. It would kill him.

For the last rescue of his long shift, he and Logan were called to the south side of Denton. Logan flew the

helo, while Wyatt rappelled out to rescue a trapped eld-
erly couple. Their creek had risen and overflowed into
their farmhouse, which had been built below the flood
line. With Dominic's help, Wyatt got the two of them
into the helo, and tried to wrap a blanket around the old
man, who had the only injuries of the two. He refused
the blanket, insisting Wyatt care for his wife first. She
called her husband a stubborn old coot, then hauled him
close in her arms, where together they remained until
the end of the flight, reminiscing about the "old days"
of their sixty-year marriage.

Wyatt watched them interact, each of them displaying loving concern and even a sense of humor in the face
of their ruined crops and house, and marveled.

What would it be like to have that much history with
someone, that much love?

He'd loved like that once, and he'd lost her. But as
he watched the woman cup her man's face with old,
wrinkled hands and smile so sweetly into his eyes,
Wyatt realized something a little unsettling.

Yes, Leah had walked away, and for a good long
time he'd blamed her for letting their relationship go.
But he hadn't fought for her, not once.

At the realization, he had to wonder exactly who was
to blame for letting their relationship go.

CHAPTER TWELVE

LEAH GOT HOME to a relatively unscathed house. Her spring flowers were flooded and she'd lost a tree in her backyard but other than that, things were shockingly… normal.

Mail was waiting for her on the foyer floor from yesterday, before the storm had hit. She walked by all the boxes she hadn't yet unpacked and flicked on her answering machine, listening to her boss tell her that Wyatt had called him, telling him of her safety. She'd been given the rest of the day and tomorrow off. For combat leave, her boss joked.

Combat leave. Sounded right, since she felt as if

she'd been at war. She turned on the TV and listened to the reports of people trapped or drowned, of those still missing, of the mayhem and damage. Wyatt was still out there, she thought, saving as many lives as he could, helping people.

Pride filled her, and something else. Affection. Need…

As she sat there in her rented farmhouse, suddenly, or maybe not so suddenly, nothing seemed right. Not her house, not her single lifestyle, nothing.

Not after yesterday, when, as unbelievable as it seemed, being trapped on a houseboat with an ex-lover in a horrifying storm had been the most right thing to happen to her in far too long.

She turned off the news, ate and then stripped out of every stitch of her clothing and got into a scalding shower. After drying off, she got into bed. She needed rest, that was all. A little sleep would get her back on track. Too bad she couldn't possibly…fall…asleep….

SHE AWOKE WITH A JERK. The sun was shining in her eyes from the open blinds. Obnoxiously cheerful birds sang on the other side of the glass. Her clock said 10:00 a.m.

She'd slept all of yesterday afternoon and the entire night without even moving. Stiff, she sat up and realized what had woken her.

Someone was at her front door.

She got out of bed and grabbed her robe from the foot

of the bed. Belting it, she headed to the living room, wondering who would be looking for her. Was it a neighbor needing help? A delivery? She looked out the peephole and froze.

Wyatt stood there looking tall, fierce and impatient, making everything within her quiver. He knocked again and her heart nearly came out of her throat.

"Leah," he called.

She put a hand on the doorknob, drew a deep breath and slowly opened the door. He held a box from the local pizzeria in one hand, a six-pack of Coke dangled from the other, and he looked more tired than she'd ever seen him. He wore a dark blue T-shirt with a SAR patch on his left pec, the hem untucked from his softly faded jeans. He looked ragged and beat, and her heart rolled over because he also looked like the sexiest thing she'd ever seen.

"I got your address from Jimmy," he said. "Is that okay?"

Unable to speak, she nodded.

"I'm hungry. You?"

"Ravished." She looked deep into his eyes.

Something in them flickered hot and the flames licked at her insides. She opened the door wider to reveal her silky robe. His gaze swept over her and he stepped close.

She met him halfway. "I was worried about you and how hard you must be working."

"I'm okay." His hands were full but he dipped his head and brushed his mouth across her temple. She leaned into him, loving how solid he felt, marveling at how glad she was to see him. Wanting to show him, she tipped her head up and kissed him gently, but he pulled back.

For the longest moment, he just looked at her, and she held her breath. Finally he stepped over the threshold and nudged the door closed with his shoulder. She turned and led him into the kitchen, where he set the pizza box and sodas on the counter.

She reached for him at the same time he reached for her, tunneling his hands into her hair, holding her head still as he took her mouth with his.

Relief filled her at his touch, which was quickly chased by a blaring heat and hunger. When he pulled back this time, neither of them were breathing steadily. "I have no idea why I'm here," he murmured, touching her jaw.

"Because this is right." She pressed her face to his throat and breathed him in. "So right."

He closed his eyes and sank to a chair. "I only have a few hours before I have to go back out."

He was hollow, exhausted and starving, and he'd come here. To her. "You work so hard." She sat in his lap. "Let me take care of you for a change." When he opened his mouth to protest, she nibbled at his lips. "You're there for everyone else..." She spread warm kisses over his rough jaw to his ear, which she also nibbled, eliciting a delicious growl from him. "Let me be here for you."

"Leah." His hands went to her hips. "Don't start what you can't finish."

"Oh, I can finish this." She cupped his face and kissed him again, giving him everything she had, going so dizzy from the sweet rush of affection and hunger, she had to hold on to him for dear life. He held on to her, too, sliding his big hands to her hips, grinding her over an impressive erection, kissing her back until she couldn't remember her own name.

"You can still drive me crazy with just a kiss," she said, hot and trembly. "Nothing's changed."

"Everything's changed." Low on her spine, he fisted the material of her robe in his hands, skimming it up until cool air brushed over her bottom. When he cupped bare skin, he groaned and kissed her harder, thrusting up against her, his denim to her naked, already wet flesh. "You still drive me crazy, too," he admitted. "Loony-bin crazy. You'll come visit me won't you?"

She smiled. "I'll bring you pizza and soda."

"That's a girl. Leah, kiss me again."

"I will." She lifted his T-shirt, tugging until he raised his arms for her so that she could pull it off. His body took her breath away. Strong, broad, pulsing with life… She kissed his shoulder as she tossed the T-shirt behind her, then dragged hot, wet, openmouthed kisses down a sinewy pec and licked his nipple.

He sucked in a breath and stood so suddenly she squeaked. Holding her bare bottom in his hands, he shifted and set her on her kitchen table, looking down at her as if she were his dinner.

Her tummy quivered. Her everything quivered.

With characteristic bluntness, he unbelted her robe and pushed the silky material off her shoulders to the floor, running his hot, hot gaze over her. "Your body always made me want to sink to my knees and beg."

"No begging required."

His gaze met hers as he settled his hands on her thighs, opening her legs, baring her to him. "I want you. In a bed."

"I don't have a condom, Wyatt."

"The pizza and soda weren't my only purchases." Reaching back, he flipped open the pizza box. Inside was a large loaded pizza, and tucked in the corner was a box of condoms.

She stared at them, her thighs trembling. "What if I'd only wanted pizza?"

"Then these would have been lonely." The half dozen condoms dangled from his fingers.

"I don't know whether to be nervous or excited."

"Be both." He slid an arm around her and lifted her against him.

He followed her directions to the bedroom. Near her bed, he released her so that she slowly slid down his body until her feet touched the floor. Then he crowded into her space, pressing her backward until the backs of her thighs hit her mattress. She sat, and with the excellent vantage point that position afforded her, went to work on his jeans. The waistband was frayed and loose enough that she could skim her fingers just inside. His belly quivered and she bent to kiss his skin while she slowly popped open his buttons.

With the same bluntness he'd used on her, she shoved the denim down his thighs, freeing him. "You're happy to see me," she murmured when the proof bounced near her face.

"I'm something— *God*," he managed to say when she took hold and stroked the length of him. He locked his knees and gritted his teeth. "Leah—I'm not going to last."

"That's okay." She leaned forward and kissed him on the very tip. "You have six condoms…."

He sank his fingers into her hair and tipped her face up. "Open one."

Because he sounded so very, very tense, her poor abused warrior, she did as he asked. The second she finished sheathing him, he let out a growl and pressed her back, deep into the mattress, coming down over her.

The feel of his hot, heavy body holding her down, his

thighs spreading hers, his hands skimming along her arms, made her heart sing and her body weep. "Now," she whispered as he ravaged her mouth, taking nips out of her lips, raking his teeth down her throat before shifting lower to a breast. He had such a wonderful mouth, and such a way of using it. "Now, Wyatt," she begged.

"No, let me—"

"No. Let *me*." She rolled him to his back, bracing her hands on his shoulders, staring down at his glorious body, her own melting at the sight. "Where were we?"

His fingers dug into her hips for purchase. "Leah—" He choked off the words when she lifted up, wrapped her fingers around him and guided him home. As he sank into her to the hilt, he let out a rough oath and then shuddered. So did she, already halfway gone. "Wyatt…"

His eyes speared hers and for one shocking moment as they stared at each other, something soul-deep and very scary happened.

"Don't move." His every muscle was taut and quivering as he held her still, his face in a grimace of pleasure. "God, don't move—"

"I won't." But staying still in that moment was the hardest thing she'd ever done. She wanted to arch and rock and stroke… But somehow she remained utterly still, swamped in the delicious, hungry, hot emotions racing through her body. "Wyatt," she whispered, loving the feeling of him inside her, filling her almost to the bursting point. "Why did I ever walk away from this?"

"Damned if I know." Eyes locked on hers, he brushed the pad of his thumb over the damp curls between her spread legs, unerringly finding her sweet spot.

With a gasp, she clutched at him. "I can't stay still if you do that."

"No? Okay, then." He rolled her over, tucking her beneath him again, where he thrust in deep. Their twin moans floated in the air.

"More," she demanded.

"More," he promised, and rode her hard and fast and well, until she came explosively, twice, until her breath sobbed in her lungs, until he wrung out his own climax…until neither of them had anything left to give.

THEY USED A SECOND CONDOM in the shower.

And a third on the kitchen table after they'd eaten the pizza.

Wyatt told himself he was still running on pure adrenaline. But deep down he knew it was more than that, much more than basic need. More than he wanted to face.

It was two in the afternoon and he still lay in her bed, holding her so close to him he couldn't tell where he ended and she began. He stared down into her sleeping face and felt his heart catch.

God, how smug he'd been. Telling her she could have another shot at tearing him up. He'd been so sure that was impossible.

Seemed the joke was on him. Again.

CHAPTER THIRTEEN

LEAH WOKE UP WITH A SMILE on her face, which faded
when she realized she was alone. She'd known Wyatt
had to go back to work, but that didn't change the fact
that her body yearned to still be wrapped around his.

When he didn't call that night, she tried to put him
out of her head. But since he was already back in her
heart, that didn't help.

He didn't show up at the TV station the next morning to pilot her around. He was still flying SAR for
storm pickup. She and Jimmy reported from the ground
all day.

That night she spent long hours unpacking, and

slowly her house began to look like a home. She felt good here, even happy. But then she lay in her bed, alone. Aching for more.

Wyatt still didn't call and she knew why. He thought he needed the distance, needed to protect his heart. But he was wrong, and the next morning, Saturday, she sought out Jimmy at his house. "I need a favor."

"For you sweetcakes, anything."

"Where are SAR's headquarters?"

He lifted a brow. "You going to make a move on our boy?"

"The address, Jimmy."

"He flies out of the private airport at the end of Fitch Drive. There's a hangar there, which SAR has taken over." He watched her move down his steps toward her car. "Leah? He's a good guy. I'm happy for you."

"There's nothing to be happy for yet."

He nodded. "Good luck, then."

She was going to need it. She drove out to the airport, which was small, well cared for and relatively busy. She parked in the lot and walked to the large hangar, which had a Search and Rescue sign on the door.

Inside was a black helicopter with a yellow stripe, one she recognized all too well, and a man standing next to it with a clipboard. He had dark hair, dark eyes and wore the same T-shirt with the SAR patch that Wyatt had worn the night he'd come to her house. At the sight of her, his eyes widened slightly. "Leah Taylor."

"Yes," she said, surprised. "Do I know you?"

"Logan White." He offered his hand as a broad grin crossed his face. "I'm the guy who deserted you and Wyatt on that houseboat."

"Ah."

He laughed. "You look like you're not sure whether to thank me or slug me."

She felt a blush creep up her cheeks. "Is Wyatt around?"

"No."

"Oh." Disappointment was like a vise around her heart. "Could you tell me where he lives?"

"Sorry, that's against the rules. Would you like me to tell him you came by?"

"Please." Disappointed, she turned and headed for the door.

"You're going to be gentle with him, aren't you?"

She stopped and glanced back, and saw that Logan's amusement had vanished, replaced by a genuine worry. "You…know our history," she said flatly.

"Some. Wyatt isn't exactly an open book. But I know he's been messed up since you came back."

"I'm hoping to fix that, actually," she said with a small smile. "If he'll let me."

"Then maybe you'd like his address."

"But the rules…"

"I never was that fond of rules." His smile went kind as he scribbled down Wyatt's address for her. "He's going to be pissed at me for meddling, so maybe you could tell him Jimmy gave you the address."

Jimmy could have told her where Wyatt lived…. She didn't know whether to laugh or cry, so she did neither but clutched the piece of paper to her heart, kissed Logan on the cheek, and ran to her car.

SHE'D FOUND WYATT'S HOUSE, but she still sat in her car, surprised. He lived on the east side of Diamond Lake, the same lake that had nearly claimed their lives. It was an A-frame-style cottage that looked like it'd been very well taken care of, and in fact, sat right next to the large, much newer house from which he'd borrowed the rescue boat. The man who lived there had given her a ride home.

And Wyatt had never said…

Because he'd thought she didn't want to know about him now? Because he figured she'd only been toying with him?

There was some storm damage to the yard. He'd lost a few trees, and the lake was still so swollen he had to have been worried about flooding over the past few days, but luckily the weather was going to hold, and she believed the worst was behind them.

God, she hoped the worst was behind them.

He didn't answer her knock but there was a truck in the driveway so she walked around the side of the house to the back. There was a lovely open yard of grass outlined by oaks and elms, and a two-story dock. Someone sat on the upper level with a fishing pole, a silhouette against the setting sun.

Swollen as it was, the lake was eerily calm, so unlike the wild water of the lake a week ago. Her heart started hammering as she walked across the water-soaked grass, her sandals sinking in a little with each step.

She didn't know what to say, what to do.

Sure you do, said her little inner voice, out of nowhere, as if it hadn't utterly deserted her when she'd needed it most. *You know exactly what to do.*

At that thought, her heart didn't exactly settle, but she did lose the urge to throw up. She put her hands on the ladder of the dock. At the top, her sandals went *clunk clunk* on the wood planks, but still he didn't turn to look at her.

The cat at his feet did though. It was a calico, with one green eye and one brown. "Mew." It stretched daintily and came to wrap itself around her legs.

She bent to stroke its chin and was rewarded with a steady rumbling purr. Leah fell in instant love with the thing, but it was her love for the man next to it that consumed her right now. "Wyatt."

"I can't do it, Leah." With a flick of his wrist, his fishing line went flying in a graceful arch. He tipped back his head and watched it sail across the setting sun. Then he slowly shook his head and sighed. "I just can't."

He spoke with a low resonant tone that made her stomach sink. "Can't what?"

"Give you another shot at me." He turned to look at her then and his sad smile nearly broke her. "I really thought I could be casual about it, even cavalier. We could have messed around and kept it friendly. But then we made love. I watched you sleep. We made love again."

"And again," she whispered.

A ghost of a real smile curved his lips but it faded quickly. "And I realized the truth. You can't take another shot at my heart, because you already have it. In the palm of your hand." He let out a laugh that held no amusement. "How's that for being easy, huh?" He slowly reeled in his line. "I'd say be kind, but it's too late for that. All I'm asking now is that you make that same clean fast break you made the first time."

She could barely speak past the lump in her throat. "I'm sorry, but I don't want to make a clean fast break."

His grip tightened on his pole. "Leah." He let out a mirthless laugh. "You're killing me here."

"I know." Moving close, she took his fishing pole and set it down.

His cat protested with a meow, clearly not happy with the interrupted dinner hunt. Leah sympathized but she had to say this. "I don't want to make any break at all." She straddled him in the chair, lifting off his baseball cap, sinking her fingers into his hair.

He groaned, a sound she swallowed when she put her mouth to his and kissed him until their breathing got hot and heavy. When he broke off with a tortured sigh and tried to shift her away, she refused to budge. She managed a smile but it wobbled. "You know, I'd have sworn to you I was a risk taker. I mean, look at my life. I left my hometown at eighteen to find fame and fortune. I leaped at dangerous assignments in war zones, political nightmares, gang treaties…." She shook her head. "But it turns out I'm not a risk taker at all. In fact, I've never really taken a true risk, not until right this moment." She gulped a deep breath and tried to smile again. "When I left here, I tried to put it all out of my head. You, what we had, my love for this place…." She cupped his face, stroked her thumbs over his beautiful lips. "But it kept coming back to haunt me, through every job I held, through every man I dated…."

Wyatt had his hands fisted at his sides but they came up to hold her now, a tenderness filling his expression that filled her with such hope, it was a physical ache.

"I've fallen in love with being home," she said. "And I'd say I've fallen in love with you, but—"

"I understand," he said, and closed his eyes.

"But I never fell out of love."

His eyes flew open. Searched hers.

"I love you, Wyatt. And I always have." She bit her lip and ran her gaze over his, trying to get a feel for what was going through his mind, but he was not making it easy. His lashes were guarding his eyes from her, and his face gave nothing away. "I know what I'm asking," she whispered. "God, I know. But do you think you could find it in your heart to—"

"I never stopped, either."

She went very still, absorbing the way he lifted his warm gaze to hers, how his hands had come to life, stroking up and down her back with affection and heat, curving under her bottom to drag her even closer.

"I'm sorry," she said softly. "I'm tired. My mind isn't as sharp as it should be. Could you—"

"I never stopped loving you." His fingers squeezed once before skimming back up her body to tunnel into her hair. He gazed at her, feeling as if his heart could burst right out of his chest. "All week I've been trying to figure out how to pilot you around for your morning reports without having you rip my heart in two."

"No more ripping," she said solemnly, gliding her hands up his chest to fist into his shirt. "Unless it's the stripping-someone-naked kind of ripping."

Wyatt felt a little stunned by the love shining in her

eyes. Love for him. He stood, still holding her wrapped around him. "Speaking of naked…"

"Yes." She began to unbutton his shirt, reverently kissing the smooth skin she exposed. "You're so gorgeous."

He stared down into her rapturous face. "We're not going to make it to my bed if you keep that up."

"I don't need a bed. I just need you." She set her head on his shoulder. "I love you, Wyatt. We're going to make it this time."

"I know." He kissed her temple, the tip of her nose, and then nipped her chin, figuring he was the luckiest son of a bitch on earth. "We raced through this thing once, Leah. What do you say we take our time this round, and do it right?"

She blinked, then bit her lower lip, dismay chasing the elation off her face. "Yeah. You probably need time to make sure—"

"No." He kissed her softly. "I didn't say *slow* down. I said take our time. And I meant the rest of our lives, with my ring on your finger, and you in my bed every night, and the kids waking us up at the crack of dawn, and—"

Her face lit up with such love his throat threatened to close. "You mean like 'I do'?"

"I do." He grinned, feeling lighter than he had in a good long time. "What do you say?"

She grinned back. "I say I do, too." Her fingers tightened in his hair until he brought his mouth back to hers. "I do, I do, I do...."

*Everything you love about romance...**and more!***

Please turn the page for Signature Select™
Bonus Features.

Bonus Features:

BONUS FEATURES

MEN OF COURAGE II

EXCLUSIVE BONUS FEATURES INSIDE

Tribute to our Real-Life Heroes

For military men everywhere, being a hero isn't something learned. It isn't about training or duty. It's an integral part of who they are, at the very core of their basic nature. Whether in uniform or not, during war and peace, with soldiers and civilians, they are the men who care—about family and country, about me and about you. So here's to the guys who keep us safe, who put their lives on the line to ensure our way of life—not because they have to, but because they want to. Here's to the real-life heroes, the military men of the U.S.A. From the bottom of my heart: thank you.

Lori Foster

The hero of my story, Cooper Harrison, is modeled after the real storm researchers out there. These are the kind of guys who would probably be the first to tell you they aren't particularly courageous. In fact, considering their work, they might well tell you they are foolhardy! But there is nothing foolish about the important work they do. They have deep respect for how volatile Mother Nature can be, and they have no qualms about taking her on—they simply do what has to be done. They intentionally place themselves in a volatile, unpredictable, life-threatening situation, in hope that someday they will be able to better predict how and where these deadly and destructive storms might strike, and warn those in their path early enough so they may reach safety. Sounds pretty heroic to me!

Donna Kauffman

Wyatt Stone in *Perilous Waters* is a fictional character, but I based him on real people who put their lives on the line every day for their chosen professions. In Wyatt's case, as a search-and-rescue expert, he's rappelling out of helicopters and dropping into unknown and dangerous locations to make sure perfect strangers make it safely out of tornadoes and floods. The strength and courage this takes amazes me, and so I dedicate this story to all the real-life heroes out there.

Jill Shalvis

Behind the scenes with
Real-Life Heroes

You've just finished reading three gripping stories involving men of incredible bravery, strength and courage. Now read about the real-life heroes who helped to inspire these stories.

Lori Foster caught up with her friend Lieutenant Colonel Rob Mann to ask him a few questions about his career serving his country.

Why did you decide to become career air force?
I can't remember ever wanting to be anything other than a soldier. When I was younger, I thought I might want to be a marine or army officer. Then when I was fourteen, I joined the Civil Air Patrol and got my first chance to fly an airplane. I was hooked immediately and changed my focus to the air force. I attended college at the Citadel and completed the ROTC program. I came on active duty in 1988, so this May I will have sixteen years of active-duty time.

Can you describe the trials and rewards of serving your country?

Separation is by far the greatest trial of military service. In addition to regular military duties that take me away from home, I have deployed for four different wars and two temporary assignments that were over three months, including a six-month stint at the USAF Weapons School (the air force's Top Gun school). While I am gone, the family has to do everything I do when I am home. Lawns have to be mowed, driveways shoveled, cars fixed, repairmen dealt with.... I worry about them and they worry about me. It can be very stressful. But bottom line, my wonderful family seems to understand that this isn't just a job for me. It's a calling to protect and serve my country, a calling I've felt compelled to follow since I was a kid.

What are your current duties?

I am now a lieutenant colonel, and the chief of the B-2 branch of the Air Combat Command Systems Office—Aero at Wright-Patterson Air Force Base, Ohio. After training, I began my career in the cockpit of the B-52, later shifting to work in bomber weapons flight testing. My job is to ensure that the B-2 stealth bomber is upgraded and modernized according to the needs of the war fighter.

Being in the service requires a lot of moving. Where was your favorite place and your least favorite?

We have lived in California twice, Michigan, North Dakota, Louisiana, Alabama, and now Ohio, soon to transfer to Florida. Barksdale AFB in Louisiana was my favorite—amazing culture, good weather, and mind-boggling food! I think that most people would probably guess that Minot AFB, North Dakota, was my least favorite but I actually enjoyed my time there, too. My wife will tell you that I liked it because as soon as winter hit, we crewdogs jumped in our bombers and deployed to Guam. There may be truth to that.

I guess that means I don't have a least favorite. After so many moves, we've learned that enjoying an assignment actually has more to do with the people than the weather or locale. My family and I have made friends from all around the country—and around the world, as well. And I'm here to tell you, partying with a Mongolian fighter pilot and his family is an experience to remember!

What is the most dangerous situation you've ever been in? And what is the most rewarding?
My most dangerous situation is one that I can't talk about (how cliché!) but I did fly a few missions in Desert Storm that were a bit more hairy than most. On my fourth combat mission, my crew led a four-ship formation of B-52s to Tikrit, Iraq. Tikrit was so far north that we out-flew our fighters and wild weasels, which left us out there with no support for about an hour. My crew also led a huge twenty-four-bomber formation over Baghdad twice and the missiles and antiaircraft fire were thick!

The most rewarding thing I have done in my career? That would be when I was in a test squadron during the war in Kosovo. I was tasked to develop a method to deliver food packets, called "Humanitarian Daily Rations," to trapped refugees—dropping the food from a B-52. Over a week-long period, I developed a plan to utilize leaflet bomb canisters, flight-tested the plan, and flew to Germany to brief the USAF Europe staff on the results of my test. After that I flew to England where the B-52s were based to train crews how to employ the "food bomb." Like I said earlier about what makes an assignment good, it's all about the people and this offered an incredible opportunity to help countless people.

Interview of Lieutenant Colonel Rob Mann by Lori Foster.
Used with permission of Lieutenant Colonel Rob Mann.

From her home in Virginia, Donna Kauffman interviewed Allan Detrich, full-time photojournalist, part-time storm chaser.

How did you become interested in chasing tornadoes?
It was April 3, 1974. I was eleven years old. My mother was cleaning the house, and I was watching *Dark Shadows*, a soap opera about a vampire.

The network interrupted the show with a bulletin that said the town of Xenia, Ohio, in southern Ohio, was hit by a devastating tornado.

My mom was in the backyard nervously staring at the sky. Off in the distance was the darkest cloud I had ever seen. There was a very distinct bottom to the cloud, with amazingly clear skies below it.

As we watched the storm front, three small
10 V-shaped funnels formed in a row across the dark cloud. They seemed to stretch and grow. The three funnels swirled and danced as they got closer to my small town. Soon the three became two, and the two became one large tornado dancing on the ground, just to the north of us.

> "The three funnels swirled and danced as they got closer to my small town."

The tornado sirens sounded in our neighborhood, and I thought to myself, *Any dummy could have told a tornado was coming ten minutes ago. What took them so long?* I stood mesmerized by the sight of the tornado, and refused to retire to the safety of our basement.

The tornado headed west and north toward Willard, the town where my father had just gone to work. We turned on the radio after my mother tried to reach Dad on the phone.

The radio said that it looked like Willard would take a direct hit, and it did. The twister took out several trailer parks, and did severe damage to the industrial plant where my father worked.

But he was safe.

Little did I know how that day would influence me. From that day on I loved watching the stormy skies and I knew that one day I would see a twister up close and personal.

I ended up working at the *Xenia Daily Gazette*, where I was assigned to cover a group of storm chasers. As a result of these events, I became a founding member of the MESO group (Multi-community Environmental Storm Observatory) (www.mcwar.org).

The more I learn about storms and tornadoes, the more I discover how little I do know.

Does being a chaser require special training?

I learned by studying the storms and storm motions, and by listening closely to my friends who at one point in time knew more about storms than I did. Over the years, I have learned how the storms form, in what directions they move, and what certain looks, as far as cloud formations, mean in terms of danger. This has given me a knowledge that has let me find several tornadoes without much outside aid.

What is the greatest risk you've taken while chasing a storm?

I have had several close calls. Five years ago, when I lived in Columbus, Ohio, I was watching radar at home when I spotted a huge cell (isolated storm) heading toward the northwest of Columbus. It was in an area that I could get to quickly via interstate roads. I went west on I-70, then north on a secondary road, and this put me slightly southeast of the storm. I was privy to an amazing lightning storm and dime-size hail. As the storm passed, the wind was much higher, and swirling. I knew I was in for quite a ride. I stopped my truck and decided to wait out the storm in a stationary position for safety. My truck was rocking back and forth and started to move sideways. The wind was probably over 110 miles per hour. All in all, my truck blew about two feet sideways, nearly into a ditch. After I got home, safely, but scared, I found out that there was a tornado embedded in the storm.

Also, on November 10, 2002, I got a call from fellow photographer Lisa Dutton at about 3:00 p.m. She told me that Van Wert, Ohio, had been hit by a large tornado. I had just checked radar and saw some interesting cells out in front of the main squall line. One particular cell was growing by leaps and bounds and was heading just south of Findlay, in a northeast direction toward Seneca County and Tiffin, just fifteen miles from where I lived.

I talked with the editors at *The Blade* and they decided to put me on overtime and get my "storm-chasing butt" into the field to see what I could come up with.

I headed south on SR 53, a direct route toward Tiffin, and was met by some amazing cloud-to-cloud lightning and wind gusts to about fifty miles per hour. As I approached Tiffin, I skirted the north part of town along Second Street and stopped quickly to photograph a group of bar patrons looking up at the ominous sky. As I was shooting that, I got knocked on the head by what I thought was a walnut, but discovered was hail. I looked to the south and saw several funnel clouds swirling around each other. In the distance, two funnels pulled down from the cloud base and formed one. I slammed on the brakes and leaned out of my truck window and got about ten frames off of the tornado before the whole town went black. The tornado turned black instantly the second it touched the ground. I tried to get in behind the tornado but was blown from one lane of road to another in a second.

I headed in the direction of the first hit of the tornado and as I topped a hill, a tree blew down over the road. I slammed on the brakes and skidded into the outer branches. I backtracked and found the initial touchdown; it had hit a subdivision and completely demolished several homes. I was there before the rescue personnel and photographed people digging through the foundation for survivors. Fortunately, the only fatality was a dog.

My tornado photo ran in the next day's paper and then ran in newspapers and magazines all over the world. It was published in December's *Life* magazine's pictures of the year edition.

Have you ever "core punched" into a tornado?
You never want to core punch into a tornado!

What recommendations can you give to someone who is interested in learning how to become a chaser?
Well, there are groups such as MESO that you can join, but our group will not let a new member go out on our yearly chase until they have proven a knowledge of storms and responsibility to the chase team, so you don't do something stupid and put all your fellow chasers at risk. Also, a sensitivity toward victims of storms, and basic search-and-rescue skills help.

Is there anything else you'd like to share with us?
You can check out these Web sites to learn more about me, MESO and storms:

14

Allan Detrich—www.allandetrich.com
MESO—www.mcwar.org/
Storm Prediction Center—www.spc.noaa.gov/

Interview of Allan Detrich by Donna Kauffman.
Used with permission of Allan Detrich.

Harold Hoffmaster, Aviation Survival Technician Chief, Air Station Cape Cod, Massachusetts, talks to Jill Shalvis about what it takes to be SAR.

How did you become interested in search and rescue?
My father found an ad in the newspaper for law enforcement and search and rescue. I had no idea what the coast guard was or what they did. I was more interested in the law enforcement aspect until I graduated boot camp and realized exactly what search and rescue consisted of. While stationed and working at a small boat unit, I remember pulling two people out of the water after their boat caught on fire. I still remember the look in their eyes. Jodi, my shipmate (later to be my wife), was on that same case with me and suggested I try to be a rescue swimmer.

Do you have special training?
I trained in Oregon for my Advance Helicopter Rescue Swimmer. I'm also a personal trainer.

What is the greatest risk you've taken while on a rescue?
One would be when I was left on the roof of a house during a flood just south of Houston, Texas. I was deployed from a smaller coast guard helicopter, with limited fuel. They put me on the roof and had to leave to refuel. I jumped off the roof into five feet of water. I stayed with the two stranded farmers until the helicopter returned to pluck us from the floods. While we waited in the flooded area, the farmers told me of the alligators they saw earlier in the week. All I could

think of was how our legs were going to be alligator bait. Another would be recently trying to retrieve a victim in heavy surf. There were large rocks close by. I kept wondering how close I was to being smacked down onto one of those rocks by a large wave. When you are in the ocean, you really can't tell where you are. Limited visibility is also a great risk we face when searching in very inclement weather.

Have you ever rappelled out of a helicopter with a wild storm around you?
One of my first cases consisted of getting lowered down to a dive boat to retrieve an unconscious woman. The boat was being tossed around and the waves reached over twenty feet.

What recommendations can you give to someone who is interested in learning how to become SAR?
You must be willing to put your life on the line for someone you have never met! There are a few different ways to get involved in SAR:
• You can volunteer to work in a mountain rescue.
• You can work with dogs to find people in rubble after an earthquake or other disaster.
• You can join the United States Coast Guard (the premier search and rescue service).

Is there anything else you'd like to share with us?
I would not be doing what I am today if not for my parents (especially my father for finding this career for me in the classifieds). I'd like to thank my wife, Jodi, for in-

spiring me to attend and succeed at Rescue Swimmer school.

With all the conflict in the world going on, it is nice to be part of a service that saves lives everyday!

Interview of Harold Hoffmaster by Jill Shalvis.
Used with permission of Harold Hoffmaster.

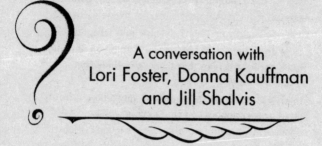

A conversation with
Lori Foster, Donna Kauffman
and Jill Shalvis

*Our three authors share some personal history, some chal-
lenges and some of their writing secrets in the interviews
they've generously shared with us below. Find out in the
following conversations which author married her high
school sweetheart, which one hates chick flicks, and who
loves to nap on her deck.*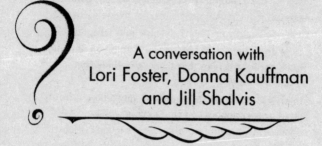

Lori Foster

**Lori, tell us a bit about how you began your writing ca-
reer.**

I was always a daydreamer and I always had stories in
my head. But I didn't know I wanted to write until I was
grown and already had three sons. Then I got sick with
pneumonia and because I felt too yucky to even get out
of bed, my sister brought me over a bag of romance
novels. I was instantly hooked! Almost immediately,
probably within two years, I went from being a reader
to wanting to write the same type of books I loved to
read. I wrote at least ten complete romances that never

sold—and I submitted them everywhere, so I got three times as many rejections. I wrote for five years before finally selling my first book to Harlequin Temptation.

Was there a particular person, place or thing that inspired this story?
Yes. The current political climate is very different from what I'm used to, but knowing that our military is the very best in the entire world brings me great comfort. Catherine Mann is a super talented, lovely woman who not only writes some of the best military romances around, she lives the romance with her air force hero husband. Knowing her has only made me appreciate our military that much more. She's shared wonderful stories about her husband, and that inspired me to want to thank our military men who so bravely work to keep us safe. Thank you, Catherine and Rob.

What's your typical writing routine?
That differs from day to day, depending on what's happening in my life. I'm usually up somewhere between four-thirty and five-thirty, depending on my husband's schedule. I get my coffee and attack e-mails. I generally get about 250-plus e-mails a day. After that, I check out the Web sites that interest me. (I go to my own message board every day, and the Romantic Times message board and the eHarlequin message board.) Around 6:45, I see my kids off to school, then I get food (I'm a grazer—meaning I eat small amounts of stuff all the time, all day long). I let the dogs out a million times, play with the dogs a million times, do at least two loads of laundry, make

beds, answer phone calls, and in between all of that, I write.

I write for however many hours it takes to get all the scenes out of my head. That might be two hours or ten, or not at all. I do everything fast. I'm not a person who does well with idle time, unless I'm watching a movie. I love movies. My brain always seems to be on Mach speed, so my fingers try to keep up. Every author does things differently. For me, I write fast, when the mood strikes me, and when I don't have anything else taking priority.

How do you research your stories?

I hate researching books. Boring! I prefer to ask someone who has the information I need. I like to talk with cops and firefighters and forensic experts. I like to chat with coroners and school teachers and vets. I like picking a doctor's brain and bugging my friend who is a nurse. Talking with someone and getting their personal take on careers and experiences is always more interesting than reading it in a book.

Could you tell us a bit about your family?

I've been married twenty-six years, and I have three sons—twenty-two, eighteen and seventeen. The boys are very nice, independent and motivated. They're into sports and fitness, and I'm very proud of them. My husband is a great guy, super funny, and incredibly supportive of me and the boys.

When you're not writing, what are your favorite activities?
I love watching my sons in any of their sporting activities. When they're not in sports, I love going to the movies. Kick-butt movies, action flicks and monster movies are my favorites. I detest chick flicks. And of course, I like to read!

What are your favorite kinds of vacations?
I like to be near water, but not in it. Like on a beach, but not swimming. (Fear of things in the water!) I like any place that is warm, while my husband loves the mountains. Actually, any place we go together is always a lot of fun.

Could you tell us about your first romance?
My first serious romance was with my husband. We dated all through high school, then got married when we graduated. Through good times and bad, he's kept me smiling.

How did you meet your husband?
The third day of our sophomore year of high school, he got transferred into my history class. And ironically enough, the rest was...history.

Any final words to your readers?
I'd like to give a giant thank-you to everyone who generously send me e-mails and letters, and who post online reviews and share their enthusiasm with other readers. Readers make this business even better than it already is. They're the icing on the cake, and I appreciate them all.

Donna Kauffman

Tell us a bit about how you began your writing career.
I've always enjoyed reading and writing stories, but it
wasn't until I was pregnant with my first child that I decided to tackle writing a novel. I was certain this obvious dementia had been induced by my being in my
third trimester during the hottest summer on record.
After my son was born, I quickly stuffed my effort
under the bed, never to be seen again. It was only
when I was pregnant with my second son a year later
that I uncovered that dusty legal pad while searching
for a tossed pacifier. Cringing, and certain I was in for a
good laugh, I read my dementia-induced efforts. Perhaps it was because I was once again in my third
trimester (during the coldest winter on record—are
you beginning to detect a pattern?) that I thought the
story had merit. After my second child was born, I
signed up for a writing class at the local college and my
instructor noticed my interest in romance. She happened to be a member of RWA and pushed me to join
both the national and local chapter. My local group was
a wonderfully talented bunch and they encouraged me
to finish that story. I was soon involved in learning all
about the industry I was now determined to be part of.
Eighteen months (and untold revisions later) I sold
that first book to Bantam Loveswept. Thankfully, I
had discovered by then that I could actually write
books without being pregnant. Thirty published books
later...well, it doesn't really bear thinking about,
does it?

Was there a particular person, place or thing that inspired this story?

I became fascinated by tornadoes as a child when I saw the *Wizard of Oz* for the first time. Even at six, I knew Dorothy and the munchkins were pure fantasy, but I soon made the discovery that there really were twisters that could actually lift a house off its foundation and spin it around in the sky! I was immediately entranced (not to mention terrified) by the very notion. Growing up on the East Coast, we didn't have many tornadoes. This fueled my imagination (and more than one nightmare) for years to come. So it's been exciting to finally find the time and place to indulge this particular interest and write about the kind of hero and heroine who are doing something I've always dreamed about doing myself.

What's your writing routine?

My sons are in high school, so I am fortunate enough to have peace and quiet during the day (well, if you don't count the constant chatter from my three parrots). I generally work from around eight-thirty in the morning until four in the afternoon. Weekends and evenings are for family. Unless I'm on deadline, then all bets are off. But everyone gets pizza and soda, so they don't complain much!

How do you research your stories?

Any number of ways. I gather information online, read research texts, interview people, and if I'm fortunate enough to have the time, travel to the locations in which my stories are set. I try to choose professions, locations and other plot hooks that interest me. So the biggest challenge isn't gathering enough information, it's forcing myself to stop reading everything I get my hands on and get on with writing the book!

When you're not writing, what are your favorite activities?

My family is very sports oriented, so weekends and evenings usually find me sitting in the bleachers watching a ball. Hobbies, when I have the chance to indulge them, range from gardening, to cross-stitching, to scrapbooking. And of course, I read every chance I get.

What are your favorite kinds of vacations?

As I said earlier, I try to travel to locations I want to set future books in. Sometimes business opportunities arise—giving workshops, etc.—that take me to new places I'd never thought of using as a setting, but quickly find all kinds of interesting tidbits that draw me in and get the juices flowing. My family both snow skis and enjoys the beach, so family vacations are usually in the mountains or on the shore.

How did you meet your partner?

I met my husband while doing research on a book. He was commanding a SERT team at the time and after numerous phone conversations he eventually invited me to meet him by coming to watch a SWAT competition at the Quantico marine base, where his team was competing. We went out afterward (ostensibly so I could ask him more questions, but by then my "research" had taken on a decidedly personal slant) and well...that led to other dates and a lot more "researching." Three years later we were married!

Any last words to your readers?
Men of courage come in all kinds of packages. It's not always an obvious one. His uniform could include a flak jacket or a hard hat, a pocket full of pencils, or a sword strapped to his side. I like writing about all kinds of heroes.

Jill Shalvis

Tell us a bit about how you began your writing career.
I began my writing career as a journalism major in college. A few years later, making less money than I would have made slinging burgers at a fast-food joint, I switched hands and tried fiction instead of nonfiction. I started with what I love to read, romance, and never looked back. When I sold my first romance, it was a true dream come true, and though I've branched out a bit now, I still love what I do with all my heart.

Was there a particular person, place or thing that inspired this story?
First, I'm attracted to a bigger-than-life hero or heroine, one who puts their life on the line willingly to save others. My husband used to drive an ambulance. In fact, some of our closest friends are firefighters, cops, doctors, nurses, search-and-rescue experts...so they all inspired me to write a story like this.

What's your writing routine?
Brutal, as it starts before the crack of dawn. With three children I don't have much choice. Getting up before everyone else (not easy with my youngest being an early riser) is the best way for me. I get a few pages in, then have to take a break to do the roundup on the family. Once I get everyone out the door, I have a few hours of peace again, and spend all that time writing so that by the time they come in looking for food and homework help and everything else, I'm done. And if I'm not, well, then, it's time for pizza takeout.

How do you research your stories?

In this story's case, all my research was done with real people. Live interviews, telephone calls, e-mails. I was lucky to have plenty of friends with experience to help me. I really wanted to jump out of a helicopter for "research" on this one, but I recently had shoulder reconstruction surgery and no one would let me. Next time, I hope. But with other stories, and other research needs, I use the Internet and the library.

If you don't mind, could you tell us a bit about your family?

I have three lovely daughters, all of whom are a bit baffled by my job, which is willingly putting words on paper. I have an equally lovely husband who hardly bats an eye at his wife who talks to herself and hears voices inside her head.

When you're not writing, what are your favorite activities?

My favorite activity is taking a nap on my deck in the Sierra sunshine. But I also do a lot of skiing, hiking, reading, and shall I admit it? Eating. Eating is a big favorite.

What are your favorite kinds of vacations?

Traveling isn't something we do a lot of. First of all, three kids. Need I say more? But if we go anywhere, it's often up and down the California coast, or Mexico or Hawaii.

Could you tell us about your first romance?
My first romance... I was working as an accountant in Southern California, in the offices where the emergency dispatch for that city was. There was this certain ambulance driver, who had been injured on duty and put to work in the offices filing for me. He asked me out, and I, having heard of the reputation of these guys, turned him down flat. He asked again. And again. Four months later, long after he'd been put back in the field, I finally agreed. And we've been together ever since.

Any final words to your readers?
I just hope you enjoy this story as much as I enjoyed researching and writing it.

Marsha Zinberg, Executive Editor, caught up with all three women this past April.

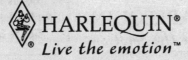

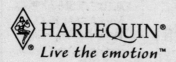

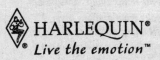

If you enjoyed what you just read,
then we've got an offer you can't resist!

Take 2 bestselling love stories FREE!

Plus get a FREE surprise gift!

LORI FOSTER

first published in January of 1996 and has since sold over forty-five books with six different publishing houses, including categories, novellas, online books, special projects and, most recently, single titles. Lori's second book launched the Temptation Blaze miniseries and her twenty-fifth book launched the new Temptation Heat series. Lori has brought sensitivity and sensibility to erotic romances by combining family values and sizzling, yet tender love. Though Lori enjoys writing, her first priority will always be her family. Her husband and three sons keep her on her toes.

DONNA KAUFFMAN

was first published with Bantam's Loveswept line in 1993. After fourteen books, she went on to write contemporary single titles for Bantam. In 2001 she returned to her category roots and had her first release with Harlequin's Temptation line. Donna is also currently writing for Harlequin's Blaze line. She enjoys creating characters that like to push the edge a little! Donna lives in Virginia with her husband and rapidly growing sons. She also has a rapidly growing menagerie of pets.

JILL SHALVIS

has been making up stories since she could hold a pencil. Now, thankfully, she gets to do it for a living, and doesn't plan to ever stop. She is the bestselling, award-winning author of over thirty novels. She's hit the Waldenbooks bestseller lists, was a 2000 Rita® Award nominee and is a two-time National Reader's Choice Award winner. She was nominated for a *Romantic Times* Career Achievement Award in Romantic Comedy, and for Best Duets and Best Temptation, and writes series romance for both Silhouette and Harlequin.